It's hurricane season.

An airplane en route to the States has just been forced to land on the island of Puerto Rico—and onboard is **AINSLEY WALKER**.

Stranded in torrential rain, she is guided by another passenger towards a rickety plantation house in the island's tropical interior, where she meets an elderly woman who has lost a precious family heirloom.

It's a pearl brooch that had once belonged to an actual pirate of the Caribbean—and the old spinster needs her to find it ... *fast.*

Soon Ainsley finds herself on another runaway adventure—one that propels her across Puerto Rico, from wealthy art museums to abandoned sugar mills, from colonial-era cities to buried pirate chests on abandoned naval bases.

Along the way, she discovers joy, pain, friendship, danger, the limits of her endurance—and the fact that things are never quite as they seem.

THE PUERTO RICO PEARL

Praise for **AINSLEY WALKER**

"Well-paced and skillfully told, with an outstanding sense of place, an enjoyable main character, and entertaining supporting cast.... *The Uruguay Amethyst* swept me off my feet."
　　　　—Venus de Hilo, 5-star review

"*The Uruguay Amethyst* is a delightful book – it will enchant you with exotic places and interesting characters."
　　　　—Linda Osborn, 5-star review

"I recommend *The American Turquoise* to anyone ... it is definitely worth the money."
　　　　—J Bronder, 5-star review

"Vivid and exciting ... *The Argentina Rhodochrosite* made me feel like I had just watched a great Travel Channel episode."
　　　　—Mel Collins

"Sketching a country with historical and cultural strokes, and tying this in with a fast storyline, is something that Jernay does well..."
　　　　—B. Till

"For anyone who has ever hoped for a whole new life, this is sheer fun..."
　　　　—Kenetha Stanton

Other **Ainsley Walker Gemstone Travel Mystery**
titles:

The American Turquoise

The Uruguay Amethyst

The Argentina Rhodochrosite

The Puerto Rico Pearl

The Portugal Sapphire

The

PUERTO RICO PEARL

AN AINSLEY WALKER GEMSTONE TRAVEL MYSTERY

J.A. JERNAY

The Puerto Rico Pearl: An Ainsley Walker
Gemstone Travel Mystery
Copyright © 2012 by J.A. Jernay.
All Rights Reserved.

ISBN: 978-1483984773

To contact the author, visit j.a.jernay.com or email
j.a.jernay@gmail.com.

Cover design: Heather Kern at Popshop Studio
Book ornament design: David Moratto

The
PUERTO RICO
PEARL

1

AS THE STORM RAGING OUTSIDE VIOLENTLY shook
the airplane cabin, Ainsley Walker kept her eyes
focused on the touchscreen embedded in the seat in
front of her.

She was playing Gemcraft. The game was a
simple test of memory. Her task was to match the
ruby to the ruby, emerald to the emerald, opal to the
opal. It was made for the lobotomized. A pigeon
could've pecked its way to victory.

But it was keeping her mind off the disaster this
flight had become.

First had been the medical emergency in the
back row. Earlier in the flight, Ainsley had been
seated next to a heavy woman who'd suffered what
seemed to be a severe heart attack or stroke. Her
skin had turned a sickly yellowish-gray.

Ainsley had been asked to change seats, which is how she'd ended up here, in first class. Then the pilot had announced that the woman's illness was forcing an unscheduled stop at San Juan International Airport.

In Puerto Rico.

Ainsley had nothing against stopping on that island, but there were two problems with this scenario.

One, Ainsley really wanted to get home. Her previous gemstone adventures had left her professionally fulfilled but feeling as worn out as a two-month-old kitchen sponge. She had begun dreaming of the simpler pleasures in life. Two nights in a row in the same bed. Making a ham-and-cheese omelet for breakfast. A pedicure.

Two, an enormous weather system raging just outside the skin of this airplane, Hurricane Hannah, was threatening to pounce on the island. That could screw up everything once they landed.

Ainsley matched the final pair of emeralds on-screen, entered her initials for fastest time, and shut off the game. She tightened her seatbelt and stared up to the bulkhead, thinking. Before she'd been drawn into the world of gemstone investigation, her home life had seemed empty and dull.

Now she understood the allure of an ordinary existence. Home. It would be good to get back.

A soft voice interrupted her thoughts. "Excuse me, but do you mind if we talk?"

Ainsley turned her head. The woman sitting next to her was about Ainsley's age. The difference is that she was stunningly beautiful. She had been blessed with dark hair, glowing skin, a wide mouth, and almond-shaped eyes.

"What do you want to talk about?" said Ainsley.

"It doesn't matter. I just get really nervous flying in bad weather and talking helps me forget."

Ainsley could play along with that. "Sure, it helps me too. Where are you from?"

"New York. But my family is Puerto Rican."

"So this is a homecoming?"

She smiled, an explosion of white teeth and lip gloss. "Oh my *God*. I haven't been here in *years*. But being in Puerto Rico makes me so *happy*, even if it's only for a few minutes."

The woman had fixed Ainsley with her huge brown eyes, which were moistened at the edges. Ainsley felt her stomach sink. This woman wasn't merely beautiful. She was stupendously, jaw-droppingly, quiveringly gorgeous. A perfect ten.

"Thank you," she said.

"For what?" Ainsley replied.

"For talking to me," she said. "My family raised me to believe that everyone is a friend. I'm Amaryllis." She offered her hand.

Ainsley shook it. "I'm Ainsley Walker. Do you want to keep talking?"

"Do you?"

"Of course."

"Do you have a husband?"

Ainsley didn't especially want to go there. "Not really."

"Why 'not really'?"

Ainsley hemmed and hawed. "I don't know where he is."

3

Her seatmate's beautiful forehead crinkled in a look of concern. "I'm kind of confused."

"Me too. It's complicated."

Ainsley found herself starting to explain. How she referred to her ex-husband as The Legal Weasel. How she'd supported him all through his years in law school, after which he'd silently retreated backwards out of the marriage.

Eight months ago he'd totally disappeared. Ainsley didn't have a clue as to his whereabouts. They were still technically married, but their relationship had become like one of those light-as-a-balloon wartime marriages in which husband and wife lose gradually lose track of one another's whereabouts.

She hadn't wanted that kind of marriage, but she hadn't been in control. The Legal Weasel had held the reins. That was because she had cared more about the relationship than he had. It sounded contradictory but wasn't. The person who cares *less* controls the relationship. Ainsley knew that now.

When she finished, Amaryllis was nodding. "I'm divorced."

"What happened?"

"He cheated. We Puerto Ricans aren't supposed to lie to each other, but he didn't care."

That sounded painful, so Ainsley switched the subject. "So what do you do for a living?"

"Telecom sales." She shrugged. "It's a living. I didn't have to work when I was married. What about you?"

Here it goes. Ainsley took a deep breath. "I'm a gemstone detective."

It felt weird to speak the words out loud. Something in her still didn't believe that she had managed to eke out a living this way lately. The high four-digit figure in her bank account proved otherwise.

Her seatmate's face expressed shock—then excitement.

"That's incredible!" she said. "Tell me, how did you get such a job?"

"Mostly luck."

"You must know a lot about jewelry."

Ainsley shrugged. She didn't like tooting her own horn, but the answer to that question was an unqualified yes. She'd been obsessed with gemology as long as she could remember.

Suddenly Ainsley felt her stomach rise into her throat. The airplane had plunged again. This was going to be a rough landing. Amaryllis's hand gripped hers on the armrest.

The pilot's voice came onto the microphone. "Sorry for the turbulence, ladies and gentlemen. That was a little taste of what Hurricane Hannah has in store. Flight attendants, cross-check the doors for landing."

A short few minutes later, Ainsley felt the wheels touch down on the tarmac. It was a gentle landing. As the airbus rolled to a stop, Amaryllis lifted her arms into the air and screamed.

Ainsley heard a few others do the same.

Her seatmate leaned over. "Natives always cheer when we land. It's an island tradition."

Then she touched Ainsley's hand again. "Welcome to Puerto Rico. I just wish we could get off the plane for a few minutes."

2

Ainsley looked out the window. She could see an ambulance waiting next to a set of mobile stairs. She heard a commotion behind her, then glimpsed the heavy woman on a gurney. She was being loaded into the ambulance. A minute later, it tore off.

Case closed. Ainsley waited for the doors to close, the airplane to back out. Nothing happened. Twenty minutes passed. There were signs of restlessness, small comments, conversation growing louder. The flight attendants wheeled the beverage cart down the aisle, hoping to bribe soda for peace.

"What do you think is happening?" asked Amaryllis.

"I don't know."

Forty minutes passed. The passengers were becoming audibly disgruntled now. A man's voice shouted about a passenger bill-of-rights.

At last the pilot's voice came onto the system. "Ladies and gentlemen, this is your captain. As you know, this was supposed to be a temporary stop on our way to Miami. But Hurricane Hannah is arriving sooner than anticipated, and the authorities here at San Juan International have decided to close the airport."

There was a loud outcry from everyone cabin.

"I hear you," the pilot continued, "and I've just spent fifteen minutes arguing with traffic control. They are adamant. They've locked down the tarmac. We were the last flight in."

Ainsley looked around. Other passengers were throwing their arms into the air. Some were swearing loudly.

"We understand that this is a massive inconvenience," the captain was saying, "and please rest assured that this airline is going to make every effort to make your stay in San Juan pleasant. The gate agents are contacting hotels as we speak. We will get you more information just as soon as we have it. In the meantime, let's begin to deplane."

Ainsley looked at her seatmate. "You got your wish."

Amaryllis was already on her telephone. "I know, it's great, right? I should call my relatives. They are going to be surprised to see me."

Ainsley gathered up her belongings and dumped them into her bag. Her spirits were murderously low. She felt like a garbage can.

A few minutes later, she was stumbling down the narrow extended gangplank, the thin floor creaking underfoot, the low ceiling mere inches above her head. She was also feeling dirty and sticky. She'd slept in her makeup, which was always a reliably lousy way to begin her day.

The only thing making her feel somewhat human right now was her favorite handbag, a white Marc Jacobs number with killer hardware, slung over her shoulder. It went everywhere with her.

The hallway emptied out into the terminal. The rest of the passengers were milling around with reddened eyes, pecking or barking angrily at their mobile phones. Two gate agents had phones cradled between their shoulders and ears, waving away the passengers who periodically assaulted them with questions.

This was going to be ugly, Ainsley guessed. Finding over two hundred hotel rooms in San Juan on an hour's notice was probably a difficult assignment on a normal day. She imagined how much more difficult it would be under threat of an impending hurricane.

"This is going to take hours," moaned a woman.

"If we're sleeping here tonight," said another, "I'm taking the best seats right now." She dropped her bag and coat across the only three seats without armrests.

Outside the angry scrum, Ainsley found an open piece of railing and stared out the window at the tarmac. The sky was dark gray, even though it was only seven in the morning. The palm trees were bent like parentheses in the tropical gales.

The gate agent clicked onto the speaker. "Ladies and gentlemen of flight four-five-seven-zero from Buenos Aires, thank you for your patience. We are attempting to locate hotel rooms for each and every one of you. We will let you know as soon as those arrangements are made, so please be patient, and stay near the gate so that you do not miss our announcement."

The gate agent began to repeat the announcement in Spanish. Ainsley looked over. The angry knot of passengers had relented slightly, backed away from the desk. Ainsley felt a little sorry for the gate agents. They were swinging torches against an angry mob.

This was looking grim.

Then Ainsley felt a hand on her forearm. It belonged to Amaryllis. "They're never going to find enough hotel rooms for us before the hurricane hits," she said.

"How do you know?"

"I just called my aunt and uncle. They live here in San Juan. They said that many of the hotel workers won't leave their houses in bad weather. And country people check into the rooms too because their homes are too flimsy."

"So what are you saying?"

"You should come with me."

Ainsley lowered her eyes. "I really couldn't do that."

"No, you must. Please. Do you really want to spend the night on the floor of the terminal like most of these people?"

"Shouldn't you ask them first?"

The beautiful woman looked at Ainsley as though she were stupid. "They're *family*. We don't even need to ask."

"But I'm not—"

The seatmate put her hand on Ainsley's forearm again. "You *talked* to me on the plane—talked like we had known each other for years. I *like* that. Come with me." She paused. "I trust you, Ainsley."

I trust you. Ainsley looked at her. The cynical part of her was wondering if perhaps this woman was a lesbian, that she was treating Ainsley's vulnerability in this hurricane as a pickup opportunity, a piece of amazing sexual serendipity. That would explain the divorce too. Truth be told, if Ainsley were to cross over to the other side of the field, she couldn't ask for a more gorgeous welcome.

But Ainsley didn't think that was likely. Amaryllis just seemed to be the rarest of birds—an authentically warm and generous person.

Ainsley wasn't used to this. After all, she'd grown up saddled with a grim Puritan heritage. A stepfather who had never offered more than a handshake. A Methodist aunt who spent an hour every morning in sober Bible study. A cousin so straight edge that he turned his nose up at beer-battered fish tacos.

She looked back at the agents' desk. The angry scrum had surrounded it. She could hear the voices rising, could see the hackles raised, could feel the anger. This wasn't going to end nicely.

Ainsley knew her answer. "Okay. Let's go."

The beautiful woman clapped. "Excellent. First I have to rent a car." Then she beamed another blinding smile. "I can't *wait* to introduce you to my family, Ainsley."

That settled the question. This woman wasn't a predator. She was just a living, breathing, walking piece of evidence for the existence of good karma.

3

THE RAINSTORM BEGAN BEATING THE WINDSHIELD almost from the moment they left the airport.

The two women were parked on a congested freeway that, truth be told, felt a lot like any ordinary rush-hour highway back home.

In the passenger seat of the sedan, Ainsley sat hypnotized by the car's windshield wipers as they performed their rhythmic dance. She listened to the tires slish through the deep puddles at intersections. She watched the arcs of water fling themselves out of the wheel wells on either side of the car like iridescent fish leaping out of buckets.

Amaryllis was at the wheel, talking excitedly. "I used to spend all my summers here with my relatives. Look, see those?" She pointed at a lagoon, on the other side of which rose a row of high-rise towers out of the dark grey mist. "That's Condado. It's where the tourists go, to the casinos, the clubs. The parties there are amazing."

Ainsley nodded. She couldn't see much more than vague shapes through the rain. "It feels a lot like America."

"That's because Puerto Rico is part of America," said the woman. "This is a territory. They use the U.S. dollar. They drive all the same cars. Most of them speak English perfectly."

"So what's the difference, really?"

Amarylis thought about that. "I don't know. Probably the tropical weather. They don't really have political representation. But they don't have to pay any taxes either."

It sounded to Ainsley like Puerto Rico existed in a gray area—it wasn't a U.S. state, but it wasn't independent either. She guessed that there were benefits to being suspended in the middle.

Ahead, a group of people scurried across the overpass, holding jackets over their heads.

"The hurricane is supposed to hit at midnight," said Amaryllis. "I wonder where all these people are going to be."

Ainsley shook her head. "I'm wondering where *we're* going to be."

"That's easy. We'll be at my aunt and uncle's house in Santurce. They have extra rooms."

"What's Santurce?"

"The best neighborhood in San Juan."

"The rich area?"

"No, but it's the best."

"Why?"

Her friend chewed on her lip. "I don't know, Santurce just feels *real*. So full of color. You'll see."

Amaryllis turned off the freeway onto a moderately-sized city boulevard. Then she turned onto a narrow side street that led into a neighborhood, one whose history revealed itself in its three-quarters scale. There were older homes built of masonry in a vernacular style, small multifamily units constructed of stucco, narrow sidewalks, and tiny street-level *tiendas*. But the streets were mostly empty.

"Here we are," said Amaryllis. "Parking is so easy today. Normally it takes fifteen minutes."

She picked an open space along the curb, pulled in, and turned off the engine. "You don't have an umbrella?"

"No."

"Me neither. Here, I took some magazines from the plane. Let's use these. It's the old-fashioned way." She handed Ainsley an in-flight shopping catalog.

Holding the magazine over her head, Ainsley stepped out of the car. Even with a hurricane bearing down somewhere offshore, the climate felt blissful. Puerto Rico had the type of tropical ambience that made walking through rain fun.

She followed Amaryllis up the hilly street, hopping across puddles of water, avoiding overflowing sewer grates, leaping away from the runnels of water that cascaded down the steepest parts. Black cans overflowing with trash lay tipped over next to broken curbs. The decay was obvious, but Ainsley sensed that decades ago, Santurce had probably been a colorful place.

The street levelled off, the concrete turned to cobblestones, and soon they had stumbled into a plaza. Bars and restaurants ringed the perimeter, their green wooden slatted doors closed and locked tightly against the weather.

"This is La Placita de Santurce," said her guide. "And that is the *mercado*."

In the center of the plaza stood a gorgeous two-story West Indian-style building, painted a deep eggplant, with elaborate cream trim and deep eaves, underneath which was a ring of countertops. Each one had a corrugated metal gate pulled down tightly across it. A high, wide doorway welcomed shoppers inside, but that was closed too.

"That's a grocery store?" Ainsley said.

"Yes, but nobody will be there today. Do you need to use the bathroom?"

"No."

"I'll be right back. Wait here."

Amaryllis ran off towards a corner of the plaza. Ainsley found shelter underneath one of the eaves.

She was startled by the sound of rolling metal behind her. A man had just pulled up one of the open-air bars.

"Are you opening today?" she said.

"Of course," he replied. He had a gap between his teeth when he smiled.

"But the hurricane?"

He waved it off. "We'll be fine. The hurricane always teases us, then turns aside. Puerto Rico is like the girl who never gets asked to dance. It's your first time to our island?"

"Yes."

He nodded. He reached under the counter and produced a tiny plastic cup. He filled it with a clear liquid, then used a pair of tweezers to drop three dark coffee beans into the cup. He handed it to her.

"*Salud*," he said. "It's Paloma. Welcome."

Ainsley lifted the small cup to her nose. The liquor smelled like licorice. She wasn't in the mood for drinking. It wasn't even noon yet. But the first rule of travelling is to never refuse a gift.

"Thank you."

She tilted the small cup backwards. She could taste the anise flavor, feel the burning as it scorched down her throat. It did leave a pleasant warming sensation in her belly.

"Did you like it?"

"I don't know."

"It'll taste better the second time." He filled up another small cup and handed it to Ainsley.

She drank it again and set down the cup. She could feel the liquor hitting her knees. "At least the hurricane is going to be more fun now."

The bartender shook his head. "No hurricane. This island will be fine. Watch, you'll see."

Ainsley turned around and rested her elbows on the bar and gazed out at the small plaza. Raindrops bounced off the empty café tables. Four enormous bronze sculptures of avocados stood nearby.

"This plaza is very popular on Friday nights," said the bartender. "You should come back to-night."

Ainsley was about to answer when she saw Amaryllis approaching, her long legs moving aggressively across the plaza. This woman had the potential to be a real maneater.

"You making friends already?" she said.

Ainsley jerked a thumb at the bartender. "He says the hurricane isn't going to hit the island."

Amaryllis looked at the bartender, who lifted an eyebrow and hoisted a glass. "*Mucho gusto,*" she said.

"The pleasure is all mine," he replied. Then he reached under the counter and produced another tiny plastic cup. He began to unscrew the bottle of anisette. "Please, join us."

"Now?" said Amaryllis, glancing at the cup. "With that hurricane coming?"

"No hurricane. You'll see."

She took Ainsley by the arm and peeled her off the bar. "My aunt and uncle are expecting us."

"Come back tonight," said the bartender. "Friday night, La Placita. The best party on the island."

"No one will be coming tonight," said Amaryllis.

She steered Ainsley across the plaza. "You have to be more careful than that. The drinking can get out of control here."

"Really?"

"You don't know our reputation?"

Ainsley shrugged in ignorance. "No."

"Nobody parties like a Puerto Rican. *Nobody.* Come on, it's only one more block."

Ainsley was still thinking about that as they walked up the street towards Amaryllis' family's house.

4

THE RAINFALL HAD STOPPED, BUT HEAVY gray clouds still blanketed the sky.

Ainsley stood next to Amaryllis. Before them stood a modest home with a wide front porch. A knee-high basketball hoop in red, yellow, and blue stood against the fence in the front yard. A high wrought-iron fence surrounded the property. A hinged gate in the middle was the only point of entry.

In the yard, a man stood on a ladder against the side of the house. He was hammering sheets of plywood over the windows.

"Uncle Tomás!" shouted Amaryllis.

The man looked over, then smiled broadly. He stepped down the ladder and walked across his yard towards the gate. The wrinkles on his face indicat-

20

ed that he was about retirement age. He carried a heavy paunch in the front of his abdomen that suggested a lifetime of eating fried Caribbean food.

"Amaryllis, what a blessing," he said. "It's a double-edged sword."

She nodded. "I know, right? There was a medical emergency onboard, and now the airport won't let us leave."

Her uncle opened the gate and they hugged each other.

"How long has it been?" he said.

"Three years," said Amaryllis.

He shook his head disapprovingly. "I know, I know," she said. "But I've been so busy with the job and the divorce. I was planning to visit soon anyways, I swear. Is Aunt Luisa home?"

He tilted his head towards the house. "She's inside on the telephone. With Doña Pilar."

Amaryllis opened her mouth in surprise. "That *vieja* is still alive?"

"Ninety-three years old."

"Is she still living in that old plantation house? Out in Caguas?"

Uncle Tomás nodded. "She'll never leave. She is there until she dies." Then he noticed Ainsley. "Who is this?"

"My friend. She sat next to me on the airplane. She has no place to go either."

Her uncle reached out, grasped Ainsley's hand, then kissed her briefly on the cheek. "I am Tomás."

She kissed his cheek in return. "Ainsley Walker."

"You've never been to our island?"

"It's my first time."

"Usually it's more pleasant than this," he said, gesturing to the dark, stormy sky.

"I believe it," she said.

The rain began to fall more heavily. Ainsley's magazine was now a soggy mess in her left hand. He was still holding her right hand.

"That damned storm," he said. "I'd be happier with blue skies and humidity. Let's go inside."

He let go of her hand. The handshake had lasted for ten seconds. At first Ainsley had thought that he was sweet on her. Now she was understanding a bit better. Puerto Ricans were totally kinesthetic.

The front door opened as they came up the front walk. Out stepped a small, heavy woman with reddish hands. Her head was tilted sideways, a mobile phone crooked between her ear and her shoulder. She was listening, occasionally nodding, humming, tossing out bits of Spanish slang.

To Ainsley's eye, she seemed annoyed with the person on the other end of the phone. Peeved usually sounds peeved, no matter what language.

Finally the woman said goodbye. She ended the connection and threw the phone against the door. "*Ay bendito.*"

"Luisa, what's wrong?" said Tomás.

"That woman has lost her mind."

"Who?"

Her fists clenched. "That old woman needs to die. It would save everybody a lot of problems."

Tomás quickly put his arm around his wife and changed the subject.

22

"Luisa," he said, "you remember my niece."

His wife's mood changed. Her face brightened. "My favorite flower."

The two women hugged each other for several seconds. Ainsley noticed that, even after separating, Amaryllis and Luisa continued touching each other, on the wrists, elbows, shoulders, waists.

"And her friend," said Tomás. "Ainsley Walker."

Twice now, Ainsley had been introduced as a friend. She was a bit surprised at this. Then that thought was almost literally squeezed out of her, as the aunt had wrapped her arms around Ainsley and was crushing her like an anaconda. This woman was a human-shaped piece of coiled muscle.

The aunt stepped back. She beamed at the two of them. "You two are such beautiful young women."

Panting, Ainsley thanked her, but inside she felt a pang of regret. She really wasn't *that* young any more. Her thirtieth birthday was only a few months away. And though she did know all the feminine beauty tricks, she also knew that she looked about as attractive as a grouper fish standing next to Amaryllis.

"Our electricity just went out," said Luisa. "Let's sit on the porch instead and wait for the news."

They offered Ainsley a seat on a plastic lawn chair, which she accepted. On the other end of the porch, Tomás was stuffing a large group of dark tubers into a burlap sack.

Amaryllis leaned forward. "What are you doing, Uncle Tomás?"

"Well," he said, "if the hurricane hits, we won't have food shipments for a week. I had to go to the *mercado* at five in the morning. Before the crowds. Look."

He tossed a tuber at Amaryllis. She handed it to Ainsley. It felt cool and rough to the touch.

"*Yautia*," he said. "Could you hand me the *quenepas*?" He pointed to an array of fruits on the windowsill.

Ainsley was nearest to the window. "Which ones are those?"

"The green ones."

A dreamy look had entered Amaryllis' eyes. "They look exactly like I remember."

Ainsley passed them across the porch. When she was finished, Aunt Luisa brought out a tray of four plastic cups. Inside each was a reddish-orange liquid. "Do you like acerola juice?"

"I don't know," said Ainsley, "I've never tried it."

"Please try."

She accepted a cup and drank the liquid. It was tart but cool on her tongue and tasted a lot like the disks of vitamin C that she'd eaten as a child.

"It's delicious."

Aunt Luisa nodded, then sat down in her rocker with a sigh. She looked out at the soggy yard, at the raindrops bouncing against the cement beyond. "Can you believe Doña Pilar asked him to drive out to Caguas?" she said, hitching a thumb towards her husband. "Tonight? With a hurricane coming?"

"What does she want?" said Amaryllis.

"To protect her windows. Her handyman isn't answering her phone call. Now she wants Tomás to do it instead." Luisa shook her head. "It's an hour away on a good day. But today—who knows?"

Tomás cinched the sack of vegetables and joined the women. "That house is doomed anyways. A strong morning dew will collapse it."

All of these people were strangers to Ainsley. She felt as if she were eavesdropping. This shouldn't be any of her business.

Amaryllis noticed her discomfort. "Doña Pilar is a distant relative of my family. She lives on a very old plantation-style house up near the mountains."

"We don't like her," said Luisa.

"*Luisa*," said Tomás.

"Admit it, she's terrible."

Tomás took a softer approach. "The real problem, Ainsley, is that her house isn't safe in a hurricane. But she won't leave."

Luisa sighed again. "It's been in her family forever. She'll never let go."

"You don't have to go tonight," said Amaryllis.

"I don't want him to," said Luisa. "And now she's complaining about something else."

"What?"

Luisa rolled her eyes. "Somebody stole something from her. I think she said it was a pearl brooch."

That sounded about right, thought Ainsley. It was a very grandmotherly piece of jewelry. Nobody under the age of seventy voluntarily pinned brooches onto her blouse any more.

"She said it was very valuable," said Luisa. "She said it was an heirloom with great historical meaning for Puerto Rico. She says a lot of things."

A hand touched Ainsley on her forearm. It was Amaryllis. Her eyes were shining again. Ainsley knew what she was thinking.

"No," said Ainsley.

"Why not?"

"Because I want to get home."

Amaryllis ignored her. "Aunt Luisa, I have an idea."

"Tell me."

"I think Ainsley should help Doña Pilar."

5

At first, the aunt and uncle didn't compre-
hend. Their eyes were light but curious, demanding
explanation. Ainsley really didn't want to give it to
them. She was starting to regret this little jaunt.

"How can Ainsley help her?" said Luisa.

Amaryllis cleared her throat. "She is a gemstone detective."

"Really?"

Ainsley lowered her head. It was still embarrassing to boast about her career. She found it
hard to meet their eyes.

"Yes, it's true," she finally said. "I find lost gemstones."

Tomás pulled up a plastic chair and sat down.
He was leaning towards Ainsley with his elbows on
his knees and his eyes staring at her.

"What type of gemstones do you find?" he asked.

"Whatever people ask me to find."

"Such as?"

She shrugged. "I just came from Argentina. I found a necklace for a famous soccer player."

A screwdriver fell from Tomás' fingers and clattered on the floor. "*El Mono*?"

"Yes."

His eyes were bugged out. "I just heard about that. It was on the radio."

Ainsley nodded. Twenty-four hours earlier she had been in Buenos Aires, speaking to members of the Latin American media, describing the secrets of the *guerra sucia* that she had uncovered during her pursuit of Ovidio Angeletti's rhodochrosite necklace. And she'd been headed back to the States when the flight had been diverted to San Juan.

"Very interesting," said Luisa, sizing up her visitor with new eyes.

Amaryllis was surprised too. "*El Mono*?" she said. "You helped him?"

"I did."

A wicked smile crept across her beautiful face. She leaned over and whispered: "My friend slept with him. She said he's terrible in bed."

Neither of those statements surprised Ainsley. But she didn't want to talk about Argentina, or necklaces, or gemstones any more. She just wanted to get back home. A bed, an omelet, and a pedicure had been calling her.

Tomás had different plans. "I am going to take you to see Doña Pilar."

Ainsley held up her hands. "No, I'm not here to work."

He shook his head. "*Escúchame*. We will go together. I will hammer her boards to the windows. You will sit inside and discuss her missing pearl brooch. Make her feel better. She'll probably fall asleep before you finish talking."

Ainsley tried to figure out a respectful way to bow out. "You know, I don't think she would want to talk. Look at me. I'm dirty and disgusting."

"Look," said Tomás, "you don't have anything else to do. The airport is closed. You can't even go to the beach."

"And she has some money," added Amarylis.

Ainsley was scrambling for excuses. "But what about the hurricane? It could hit while we're on the road. Thank you, but it's too dangerous."

In response, Tomás reached over to a small transistor radio on the windowsill and snapped it on. It looked about half a century old. "This is my best friend when I'm working in the garden out-side. Can you believe it still functions? It was my father's."

He twisted the tuning knob. Ainsley listened to the white noise issuing from the speaker. Finally he found a station. A staticky voice became audible.

Everybody leaned in, listening closely. Ainsley had good Spanish skills, but over the hammering rain and the shitty sound quality, she couldn't under-stand very much at all.

A moment later, Tomás and Luisa suddenly threw their hands into the air and cried out. It was a happy sound.

"What did he say?" asked Ainsley.

"The hurricane is turning north," said Amaryllis. "It's heading towards the Bahamas."

"It's going to miss us," said Luisa.

Ainsley thought about the bartender in La Placita de Santurce. He'd been right. Puerto Rico was the girl who never gets to dance.

"Wait, there's more," said Tomás. He was nearly pressing his ear to the radio. "The man says three to four days of heavy rains are expected. Heavy flooding anticipated in Carolina, Isla Verde, and San Juan International Airport." He looked at Ainsley. "It's closed until at least Tuesday."

Ainsley felt her stomach plummet. That was four days away.

The beautiful seatmate from the airplane put her hand on Ainsley's knee. "See, it's like fate. You were meant to see Doña Pilar."

Tomás jumped in. "At the very least, come see her property. It's amazing. I can do my work, you can chat with her, and then we'll come right back here tonight."

Ainsley felt three pairs of eyes waiting for her response. All the doors had closed. She had been corralled.

She gave in. "Okay. I'll talk to her."

Tomás slapped Ainsley on the knee. "You're a good girl. I could feel it. Let me call her and tell her that we're coming."

The others stepped inside. Ainsley sat alone on the porch, watching the raindrops again. It was barely eleven o'clock in the morning.

She sipped her fruit juice, thinking. Resisting the natural flow of events was futile. She had to ride the horse in the direction it wanted to go. And if this horse wanted to carry her through a Caribbean rainstorm towards a cranky woman who wanted to bitch about her missing pearl brooch, then so be it.

Tomás stepped out onto the porch again. "It's all set. Doña Pilar wants to meet you. We should leave now, so we can return before the big rains tonight."

Ainsley stood up, resigned to her fate. Amaryllis launched herself through the door and wrapped herself around Ainsley. When she pulled back, there were tears in her eyes. Ainsley was starting to sense that she was a highly emotional person.

"I knew that I could trust you," said Amarylis.

Ainsley shrugged. "Thanks, but it's not like I'm saving the world."

"Tell me all about Doña Pilar when you come back tonight."

"I will."

On her way out of the house, Ainsley looked back. Amaryllis and her aunt had linked arms around one another's waists, waving happily.

To Ainsley's sensibility, this was an odd send-off, especially for a stranger. After all, she was only leaving for a few hours. Soon she would return, and after that she would be back on an airplane.

But there was one thing she hadn't counted on. An old saying.

Life is what happens when you're busy making other plans.

Caguas

6

A HALF HOUR LATER, AINSLEY WAS in the passenger seat of Tomás' pickup truck. They were headed south.

She stared out the side window at the rain dancing across the freeway, towards the green hills cloaked in a silver veil of rain and mist.

Tomás drove easily. His left hand rested casually on the top of the steering wheel, his right hand hooked around a thermos. "These *vaguadas* are too much," he said. "Even before this week, it's been the wettest year in our history."

"Really?"

"San Juan was always drier than the west side. It rains there constantly. And El Yunque too, of course—that mountain range is wetter than the ocean. But for us in the capital, all this rain is new."

"What do you think it means?"

He shrugged. "I guess the climate is changing."

Ainsley thought about that. It seemed reasonable. As the atmosphere worked to absorb excess carbon dioxide emissions during the last century, some parts of the world were growing drier, and other parts were growing wetter. San Juan was becoming one of the wet spots.

"So you should know something else about Doña Pilar," Tomás said.

"What's that?"

"You can't speak English to her."

"Okay."

"You speak some Spanish?"

"*Claro.*"

Tomás nodded. "You'll need more Spanish than that, though."

Ainsley knew that he meant well, but Tomás had little idea of the struggles she'd just endured in South America, not only in bringing her Spanish up to speed but also in adjusting to the unusual idioms and usages found only in that region. In fact, Ainsley felt like she'd just emerged from a linguistic war.

By contrast, being here in Puerto Rico, where everyone spoke both a more familiar Spanish and good old American English, felt like slipping into a warm bath. But she didn't want to sound cocky.

Instead, Ainsley just said, "Don't worry, I'm good."

"There is something else too," he said. "I don't like to be very direct about unpleasant things, but we don't have much time."

"I'm listening."

He looked uncomfortable. "Doña Pilar has ... a reputation."

"For what?"

"Being snobby."

Ainsley wasn't surprised. Luisa had already said that nobody liked her. "Is it because she's rich?"

"No, she's not that rich." He clenched his fingers around the steering wheel. "She thinks she's Spanish."

"You mean from *España*."

"Yes, correct. I'll give you an example." He held out his arm. "Look at my skin. Would you call me white?"

Ainsley looked at him. He was tanned, olive-skinned, slightly swarthy.

"You're a little darker."

"Of course. We call this *trigueño*. Many Puerto Ricans look like this. But not Doña Pilar." He laughed. "She's whiter than milk and proud of it. Watch, you'll see."

"So how are you related?"

"Very distantly. There is no shared blood. She's my wife's great aunt. All the others between us have passed away. Now Luisa is the only family she has left." He squinted ahead, trying to peer through the raindrops. "Here it is."

He turned onto a four-lane surface street and drove the truck through a commercial area. Ainsley saw broken-down storefronts flashing past the window. Long-dead restaurants. Auto repair yards advertising with hand-painted signs and piles of tires in the weed-choked lots.

Then the commercial center gave way to a rural landscape, with more rolling hills. Tomás slowed the vehicle to navigate across a low-lying piece of road that had already flooded. She heard the water sloshing up against the undercarriage.

Then he accelerated again, and a few minutes later turned the truck onto a two-track dirt road. It was lined with tall silk cotton trees, their smooth, bare trunks at least forty meters high. Each was crowned with a spray of red branches at the top, like nature's biggest matchsticks.

Beneath them, the truck bounced and jutted over the road.

"I see why you didn't want to come out here," said Ainsley.

"Doña Pilar won't live anywhere else," he said, "and there is nobody to take care of her. Look, do you see that tree?" He pointed at a branch with dangling seedpods. "Those are called women's tongues because they always whisper as you pass by them. It sounds like gossip."

Ainsley smiled at that one. Then the road careened around a bend, and she forgot all about women's tongues, because Doña Pilar's house came into view.

It looked like it had been lifted out of the nine-teenth century. Ainsley guessed that it hadn't seen a coat of paint in almost that long.

It had been—and still barely was—a classic plantation-style structure. The porch boasted a white trellis-style railing that engulfed the front door. On the upper floor, a row of four shuttered doors opened onto a long, narrow balcony. That

36

was the best that could be said for the place. The house was made entirely of wood, and the white paint had peeled off in huge sickening strips, exposing the gray, weather-beaten boards below.

"It survived the 1928 hurricane," said Tomás. "I don't know how. Doña Pilar says that she slept all the way through the storm."

"But it's all wood."

He shrugged. "I tell Doña no candles in the house."

"You could charge admission," she said.

Tomás nodded thoughtfully. "After she passes away, we're going to turn it into an eco-lodge. Or maybe a museum."

"Good idea. Is she okay with that?"

"She doesn't care. All she wants to do is die."

He parked the truck and stepped out into the grass. Ainsley followed. She inhaled deeply. The fresh, tangy smell of wet greenery engulfed her senses. She listened to tiny sounds of rain dripping from the red leaves of the royal poinciana flowers that dotted the ground.

"Wait here," said Tomás.

He shuffled across the grass, head down. This was a chore for him. Ainsley watched him step onto the porch. He gingerly pressed the sole of his left boot onto a board before the front door. It held. Then he did the same with more pressure.

"Okay," he said. "Somebody fixed this one."

She joined him. He rapped on the front door. Ainsley quickly ran her fingertips along the lintel. It felt rough, old, textured.

"I painted this house thirty years ago," he said. "Nobody's touched it since."

They waited for a minute. Nothing was moving within the house. He stepped back and cupped his hands around his mouth. "*Doña Pilar, es Tomás. Abra la puerta.*"

Ainsley waited. From inside, she heard a tiny voice, almost imperceptible. Then there was nothing.

"I think she said something," Ainsley said.

"She's probably in bed," said Tomás. "Ninety-three years old, you know? We'll just go inside."

He opened the shutters. Behind them stood the door, an imposing slab of wood with Spanish scrollwork. The doorknob had been placed in the center. It looked as though it had been imported from Madrid.

Ainsley hung slightly behind as he turned the doorknob. An unreasonable fear had gripped her heart. She couldn't explain it.

Her guide walked inside and was swallowed into the darkness. It was midday, but the dark rainclouds that rumbled and echoed overhead seemed to have blotted all the light out of her home.

"Ainsley," said Tomás, "come inside."

Tensed and anxious, Ainsley put a hesitant foot into Doña Pilar's house.

7

OUT HERE IN THE LUSH FIELDS, blanketed beneath the impending thunderstorm, Ainsley felt like she was in the dying end of twilight. Ordinary objects took on supernatural overtones in the gloaming.

Ainsley took a deep breath and stepped into the plantation house. Even with the windows open, the front room was mostly dark, and the damp smell of rain wafted into her nostrils. She waited for her eyes to adjust.

Soon she glimpsed the outlines of things from the corners of her eyes. A tatty lace curtain fluttering. A Spanish credenza against the wall.

These things vanished when viewed directly. It was hard to believe that it was barely noon.

"Don't worry," said Tomás. He was merely a voice in the darkness. "I know this house like I know my own children."

"Can't you turn on the lights?" said Ainsley.

"There aren't any lights. Doña Pilar prefers it this way." He lowered his voice. "I told you, she is very difficult. Oh look, here is a picture of her family."

He pointed to a mounted sepia photo of a crowd of stiff, unhappy looking white people. If that's what nineteenth-century Spanish colonists looked like, Ainsley was glad she'd been born in twentieth-century America.

Tomás began walking deeper into the darkened house. Ainsley followed him by listening to the floorboards squeaking beneath her shoes. The light had almost completely disappeared now. She dragged her fingertips along the bare wall to her left, feeling the tiny splinters of wood stabbing into her fingertips like small blunt daggers.

"Doña Pilar's bedroom is on the second floor," said Tomás. "We're going to go up the stairs on your left."

Her left hand found the banister, and she circled around the endpost and began climbing the stairs. Each stair was very narrow and shallow. One of Ainsley's most embarrassing features was her large feet. On this staircase, she had to turn her feet diagonally.

Tomás was waiting for her when she arrived at the top. She could hear the timber creaking. It sounded like an old-school roller coaster. It didn't feel particularly safe up here.

"Are you doing okay?" he whispered.

"I'm fine," said Ainsley.

"Good," he said. "Let me do the talking at first. Then I'll leave you alone with her while I work outside."

He crooked a finger and walked stealthily down the hallway to a decrepit but proud door. It stood as though daring the world to knock upon it.

Tomás did exactly that. He also switched to Spanish. "*Doña Pilar, estamos aqui para ayudar. ¿Puedo entrar?*"

Ainsley waited with baited breath. Behind the door, she heard the pustulent sound of someone loudly clearing her throat.

He gestured to Ainsley to stand beside him. She obeyed. Tomás wrapped his arm around her shoulders. Then he knocked again. "Doña Pilar, it's Tomás. I have a visitor for you."

There was more clearing of the throat. Then the voice finally sounded, as harsh as a machete swinging into a sugarcane stalk.

"Don't stand outside breathing like criminals. Come in."

The voice was delivered in perfect Castilian Spanish. Tomás pushed the door open, and Ainsley peered around the edge of the frame.

8

PROPPED IN THE MIDDLE OF A large Spanish-style four-poster bed was one of the oldest living humans that Ainsley Walker had ever seen.

Doña Pilar.

Her face was extraordinarily wrinkled. Her arms were laden with golden bracelets. She looked like one of those decayed skeletons that archaeologists have unearthed, the corpse of some former ruler still wearing the hoops and necklaces of a long-dead primitive civilization.

But her hair had been permed, and it was a bright lemon-blonde. She seemed like the type of woman who had dyed her hair into submission for so hard and for so long that even she had forgotten its true nature. A hand mirror, one of those gilded vintage ovals, lay on the bed within arm's reach.

Ainsley smiled. The old woman still enjoyed her moments of vanity.

Then she noticed Doña Pilar's eyes. They were green—an intense green, with heavy saturation, the type of color that seized you by the throat and challenged you to forget.

Then Ainsley tore her eyes away from the old woman's face and scanned her room. It felt like a shrine, lit by several candles flickering on the dresser and nightstand. A pair of cordoban chairs had been placed at the foot of the bed, their burgundy leather cracked with age.

Tomás stood between them with his feet planted far apart. He made no attempt to touch the old woman.

"Why did it take you so long?" gasped Doña Pilar.

"We drove from San Juan. Did you call Luis again?"

She frowned. "He isn't answering his phone."

"Luis is useless," replied Tomás. "There has to be somebody else you can hire."

Doña Pilar cackled, which quickly turned into a coughing fit. When it had passed, she said, "No, he needs me. I have an obligation to the lesser people. The humble people. The darker ones."

Ainsley cocked her head. She wasn't sure that she heard that last one properly. The *darker* ones? Here, on this island, where African, European, and natives had mixed freely for hundreds of years?

But the *faux pas* didn't even register on Tomás. Maybe it was like white noise by now. "There won't be a hurricane tonight," he said, "but there will be a

43

lot of rain and wind. Is there anything in particular that I should check?"

"Check everything."

"You still have the boards in the shed?"

"I don't know."

"I put them there two years ago."

"You have to ask Luis," she said, "only he knows." She paused. "You didn't have come out here to help me."

"It's my pleasure."

"No, it's not." Her eyes were a pair of fiery coals. "You and Luisa hate me. I can tell."

"Please, no, Doña, it's not true—"

The elderly woman waved her hand to silence him. He shifted his feet. For a moment, nobody dared to speak. The atmosphere was tense.

Ainsley found herself wanting to edge towards the door, regretting that she'd come. She had always imagined what happened to a person with a really difficult personality as she grew older. The answer was laying here, wrapped in a bejeweled nightgown and swaddled in hand-stitched quilts.

"Luisa told me you lost a piece of jewelry," said Tomás.

"I didn't lose it," she replied, "someone stole it."

"This is the woman that Luisa told you about on the phone. Finding lost gemstones is her specialty. She came to talk to you."

Ainsley felt the old woman's gaze sizzling up and down her body. She remained standing with her hands folded politely, waiting.

"What's her name?"

Tomás looked at Ainsley and nodded. That was the sign. Ainsley stepped forward and summoned her best formal Spanish.

"Doña Pilar," she said, "I am called Ainsley Walker."

Ainsley had to stop herself from curtseying. That was ingrained in her from a lifetime of watching Merchant-Ivory movies. She reminded herself that no matter how imperiously she acted, Doña Pilar wasn't royalty. She was just an old Puerto Rican woman lying in a dark house made of matchsticks.

"Ainsley Walker." The old woman's jaw began working itself. It looked like she was literally grinding the name into bits between her teeth. "Are you Puerto Rican?"

"No."

"Where is your family from?"

"The United States."

"Before that."

"I don't know."

The old woman looked at her sharply. "You don't know?"

"I'm a lot of different ethnicities."

"Spanish?"

"Maybe."

Doña Pilar softened. "Luisa likes you. Your accent is good."

Ainsley tried not to downplay that. "I do my best."

Meanwhile, she secretly felt vindicated. She had always prided herself on her ability to reproduce accents. In fact, languages had always come second nature to her, the conjugations, the idioms, the syntax. Over the years she'd dabbled in learning Spanish, Portuguese, Italian, French, Polish, Hungarian, Japanese, Tagalog, and Russian. Of course, she'd always shied away from German and Mandarin Chinese, but life was long. She probably could've had quite a career as a mimic, or an actor, but she didn't need that much public attention.

The bedroom door closed shut. Ainsley realized that Tomás had slipped out of the room. Now she was left alone with Doña Pilar.

"You can sit down," the old woman ordered. She was gesturing to one of the cordoban leather chairs.

Ainsley felt the subtle struggle for dominance in the room, the tide of power flowing between them. There was no point to it. The old lady had nothing to offer. In fact, there was only one thing that Ainsley really wanted right now, but it was the one thing nobody could give her.

A plane ticket home.

It was good to know that she held all the cards. Ainsley set her bag on the floor and settled into the chair. She leaned back, ready to listen. And maybe, if she felt so inclined, she might assist this elderly woman in her quest.

"Now," said Ainsley, "please tell me about the pearl brooch."

9

"My family came here from Spain three hundred years ago," Doña Pilar began. "We have always been pure Spanish."

"One hundred percent?" said Ainsley.

"Yes. We never mixed with the *negritos*, the *mestizos*, the *jabas*, the *grifas*. Just whites. Here, look at me. You can see it."

The old woman held up a bony hand. Ainsley glanced at it. It was covered in so many gnarled green blood vessels and brown liver spots that she couldn't tell.

"I guess you look white to me," said Ainsley.

"My first ancestor on the island was Francisco Fernando Cestero Cruz II. A very respectable man. He owned an *ingenio*, inherited from his father."

Ainsley didn't dare ask what that meant. She just played along as though it were a fact so obvious that it didn't even need acknowledging.

"This sugar mill was the pride of San Germán. He was carried around on a litter by the *negritos*. Like a king." A big smile came across her face as she pictured her ancestor in regal splendor on the shoulders of his slaves.

"And his wife was so beautiful. There was never another *peninsulare* as gorgeous as Don Francisco's wife."

"Is that so," said Ainsley.

"Yes. Are you going to write this down?"

She looked legitimately angry. Ainsley rummaged for a pad of paper in her bag, then began to take notes. She was feeling like a stenographer.

Doña Pilar hoisted herself up in bed. Her eyes were locked above her as though the myth had been written into the ceiling, and the stars, above. "Don Francisco went to Jamaica for his business. He returned home a month later and presented his wife with a gift."

"The pearl brooch," said Ainsley.

She nodded. "It was beautiful. And enormous. He had bought it from the captain of an English schooner who'd just returned from the South Pacific. It is one of the most beautiful pearls in the world."

"She was a lucky woman."

"Oh, and she deserved it. She was so light, so beautiful—"

Ainsley grew bored of this woman's boasting about the skin color of her dead ancestors. "Keep going. What happened?"

"It didn't stay hers for long. Olayinka heard about it."

The old woman looked at Ainsley. There was a wicked fire burning in her eyes. Ainsley got the distinct impression that she should be shivering in fright at the mention of that person's name. But she decided to play it straight.

"Who was Olayinka?"

The old woman's nostrils flared. "You don't know?"

"No."

"She was one of the most famous pirates of the Caribbean."

"Oh."

Doña Pilar leaned forward, lifted a finger, and whispered the next line: "She was a *black woman*."

Ainsley lifted an eyebrow. A black female pirate. She'd never heard of that one before. It was believable, of course, since black women had for centuries been more or less written out of the history books in every other imaginable way.

Doña Pilar continued. "She was an escaped slave who stole her master's ship and sailed everywhere, raiding the small settlements on the edges of this island. When she got to San Germán, she stole Don Francisco's wife's pearl brooch."

The old woman sat back on her pillows, her eyelids quivering, filled with anger at the old injustice against her ancestor.

"So what happened?"

The old woman lifted her water glass with a shaky hand, sipped from the rim, then set it back down. "Don Francisco was enraged. He sailed around the Caribbean for ten years tracking Olayinka. He finally found her on Vieques. And then"—her eyes met Ainsley's—"he killed her."

Doña Pilar pretended to run an imaginary sword through someone's belly. "My ancestor took back the pearl. It has never left the family since." A look of supreme vengeance or happiness came over her face. It was hard to see the difference.

"That's a good story," said Ainsley, "but it doesn't explain why I am here."

"Because," said Doña Pilar, "it has been stolen again."

10

"I AM AN OLD WOMAN," SAID Doña Pilar, "and I was never lucky enough to bear any children. Believe me, I wanted to."

"That's too bad," replied Ainsley.

"It's too bad for everybody," she said. "It's very important for us to lighten the race."

Ainsley felt the bile rising in her throat. Had she heard that right? Was this woman really that much of an unrepentent racist? Ainsley was regretting ever having paid her a visit.

"I don't have anybody to give the pearl brooch to. So I decided to donate it to the Ponce Museum of Art."

"That's very nice of you."

She shrugged. "My family is very important in the history of Puerto Rico. This is an important artifact. Its story needs to be told."

"I'm sure." Ainsley tried to keep her game face.

"So the museum officials came here last year. They agreed to display the pearl with the story as I have told it. And so I agreed to donate it."

"That was very nice of you."

"Of course," she said. "I'm a very agreeable person. So last week the driver from the museum arrived in a truck. We gave him the pearl. He placed it into a small box. He drove away."

"And then?"

"It never arrived."

Ainsley sat up a little straighter. "You mean he lost it?"

"The museum says he never arrived. The driver completely disappeared."

"That sounds like a problem for the police."

The old lady pretended to spit. "I don't believe the police. They're all so dark-skinned."

Ainsley had to lift her jaw back up to her skull. This was the total opposite of the complaints she'd grown up hearing in the United States.

"Are they investigating the disappearance?"

"They say they are investigating. I don't believe them." The old woman's green eyes burned into Ainsley's. "That's why I want to hire my own investigator." She lifted a bony finger and pointed at Ainsley. "That's why I want to hire you."

This was happening much too quickly. Ainsley stood up from the chair and retreated to the farthest corner of the room. "Doña Pilar, maybe you don't know, but I only arrived in Puerto Rico this morn-ing. It was an accident. I was flying back to the United States when there was a medical emergency. We were grounded in San Juan by the hurricane."

Doña Pilar waved her off. "Your sad story doesn't affect me."

"Yes, it does. Because I don't really want to work for you. I just want to go home. That's all."

A cunning look passed across the old woman's face. "I can help you do that."

Ainsley felt suspicious but interested. "How?"

"I know a pilot."

Ainsley crinkled her nose. That statement smelled vaguely like horse shit. "What's the name of this pilot?"

"Ivan Torregrosa."

That didn't smell too bad. She had answered quickly. Most liars required a couple seconds at least to fabricate something new.

"He'll take me to the mainland?"

"I'll call him to verify," said Doña Pilar, "but he can usually get to Miami in three hours. I'll make sure he takes you, as soon as the storm is cleared."

Ainsley pursed her lips. The offer that was hard to refuse, but she truly hadn't wanted to take on any assignment. She decided to play hardball.

"No," she said, "it's not enough."

"What do you mean?"

Ainsley turned sassy. "I don't really have to do this. I mean, I'm exhausted. I can sit in a resort somewhere and drink margaritas while this tropical storm blows over. Besides, your assignment seems frankly a little questionable."

The old woman's tongue snaked out and moistened her thin, dry lips. "Then what else do you want?"

Ainsley looked at her directly. "Money."

"How much?"

"What are you willing to pay?"

"Nothing."

"Then we don't have a deal."

Suddenly she knew that she'd spent enough time here. Talking to the old waxworks had been a favor to a friendly seatmate, but now she'd run out of patience.

Ainsley reached for her bag and began to walk towards the door. Doña Pilar reached both arms out towards her, the gold bracelets clinking. She looked a lot like a revivified mummy.

"Wait, wait," she said. "The museum has also offered a reward."

Ainsley stopped. "How much?"

"They told me three thousand dollars. To anybody who gave them the pearl brooch. But you can ask them yourself."

Ainsley sucked on the inside of her cheek. Three thousand dollars. That wasn't chump change. Truth be told, earning that would feel a lot better than sitting on a rainy balcony for a week, watching the ice melt in her margaritas, feeling mildew growing between her toes.

"Please help me."

Doña Pilar was looking at her imploringly, a wasted, skeletal apparition in a thin nightgown. Ainsley didn't like her personality one bit, especially not the stench of nineteenth-century racism. But

AN AINSLEY WALKER GEMSTONE TRAVEL MYSTERY

she did feel pity for anyone who'd survived the ravages of time. It was only natural.

Before Ainsley could answer, however, footsteps sounded on the floorboards outside the room. The door opened.

Tomás entered. His hair was plastered with water, and his shirt was soaked. "The rains are getting heavier. I covered as many windows as possible, but we have to go." He stood there, breathing, looking back and forth between the two women. "Is everything okay?"

"I was just telling Ainsley about the pearl brooch," said Doña Pilar. "I think she's interested in helping me."

"Are you?" said Tomás.

Ainsley looked at her shoes, feeling oddly embarrassed. "She's going to help me get home sooner."

"How?"

"A private pilot," said Doña Pilar.

Tomás lifted his eyebrows. "He'd better be good. Ladies, I'm ready to leave. Ainsley, are you coming with me?"

The old woman shook her head. "No, she's staying here."

Ainsley swiveled her head. "No, I'm not."

"I'm going to need you tomorrow. You have to meet Luis. He'll take you to Ponce to start the investigation."

"But only if the weather's cooperating."

"And if Luis is cooperating," muttered Tomás.

Doña Pilar ignored the comment. "You must stay here tonight, please. Tomorrow, start working."

Her eyes looked wide and frightened. Ainsley suddenly realized the words beneath the words. This old woman didn't want to be alone in her house during a rainstorm. She was just scared, plain and simple.

Tomás shrugged. "Doña Pilar is right. If you're going to Ponce tomorrow with Luis, it makes sense to stay here tonight."

Ainsley didn't relish the thought. A bird's nest would probably be a safer place to ride out a furious tropical storm than this house of ancient twigs. But she had always thrived on adventure.

Her decision was made. "I'm staying here," she said.

Tomás gestured to her. "Okay, but follow me downstairs. I'll show you how to seal up this place before the storm hits."

"Ainsley," said Doña Pilar.

"Yes?"

"Come see me later. I have a secret to tell you."

As Ainsley stepped out of the bedroom, she could feel the old woman's sharp green eyes blazing into her back.

11

SHORTLY BEFORE NINE O'CLOCK THAT NIGHT, Tropical Storm Hannah flung itself onto the island, and it was unlike anything Ainsley had ever experienced.

The weather system swung into Doña Pilar's ancient house with the strength of a wrecking ball. Wind and rain, rain and lightning, lightning and thunder, thunder and wind—the storm attacked with such intensity that it rattled the planked-wood walls and sent the doors shaking in their frames.

It was, more than anything, *loud*. It would have been impossible for Ainsley to hold a conversation, if anybody had been there worth speaking to.

Doña Pilar certainly hadn't been. She hadn't even been awake for most of the day. Ainsley had peeked into her bedroom once, but the old woman had been asleep, her mouth hanging open, her lemon-blond hair arranged like a meringue pastry on the pillow around her.

So Ainsley had spent part of the afternoon outside during breaks in the rain, traipsing through the property under the gathering storm clouds. She'd kicked her boots and socks off and danced barefoot through the grass, feeling like a little girl. She'd sniffed the bromeliads and touched the thick, rubbery leaves of the aloe vera plant. She'd gazed at the heavy white clouds that ringed the tops of the green mountains that surrounded the small darkened valley.

This was an astounding piece of land. It was purple and green, ripe and full. Ready to burst.

Then Ainsley had finished the tasks that Tomás had given her. Locking a few storage bins. Picking up tools from the yard. Securing loose furniture. It was sad that Doña Pilar had nobody to assist her with these basic things. Ainsley guessed that she had chased away everybody who had ever dared to love her.

Before darkness fell, Ainsley began to explore the interior of the house. She examined each and every room. Most were packed with Spanish an-tiques, and especially Spanish lace, which Doña Pilar couldn't seem to collect enough of.

In the living room she looked at the mildewed sepia family photograph once again. It showed eleven members of Doña Pilar's long-gone family. They were posed formally, the men in high collars, the women decked out in swathes of black lace. The severe faces were uniformly white.

Then Ainsley had discovered the library.

She'd felt like she was stepping into a scene from a classic novel. With the rain pelting the windows, Ainsley had lit a candle and looked at the spines of leatherbound volumes on the shelves, the soft light dancing against them. Tilting her head, she noticed that these titles were all about Puerto Rico. And they were all written in Spanish.

It was the perfect night for this type of journey. But Ainsley knew that she was going to stock up on some refreshments first.

She tiptoed downstairs to the kitchen. In a cabinet she found a jar of olives and a decent-looking piece of chorizo. In a nearby rack lay an old bottle of red wine. She opened the cork using a knife, found an acceptable glass, and carried everything back upstairs to the library.

There, she settled herself into a heavy leather chair, whose armrests were discolored and cracked. She arranged her legs underneath her, swaddled herself in a lacy quilt, then opened one of the books.

It was a history of the island. As Ainsley scanned the pages, she learned that the first inhabitants, the Taíno people, grew yams, maize, beans, squash, and manioc. They called their island *Borinquén*, which means "Island of the Brave Lord". To English they loaned the words *barbacoa* (barbeque), *tabaco* (tobacco), and *hamaca* (hammock).

Ainsley could guess what the Taíno priorities had been. Eating, smoking, sleeping. Humans hadn't really changed.

The Taíno had also coined the word *juracán*, which meant "god of the fierce winds". It wasn't hard to guess which English word came from that. A downgraded version of it was currently pounding the outside of the house.

Reading on, she learned that the Taíno also had a talent for being kidnapped, most especially by a violent tribe of people called the Carib, who lived on the nearby island of Hispañiola. In fact, Christopher Columbus had given a few Taíno a lift home from that island, which is how he came to land in an unknown bay somewhere on the western coast of the Puerto Rico in 1493. He christened the island San Juan Bautista.

Ainsley pictured the first landing. Columbus placing his silken foot on the sand. A crew member planting the flag—a long vertical banner with the royal Spanish insignia in red, and a pair of points flapping at the bottom.

Columbus ordered cattle to be sent to the island, then sailed off. For fifteen years, nothing happened. The Taíno let down their guard. They went back to their barbeque, tobacco, hammocks.

Then the Spaniards returned.

The story is sadly familiar. Seeking gold, the Europeans enslaved the Taíno and forced them to dig mines, which turned out to be a poor decision for everybody, since the island contained about as many precious metals as a watermelon.

Soon they shifted the Taíno to field labor, growing coffee, tobacco, sugarcane. That was a bust too. The natives were constitutionally unable to work. They missed their barbeques, tobacco, and hammocks.

Soon after that, all the Taíno were gone. They'd either died or fled. The Spaniards, famously averse to performing manual labor themselves, decided to begin importing their slaves from a different place.

Africa.

The storm was whipping the house even harder now. Doña Pilar had been asleep for hours and showed no signs of waking. Snuggling even deeper into her blanket, Ainsley reached onto the shelf and picked out another book.

12

Opening the second book, Ainsley learned that Puerto Rico was the highway rest stop for the *conquistadores*.

The map showed her why. It's the first major piece of land after the long ocean crossing from Europe. It was the perfect place to stop for a bath and a shave before heading onto Mexico and Peru, where the real riches lay.

The Spanish, however, weren't the only ones who needed a rest stop.

For almost four hundred years, the island withstood a constant series of raids by buccaneers from Netherlands, France, and England. They snatched cattle, vegetables, rum, and women from the unguarded settlements on the flanks of the island.

So the Spanish built El Morro, the heavy, imposing fort that draws tourists to San Juan today. It acted like the security guard who sits on a stool at the entrance to a jewelry store. There was no policing anything. Trying to control Caribbean ships was like herding grasshoppers.

By the eighteenth century, Puerto Rico had also become known as a sanctuary for black slaves escaping from nearby colonies. They often arrived in fine ships (stolen from their masters) and dressed in the finest silk (also stolen).

But there was backlash. Some families endured ludicrous trials known as *limpieza de sangre* ("blood purification") to prove that no African blood flowed in their veins. This would entitle the family members to marry into another "pure" family.

To Ainsley, all this sounded ominously similar to the famous brown bag test in New Orleans. There, if your skin were darker than a lunch sack, you weren't welcome inside certain fraternities.

But things soon got even worse for the black residents. The Spanish passed a *codigo negro* (black code) in 1848 that targeted the *prietos*. Under the new rules, blacks could be sent to prison for five years for "verbal abuse" of whites. Any black person who used a weapon to injure a white person could be executed.

Ainsley laid down the book. Her stomach felt sour. She couldn't tell whether it was from the wine or the stories of oppression.

Then a small sound caught her attention. Outside the door, there was the sound of floorboards creaking.

She put the book down and listened closely. There it was again. A low scrape, one that was distinct from the thousands of other screeches and scritches, rattles and rasps that the storm was throwing at the house.

Ainsley stood up and opened the library door. She found herself looking into the bony face of Doña Pilar. She was holding a shaky candle.

"What are you doing?" the old woman said.

"Reading."

Her eyes flicked past Ainsley into the room, as if to verify. "Those books were my grandmother's."

"I won't hurt them."

"I need to tell you the secret."

"Okay."

Her bony hand grasped Ainsley's forearm. It was ice-cold. Ainsley tried not to flinch.

"When you begin to investigate," the old woman said, "don't speak to the *prietos*. They will not help you."

The *prietos* were the dark-skinned Puerto Ricans. Ainsley tried to keep from rolling her eyes. "Thank you," she said.

But Doña Pilar wasn't finished. "If you do have to speak to them, and if you they give any trouble, there is a way out."

"Really."

The candle trembled in Doña Pilar's hand. "Tell them that you are working for me."

"For you?"

"Oh yes," she said proudly, "they know me. After all, I've helped so many. It's my duty because they can't rule themselves. They need our tutelage."

Ainsley felt her stomach churn. That was hideously familiar to her American ears. Doña Pilar sounded like a Southern paternalistic nineteenth-century bullshitter, sipping a mint julep on her front porch somewhere in deepest, darkest Mississippi. The only thing missing was a seersucker suit.

Ainsley struggled to think of a diplomatic response. "You have an interesting point of view."

Doña Pilar nodded wisely. "I turned down the covers for you in the other bedroom. Good night."

Ainsley watched the brittle woman in her nightgown teeter down the hall, the candlelight shrinking as she went.

13

THE NEXT MORNING, AS THE SMELL of frying
bacon penetrated Ainsley's slumber, she woke with
a start.

She had slept diagonally on the bed in one of
the many guest rooms. There'd been no other real
choice. The mattress was too short, having been
designed for nineteenth-century bodies. Since then,
humans had discovered things like antibiotics and
indoor plumbing.

She stood up, yawned, and pushed aside the
lace curtains on the window. Outside the rain was
falling steadily. The worst of the storm seemed to
have passed, but she could forget about tanning or
beach sports. This felt like the rainforest right now.

That smell of bacon hit her nostrils again.
Ainsley was now conscious enough to wonder who

was cooking. Doña Pilar wasn't capable of lifting a frying pan.

Wearing the same clothes she slept in, Ainsley stumbled down the stairs into the old kitchen.

A portly man was standing over the stove. He was wearing a white apron and a white chef's hat. On the stove was a pan loaded with crispy bacon. He was using the tongs to put the meat from the pan directly into his mouth.

He issued an enormous burp, then continued eating.

"Hi," said Ainsley.

He glanced at her, grunted, then returned to the bacon.

That was rude. Ainsley felt herself waking up. "You could drain those on the paper towel first."

"Then you lose the flavor," he replied.

"No, you just lose the grease."

"That's flavor to me."

She watched him finish the batch, then unpeel several more slices of fatty bacon and start to fry a second round.

"I'm Ainsley," she said.

"I know," he said.

"So you don't have to introduce yourself?"

"I was going to make you guess my name."

The second batch of bacon had browned and curled now. The man was eating that too, pan to mouth.

"Your name is Luis," she said.

"Half this island is named Luis," he said.

"That's not a denial."

His mouth full of bacon, he finally faced her.

"If you're so smart, what's my last name?"

Ainsley shrugged. "I'm not psychic."

He pointed his tongs at her. "It's Cepeda. Luis Cepeda. I'm supposed to drive you to the museum in Ponce today."

It was verified. Luis Cepeda. This was the handyman who could not be found before a hurricane.

"So I heard," she replied. "And you didn't pick up your phone yesterday."

"Of course not. There was a hurricane coming."

"Doña Pilar needed you."

He shrugged. "She's still alive."

Ainsley sucked on her front teeth. He wasn't making the most favorable impression. "Other people told me that you were irresponsible."

Luis crammed the rest of the bacon into his mouth. Then he looked up at her, a huge bulge of meat inside his cheek. He sure as hell wasn't doing anything to discourage that conclusion.

He swallowed with an audible gulp. "I'm an artist," he said. "What other people think doesn't matter to me."

Ainsley walked across the kitchen. She took the tongs out of his hands, then used her hips to knock him away from the stove. "Move it."

"This isn't your house."

"It's not yours either. And since you're not going to offer me any bacon, I'm going to cook for myself."

She unpeeled several strips of the fatty meat and began to fry them. Luis sat down at the table.

"That's fine," he said. "I had enough anyways."

His foot beat a restless rhythm against the floor. He watched Ainsley pull her sleeves lower on her arms to protect from the popping grease.

"So you're some kind of detective?"

"I find lost gemstones. Hand me the paper towels."

He passed them over. Ainsley ripped a few off the roll and removed the bacon to the towels and let the grease drain. She could feel his eyes watching her.

"Do you know who has the pearl brooch?" he said.

"Not a clue. Do you?"

He shook his head. "The museum is the best place to begin. They hired the driver."

"That's a plan."

Luis nodded. Then his eyes narrowed. "How much is Doña Pilar paying you?"

Ainsley didn't like his tone. She didn't know his wages, and she didn't want to stoke any jealousy.

"That's none of your business."

"Is it more than she pays me?"

"I don't know how much she pays you."

"Almost nothing."

"Then maybe you should ask for a raise."

An ancient Spanish voice from the staircase cut in. "He won't get one."

It was Doña Pilar. She was slowly descending the steps. First the purpled, veiny feet. Then the hem of her paper-thin nightgown.

Groaning, Luis stood up and shuffled over. Offering his arm, he helped the old lady reach the landing.

"You look good this morning," he said.

Ainsley noticed that he had switched to formal Spanish. But the old lady was in no mood for chivalry. "It's about time. You only come when you want to."

"No, Doña, the roads were washed out."

The old lady pointed at Ainsley. "She got here on the same roads."

Luis stared daggers at this American visitor. "See, that's because Ainsley didn't drive. She was dropped here from heaven."

Doña Pilar slapped his shoulder. "You're full of shit. Always." Then her eyes found Ainsley. They travelled up and down her body, from her sloppy hair down to her dirty feet.

"Look at you," said Doña Pilar. "Why aren't you ready to go?"

"I just woke up."

The old woman tsk-tsked. "You're on my clock now. Go upstairs and make yourself pretty. You're my representative."

Ainsley couldn't disagree with that, since Doña Pilar was literally her ticket home. Still, the old woman was shaping up to be an irascible client. Ainsley was happy to be getting out on her own. She was always happier as a lone wolf anyways.

Then Ainsley remembered that her bag was back in Santurce. She'd left it with Amaryllis' family, since she hadn't been planning to spend the night.

"But—"

Doña Pilar cut her off. "Your bag is by the front door. I had Luis pick it up from Tomás' house this morning."

"Yes, *señora*."

The old woman was nearly psychic. Ainsley wiped her hands on a towel and headed up the staircase. Glancing back, she noticed that Luis had scurried over to the paper towel to eat her bacon.

14

Though Ainsley had grown up calling it the "oh shit" handle, she'd never actually felt the truth of those words until now.

She was in the passenger seat of a battered Ford Fiesta, clutching the handle that was built above the diagonal edge of the door. The vehicle was a decade old but already looked twice its age.

Luis occupied the driver's seat, a single lazy finger at the top of the steering wheel. He was whipping the vehicle around the rain-slick roads of Highway 2 as it zigged and zagged over the hilly midsection of Puerto Rico.

"I've been in four accidents," he was saying, "but only two were my fault."

"What happened?"

"Two were in New York. Two were on this highway here. This road is no joke when it's raining." He casually picked some food out from his teeth.

That was disturbing. Ainsley decided to change the subject. "You've been to New York?"

"Of course. I used to live there."

"For how long?"

"Almost forty years."

Now that made sense. His English was fast like a New Yorker's.

"Interesting," said Ainsley.

"Not really. Millions of us Puerto Ricans have moved there. The only thing I did different was come back."

"Why?"

"I don't know. It was just getting too hard in the States. The winters are bad. The jobs are going away. I'm fifty-eight now. I didn't want to be shipped back to Puerto Rico in a box. I wanted to enjoy it again while I'm still alive."

"So here you are."

"Two years and counting. My kids are going to visit soon."

"How many do you have?"

"I don't know. Lots."

He winked at her. Ainsley imagined the feelings of those children, especially daughters, at having such a rapscallion for a father.

Outside the window passed a large stone sculpture mounted on the side of the freeway. It was a noble-looking peasant in a broad-brimmed hat, a machete hanging from one hand.

"That's a *jíbaro*," said Luis.

"What's that?"

"It's like a hillbilly," he said. "They're the ancestors of a lot of us Puerto Ricans. They were a mixture of freed blacks, poor whites, Taíno. But they're all gone now."

"Like cowboys in the States."

"Yes, exactly. My grandmother was a *jíbara*. We kids always made fun of her because she hated the smell of fish. She never saw the ocean, and it was only thirty miles away." He shook his head. "It was a different time."

The road was descending now, and Ainsley contented herself with watching the mountains give way to broad, lush, green plains.

"Ponce is coming up soon," he said. "My hometown."

"You sound proud of that."

He bolted up in his seat. "Absolutely. Ponce is the real capital of Puerto Rico. Ask anybody."

"I will."

"You know what we say? The rest of the island is just a parking lot for Ponce."

"So you don't like San Juan?"

He spat out the window. "I would saw off my own feet before I visit San Juan. Those *gente de la losa* are so arrogant." He drummed his fingers on the steering wheel. "Ponce is where the real *boricuas* live."

"Let me know when we get there."

"Oh, we Ponceans are so humble, you won't even know it. Look."

He extended his finger straight ahead. Ainsley peered through the windshield, down the rainy freeway. Slowly, five enormous shapes began looming out of grayness. They were arranged horizontally, were painted bright red, and were at least ten meters high.

She squinted hard. The one on the left was a letter. It looked like a P.

The second: O.

The third: N.

Ainsley didn't even need to see the last two letters. As they emerged from the gray rain, the word PONCE was spelled out in letters so huge, so bright, it could practically be read from outer space.

"See?" said Luis. "So very humble."

Ponce

15

As Ainsley ascended the steps of the Ponce
Museum of Art, a white modernist box, she suddenly remembered something.

She didn't like museums.

That wasn't to say that Ainsley didn't like art.
As a teenager, she had loved sculpture, mosaics, and
stained glass so much that she'd fantasized about
becoming a curator. It was actually a good thing
she hadn't pursued the field, because that position
would have been too constricting for her.

No, the reason was more physiological. She'd
always suffered museum fatigue. Her hamstrings,
thighs, calves, ankles, and feet just flat-out refused
to carry her across any more marble flooring. She
wondered why marble in particular made her feet
ache.

"How is the collection here?" she said.

Luis looked uncomfortable. "They have four thousand pieces of art. It's supposed to be the best in the Caribbean. But I wouldn't know personally."

"Why not?"

He made a face. "I don't like this museum. The people here just seem shady."

"You're from Ponce," said Ainsley, "so maybe it's because you know what everybody's *really* like."

He shrugged maybe.

They entered the lobby. A white pair of bifurcated ladder staircases encircled a small fountain. It looked as though some glamorous actress should be descending one side of them.

"Juana said she would meet us here," said Luis, checking his watch.

"She's the executive?"

He nodded. "But she doesn't seem to know what she's doing. You tell me what you think." Then he looked at Ainsley. "Look, this is the end of the line for me. I really don't have anything more to do from here. I'm just a handyman."

This blindsided Ainsley. She felt a touch of panic. Even though Luis was caddish, she did like having a knowledgable guide with a car. "Please stick around, Luis. I might need you."

"Really?"

"Yes."

He shrugged. "Okay."

Ainsley felt the importance of this moment. Until now, she had been merely passive, reacting to seatmates, to families, to weather, to racist old women. Now she would have to begin to *act*, if she

were to demonstrate her worth as a private gemstone investigator, not only to Doña Pilar—but also
to herself.

Meanwhile, a tall, beautiful black woman had
descended the stairs and was striding towards them
across the floor. Her smile was unforgettable. Two
rows of strong white teeth shone like beautiful
chips of ivory inside her generous mouth. Ainsley
noted the outline of her strong leg muscles inside the loose linen pants, her toned triceps in her
sleeveless silk blouse.

"Miss Walker?"

"Yes."

"Juana Barbosa," the woman said, "senior proj-
ect administrator. It's a pleasure."

They kissed cheeks. The woman seemed extraordinarily happy to see her, despite the reason for
the meeting. "This is Luis Cepeda," said Ainsley.
"Señora Pilar's assistant."

They shook hands and kissed. "From Ponce,"
he added.

Juana acted surprised. "Ah, a local boy. Keep
an eye on the staff. You might recognize some of
them."

Ainsley assumed her best game face. "So where
can we discuss things?"

Juana held her clipboard against her chest.
"Have you visited our museum before?"

"No."

"Then let's just talk out here. I'll tell you about
our collection."

Ainsley groaned inwardly. That would mean
minutes, maybe hours, of crossing marble. And

creeping up her spine was the sense that this woman didn't seem to be treating the robbery of the pearl brooch with the seriousness that Doña Pilar deserved.

Still, when Juana Barbosa gestured to her visitors to follow, she followed. The executive led them a few steps to the first gallery, a hexagonal room with oil paintings from the British Pre-Raphaelite era of painting. Ainsley had always been bored by pudgy pink cherubs floating amongst puffy white clouds. Juana was saying something about gifts to the museum.

The tour continued into the baroque Italian galleries, which were harder to object to, and finally into a gallery dedicated to the Spanish Golden Age. All of the rooms had been hexagonal, illuminated by natural light. Ainsley felt her ankles beginning to ache.

"Juana," she finally said, "can we discuss the pearl brooch?"

"If you wish," came the reply.

"So what happened?"

"Our driver is missing," she said. A worried look clouded her face. "We think he was robbed."

"Maybe he was an accomplice to the theft."

She shook her head. "That's impossible. He's been with this museum for decades."

Ainsley pressed on. "Have you talked to the police?"

"Of course. They're pursuing it."

"I'm here because Doña Pilar wants her own investigation."

"I know."

"So I'd appreciate getting the name of the driver."

Juana shook her head again. "I can't tell you that."

"Of course you can."

"No, I'm not allowed to assist you."

"But you'll assist the police."

"Yes."

"I don't deserve the same courtesy?"

She looked at Ainsley over the tops of her glasses. "Miss Walker, you're not from this island. We don't have your credentials. And as far as we're concerned, you could be gathering evidence for Señora Pilar in preparation for a lawsuit."

"So what can you tell me?"

Juana sighed. "We were planning an exhibition about the pearl brooch, and its place in Puerto Rican history. The driver picked up the brooch five days ago. He never arrived here at the museum. Neither he nor the item has been located yet."

"That's all?"

"That's all."

"And there is a three thousand dollar reward for its return, correct?"

Juana Barbosa shifted uncomfortably. "Yes, there is."

The two women were standing toe-to-toe in the middle of the gallery. The old faces of dead Spanish *conquistadores* and noblemen looked down upon the standoff.

Ainsley backed down. "Then I guess we're finished."

"It's been a pleasure." Juana beamed an enormous smile at Ainsley. "I hope you enjoy your visit to Puerto Rico. Don't forget to stop in the gift shop before you leave."

She turned on her heel and left the gallery, her heels clicking on the marble. Ainsley saw Luis standing nearby, a pensive look on his face.

"What do you think?"

He frowned. "I knew you wouldn't get anywhere with her. We Puerto Ricans know how to avoid unpleasant topics."

Ainsley drummed her fingers against her thumb. Her ankles were already hurting. Her mind was spinning. Juana Barbosa had wanted nothing to do with her.

"So you give up now?" said Luis.

Ainsley whirled. "Are you kidding? I'm just thinking of what to do next."

Luis picked his teeth. "We could go eat lunch next."

That wasn't a surprise. Luis seemed to dependably follow his appetites. But then her tummy growled, and she realized that it was a good idea.

"Where?"

He shrugged. "There's a good cafeteria downstairs."

"I'm game."

As they left the galleries, Ainsley gave a silent prayer of thanks that she wouldn't be walking across any more marble that day.

16

A FEW MINUTES LATER, AINSLEY STOOD in a long line of people waiting to ask for food. Her plastic tray lay on the aluminum tubes that ran along the lunch counter at waist level.

She was feeling frustrated by life, by the weather, and most of all by the brick wall that was Juana Barbosa, the senior projects administrator.

Luis stood behind her. "Do you want to try something traditional?"

"Sure."

"Maybe something good for a rainy day?"

"I don't care."

He pointed to a small black cauldron of stew, steam curling up from its surface. "Try that. Chicken *asopao*. One of the best things that Puerto Rico ever invented. I used to dream of this when I was in New York in the winter and the boiler in my apartment was broken."

Ainsley didn't feel like disagreeing. She ordered a bowl from the chef behind the counter, who promptly delivered it in a small ceramic pot.

She paid for lunch and chose a table near a window looking out onto the garden. Luis sat down with her, bearing his own ceramic pot. A distracted look was on his face as he glanced back at the kitchen. "I know that guy. I remember his face."

Ainsley shrugged. She studied her *asopao*. It looked like a cross between soup and paella. A juicy chicken thigh had been placed at the top of the bowl. She scooped a spoonful and placed it tentatively into her mouth. The flavors spread across her taste buds, chicken, rice, green olives, salty ham, peppers. She felt like she was being somehow reborn.

"This is miraculous," she said.

But Luis barely heard her. He was still looking at the cook. "I think we went to school together."

"Who?"

Luis stood up. "I'm going to talk to him."

Ainsley watched him approach the chef behind the countertop. They exchanged some words. Then a huge smile spread across the chef's face. He actually leaned over the glass barrier and embraced Luis.

The line had backed up behind Luis while he and the chef chatted with one another. One thing about island people was so true that it had become a cliché: they are never in a rush.

She finished her *asopao*. Meanwhile, the other bowl had cooled off. It was the perfect temperature. Ainsley couldn't resist. She pulled it to her side of the table and dove in.

Eventually, Luis trotted back to the table, a spring in his step. "I can't believe that shit-eater is still in Ponce." He shook his head, grinning, jerking a thumb back at the chef. "We used to rob cars together back in the day."

Ainsley didn't doubt that. Then she had a light bulb moment. "Do you think that guy might know the driver?"

Luis nodded. "I already asked. He told me to come to a poetry reading tonight. He said that many of the museum employees will be there. You can come too."

"Oh really?"

He nodded. "But you have to pretend to be my girlfriend."

"That's not going to happen."

Luis folded quickly. "Oh, I know," he said, "I just wanted to see if you'd play along." Then a concerned look came across his face as he scanned the table. "What happened to my *asopao*?"

Ainsley chewed her lip and tried to keep a poker face. "I don't know. Somebody must've stolen it."

She changed the subject to avoid further questioning. "So you like poetry?"

"No, but I write it anyways." Luis pounded his fist onto chest. "Luis Cepeda, proud *boricua* and failed poet, at your service."

Ainsley looked at him with new eyes. The huge appetites, the disregard for personal safety, the late-in-life poverty. It all made sense.

"You know," she said, "I've discovered something."

"What's that?"

"Maybe you're not as stupid as you look."

Ainsley grinned at him. It was hard to believe they'd only known each other for a few hours. He was making her feel feisty, especially now that there was a glimmer of a future for this case.

"You know," he said, with a philosopher's air, "I like it when people underestimate me."

"I do too."

They stared at one another. It was the meeting of wills, the recognition of equals. Finally Luis broke the tension. "So why don't you buy me another *asopao*, you stinking little thief?"

He cracked a smile as Ainsley rose from her chair and got back in line. He'd won this battle.

17

The rain clouds parted, and for a brief moment the pink Caribbean sun hovered just above the watery horizon, like a stage actress caught with her dressing room door open.

Then the curtain was pulled shut, and the gray rain returned.

Ainsley had parked herself at a covered dining area. She was at one of the kiosks at the La Guancha. It was a *malecón*, the Spanish term for a boardwalk, and Luis had insisted that this was the heart of true social life for Ponceans. La Guancha also happened to be where the poetry reading was going to be held. And they were an hour early.

They'd already wasted more time than that. With all afternoon to kill, Ainsley had suggested that they tour the historic downtown, its gaudy red-

and-black historic fire station. She'd already noticed that the downtown streets were all curved to better accommodate nineteenth-century carriages that couldn't turn at right angles.

"Why do you want to act like a tourist?" Luis had said.

"What else do you want to do?"

"Get drunk."

So they'd agreed to support each other's priorities. Ainsley had waited outside a bar while he slammed several shots of rum inside. Then Luis had followed her through the historic district, grumbling but answering her questions about the city. Yes, he said, it'd been named for Ponce de Leon's great-grandson. It boasted its own style of creole architecture based on Barcelona's swoopy art nouveau. And it was, interestingly, nicknamed "the Pearl of the South".

Ainsley had wondered if that was why the museum wanted Doña Pilar's pearl brooch.

Now they were at La Guancha, parked here on the nearly empty boardwalk, watching the occasional fat girl wearing tight jeans and wedges scurry past with her jacket held over her head. An observation deck stood to the left; an empty stage for salsa to the right. It felt like many towns along the New Jersey shore.

Ainsley had a *bacalaito*, or cod fritter, in one hand. It was heavily fried. In the other was a tall piña colada, served the right way, without any ice. This wasn't an entirely bad way to spend the day.

Luis, meanwhile, was at the next table. He was scribbling furiously on a pad of paper with a colored pencil. A small purple velvet bag lay next to him.

"What are you doing?" she asked.

"I was wrong," he said. "You *are* dumber than you look."

"Sorry, you're writing. What are you *writing*?"

"A poem."

"Can I read it?"

"No, but you can listen when I read it to the crowd. Then you can stand and vigorously applaud."

"What's it about?"

"Why American girls should be barred from visiting Ponce."

There was been a tussle over the note pad at that point, because Ainsley couldn't let that jibe go unchallenged. Luis won, and retreated to another table to finish his master opus. She noted that, even given the thirty-year age difference, they already had a sibling-rivalry type of relationship.

Ainsley went back to her piña colada and watched him work. She guessed that he'd been a poet of ordinary talent, but you could never really tell. Poetry was such a slippery, vague form of art. There was no metric to judge it.

He put his pencil back into the purple sack, then sighed. "Poems are never finished, just abandoned. This one is left to the universe."

"Great."

Luis missed the sarcasm. "It *is* great. It's the perfect distillation of what I'm feeling this very second. That's the essence of poetry. Promise me you'll listen to me read it."

"I promise."

He seemed satisfied by this. Ainsley swallowed the rest of her piña colada. "You just keep pencils in that purple bag?"

He cinched the sack tightly and stowed it in his pocket. "My pencils are very valuable to me. I can't write poetry without them."

Some people were weird about things like that, Ainsley thought. She paid for the food, then strolled down the boardwalk past the other kiosks, most of which were closed. She'd purchased an umbrella from a vendor and was watching the raindrops bounce against her boots. She wondered how much rain had fallen in the last two days.

The poetry slam was being held in small covered dining area on the edge of the boardwalk, literally against the ocean. Someone had set up a microphone and speakers at one end of the dining area. A thick woven dock rope strung between two stanchions acted as a guardrail against any drunken poet who might be tempted to pitch over backwards into the water.

There were a handful of people here already. From their friendly banter Ainsley guessed that they'd been performing to one another for a very long time.

The group roared when they saw Luis. Soon the people had surrounded him. Ainsley saw the chef, who'd changed into a t-shirt and jeans, greet him with a long bear hug. They were speaking in Spanish.

"How long have you been back now?"

"Almost two years."

"And you didn't come down to this reading?"

"I'm working in Caguas."

"So you ready to kiss the sky for us tonight? New York didn't kill the spirit?"

Luis smiled. "Never." He glanced at Ainsley. "Say hello to my girlfriend. From the States."

Ainsley rolled her eyes but decided not to challenge that. Escorting her around the island in search of a pearl brooch for Doña Pilar was probably not anybody's idea of fun, so she'd let Luis have this victory. Not that he needed the ego boost of having a younger girlfriend, but at least nobody would harass her.

"*Mucho gusto*," she said, kissing cheeks all around.

The group settled around a table. Luis casually threw his arm around Ainsley. She could tolerate the act. He wasn't totally disgusting, and she liked his repartee.

"So who else is working at the museum that we used to know?" said Luis to the group.

The chef swallowed from a beer. "Paco is with me. Tito is in maintenance. Benetín—"

Luis raised a theatrical hand to his forehead. "Benetín. That arrogant bastard."

"Benetín is one of the curators. This is his wife."

A well-dressed older woman was staring daggers at Luis. He tried vainly to recover. "I bet you changed him. You turned him into a sweet pussycat. But my question is, what about the drivers?" said Luis.

"The drivers?" said the chef.

"Yeah, the guys who make deliveries."

The chef shrugged. "I think we just use UPS, brother."

"No," said Luis, insistent now, "I was talking to a friend this afternoon who heard that a delivery man has gone missing."

Ainsley liked how he was handling this. Not that she should be judging anybody's investigative skills, but he was framing the conversation. She decided to remain quiet.

The chef swigged his beer, then shrugged. "I didn't hear about that."

Suddenly a man in the back raised his voice. "You're talking about the runner."

That caught Ainsley's attention. She craned her neck and looked around. The man was wearing a blue Yankees cap.

Luis nodded. "Yeah. The runner."

"I don't know what happened to him," said the man in the Yankees cap. "We haven't seen him in a while."

Then the conversation turned aside, the other voices grew louder, and the subject was swallowed up in an ocean of laughter.

Luis had tried the best he could. But Ainsley kept an eye on the guy in the Yankees cap.

18

OVER THE NEXT HOUR, THE TABLE broke up as more people had trickled into the reading. Somebody switched on the speaker system. Ainsley counted about fifty people, which she supposed was pretty good attendance for a poetry reading. A waitress came around with more beers.

Then the first poet took the microphone. She was a heavy woman with even heavier blue eyeshadow and red lipstick. She began reciting a poem in Spanish about her lost puppy. Ainsley listened closely. It became clear that the woman wasn't actually speaking about a lost puppy. It sounded like she was speaking about her lost sex life. The whoops and hollers from the men in the audience confirmed that.

Just before delivering her final line, the woman grabbed a piece of the air and pumped it hard with her hips. The applause was vigorous. She set down the microphone on a table and walked back to her seat, grinning at the attention.

During the readings, Ainsley counted two, then three, then four empty beer bottles in front of the guy in the Yankees cap. There was no way his bladder could hold out much longer.

When he stood up, Ainsley whispered to Luis, "I'm going to use the bathroom."

She slipped out of her seat and followed the bobbing Yankees cap as it stumbled down the boardwalk. Ainsley quickened her stride and cut him off just before he was about to enter the men's room.

"Hi there," she said.

His eyes, watery and rimmed in red, scanned her up and down. "Hello, beautiful."

Ainsley inched a little closer. "So you know that runner? At the museum?"

His eyes watery eyes struggled to focus. "Yeah."

"What's his name?"

"Roman."

"Last name?"

"Galarza."

"Do you know where he lives?"

"No."

"Do you know if he has a family?"

"I don't know." He gestured to the bathroom. "Can you let me go in there? I really need—"

Ainsley placed her hands up across the doorway, blocking it. She realized that it made her chest protrude, but she'd use anything at her disposal to keep this guy talking right now. "What else about him that you can tell me?"

The Yankees cap blew air out of his lips. "I don't know. I mean, I just see him in our break room. Sometimes he tells me about the stuff they ask him to pick up. They really trust him, you know? Then one day, *mira*, he leaves and never comes back. I think maybe he got fired."

Ainsley pushed harder. "There must be something else you can remember."

The man shook his head. "Why do you want to know all this?"

"Don't worry about it. Let me know if you remember anything else."

Ainsley finally stepped aside. The man rushed past her into the bathroom, his hands fumbling at his zipper.

There was an extra spring in her step as she walked down the boardwalk, back to the poetry reading. Ainsley had learned the driver's name.

Roman Galarza.

On an island of four million people, however, there were bound to be at least more than one Roman Galarza. Maybe twenty, thirty, forty. She could spend the next month trying to locate all of them. The immensity of the task depressed her.

She crashed into her seat at the poetry reading and opened another beer. A wiry man wrapped in a Puerto Rican flag had just ended an obviously political reading. There was polite applause.

Then a new chant began. *Luis ... Luis ... Luis*. Her guide shook his head. The chants grew louder. *Luuuuuuuuis*. Finally he stood up and took the microphone. Ainsley was excited to hear what he'd written.

As he was about to begin, she felt a hand on her shoulder. She turned her head. It was the guy in the Yankees cap. "I remembered something else." He gestured with a tilt of his head outside the group.

She followed him outside, away from the poetry reading. She heard Luis' voice begin to recite his masterpiece, but then she was out of earshot.

"I know where you can find Roman," said the Yankees cap guy.

"Where?"

"He told me about his favorite *lechonera* once. He likes to go there on Sundays."

"Okay."

"But it's not one of the commercial ones in Cayey. It's hard to find."

"Why?"

"It's held in an abandoned *centrale*."

Ainsley hadn't heard that word before, and her face must've shown it.

"You don't know what that is."

"No," she admitted.

"A *centrale* is a sugar mill. Puerto Rico is full of abandoned sugar mills. This one was called Alondra. It's near Yabucoa. It's in ruins. I've never gone myself. Roman was always saying that he would take me. He said it had the best *lechon* in Puerto Rico."

Ainsley pulled a small notepad from her purse and jotted down the information. The guy in the Yankees cap guy watched her. "You're still not going to tell me why you're searching for him?"

"Maybe later. Why are you helping me find him?"

"That's my secret," he said. "But Roman is very difficult to find. I'll be amazed if you ever do."

Ainsley thanked him. Inside, her stomach was doing backflips of happiness. This was a really strong lead.

She arrived back at the poetry reading just as the applause ended. Luis was kissing everybody in the audience.

He approached her, his eyes lit with excitement. "I know you think I'm amazing."

"Luis," she said, "I missed the poem."

His face fell. "But that was my big moment."

She had to smile at his neediness. "I was too busy getting this." She held up her notebook with the name on it. "His name is Roman Galarza. He's going to be at a *lechonera* in Yabucoa tomorrow."

Luis looked at the notebook, then back at her. "The guy in the Yankees cap told you?"

"Yep."

He nodded, as if he were just discovering what this turn of events meant for him. "Then you're probably going to want to go to the *lechonera*. And you're going to need someone to drive you."

Ainsley nodded.

He shrugged. "That's fine. I had nothing better to do tomorrow anyways."

Yabucoa

19

More rain.

She and Luis had spent the night in separate rooms at a simple hotel on the outskirts of Ponce. They'd reconvened in the breakfast room at eight am, shared a quick pastry and some coffee, then began the drive to Yabucoa.

This time, Ainsley was behind the wheel. She'd insisted, after the hair-raising trip down from the mountains the morning before.

Luis sat moodily in the passenger seat. As they drove along the southern edge of the island, he stared out at the small, dried-up towns, the crashing waves.

"I'm ready to hear your poem," she said.

"You can't," he said.

"Why?"

"It only existed for that moment. Now it's rotted. It's like a head of lettuce."

Ainsley shrugged. They continued driving in silence.

"Can I ask you a question?"

"Okay," he said.

"Puerto Rico makes rum, right?"

"Of course."

"And Bacardi is the most famous."

He corrected her pronunciation. "It's Bacar-*di*."

"But that guy last night told me that the sugar mills are all closed."

"Yes."

"How is that possible? Isn't rum made from sugar?"

"It is. But we haven't grown sugar cane in a long time. The last *centrale* closed ten years ago."

"So where does the sugar come from?"

"The Dominicans, mostly."

Ainsley hadn't known that. The more she thought about it, the more she realized how ignorant she was about the history of sugar in the Caribbean, how its care, cultivation, and price had affected everybody, at every time, on every island in the region.

Luis said he knew exactly where the Alondra *centrale* was located. After forty-five minutes, he directed Ainsley to turn off the road. Soon they were riding down a dirt track through the green hills. The mounds and vales were dotted with stiff palm trees. Despite the rain, this part of the island still felt somehow dry.

They came to a heavy rusted gate. A large sign stood next to it, its words blanketed in a carpet of rust. Ainsley stopped the car. "Hold on," said Luis.

He got out of the car and manually swung the gate open. Ainsley noticed several sets of fresh tire tracks.

He returned to the car, and Ainsley pulled forward. Formerly paved, the road was now overgrown with weeds. Brush scraped against the side of the car.

Luis craned his head forward. "Watch for holes," he said. "We don't want to get stuck." Ainsley cranked the wheel around several crater-sized potholes. Soon the ridge in the center of the road grew so high that she steered off the road to avoid getting high-centered.

Then their destination came into view: the Alondra Sugar *centrale*.

Or what was left of it. A large warehouse lay half collapsed on the ground like the carcass of a mastodon, its corrugated roof rusting under the rainy skies. A huge hopper squatted beside it. And the skeletons of three rusted cranes were arched twenty meters over the hardscrabble dirt, waiting to lift a final load of raw sugar cane into the grinding mill—a load that would never arrive.

"Wow," said Ainsley.

"There it is," said Luis. He was pointing to a collection of about fifty cars parked near the only remaining upright structure, a large warehouse with three tall chimneys behind it. "Pull up there."

She obeyed, threw the car into park, and pulled the keys from the ignition. She tossed them to him.

"Good driving," he said.

"I have one other question."

"Is it a stupid one?"

"Yes."

"Excellent. I love to feel superior."

"What's a *lechonera*?"

In response, Luis pointed to his nose. "Roll down your window. Take a deep smell."

Ainsley did so and inhaled deeply. She caught the scent of something sweet, crackly, and meaty. "It smells like barbeque."

He nodded. "Do you know what that is, exactly?"

"No."

"Roasted pig. It's going to be the best you've ever tasted. Follow me."

20

As she stepped into the abandoned refinery, the smell of roasted pork slid into Ainsley's nostrils, down her throat, and seized her belly. Her stomach instantly sprang to life.

Then there were other sensations—the dampness of rotting palms, the reddish hue of rusted factory parts, the dirt beneath her shoes. It looked to have been tracked in by wild animals.

But most arresting was the sheer amount of rusted metal in the abandoned mill. Thin railings ran sideways; thinner ladders stretched up and down. Catwalks crisscrossed the ceiling. Enormous gears, five meters high, stood on edge, their serrated teeth prepared to bite into one another and begin turning at the next word from a supervisor.

But that supervisor had gone away long ago, and this metal was probably going to last the longest in the battle against nature.

Ainsley wandered through the space, gaping. Then she noticed that Luis seemed to be moved.

She placed a hand on his arm. "Are you okay?"

"This doesn't seem real," he said. "I grew up with Puerto Rico making sugar."

"Not anymore."

He wiped his eyes. "I heard that the government spent over a billion dollars to save our sugar factories." His hand made a circle the air. "Look at the result. What a waste."

Then he straightened up and cleared his throat. "I didn't come here to cry. I came here to eat pork."

"And to find Roman Galarza."

"That's more important, of course. Doña Pilar needs that pearl brooch."

He nodded eagerly, but Ainsley knew the truth. Luis really just wanted to party. Still, this wasn't the time for that. She needed him to stay committed to the mission.

The sound of laughter and music danced lightly through the air. "They're in the back," said Luis, "by the furnaces."

Ainsley placed a finger against her lips. "So I have another question."

He sighed exaggeratedly. "So many questions."

"Is this place really popular?"

"Yes, it's one of Puerto Rico's best-kept secrets."

"Do we need a reservation?"

He sighed. "You're such a mainlander. Nobody has to be *invited* in Puerto Rico. We don't have to *call ahead*. It's never *full*. We just make room for each other. Everybody eats, everybody drinks, no matter what. Everybody's happy."

That suddenly made sense. Ainsley realized that she had to adjust her point of view. Certain social boundaries that she had been told were sacred—the products of her Protestant upbringing—simply didn't exist here. They had been drawn with chalk in the rain.

She and Luis moved through the refinery until they found the *lechonera*. At least two hundred people were seated at folding tables, milling about. Some were chatting, some were even dancing to the salsa music on a makeshift dance floor.

Beyond the tables, on an elevated dais, below a wide backdrop of metal piping that rose from the factory floor like an industrial altar, was roasting the biggest pig Ainsley had ever seen.

It was a monster, at least seven feet long, impaled upon the spit. Its skin was shiny and mottled. A teenage boy was turning the animal with a hand crank.

A smile spread across Luis' face. "I like it here already. Look, they're using natural wood charcoal."

"Is there another way?"

"There's gas. But it dries out the pork more quickly. Come on, let's make friends."

She trailed Luis as they entered. He greeted strangers with kisses on the cheek, or arms flung over their shoulders. He commented on their clothing, their children, their body parts.

Ainsley had always admired people who could work a room. It wasn't natural to her. Being the life of the party took timing, effort, shrewdness, and usually some social lubrication for everybody involved.

Soon Luis found her. He was holding two plastic cups and handed one to her. "Mojito," he said. "Island classic."

"So how do we find Roman Galarza?"

He shrugged. "I don't know. Just start talking."

At that moment, two enormous meaty hands landed on his shoulders. "Luis Cepeda," said a deep voice in Spanish. "Forty years I've been waiting for this."

Luis' eyes grew wide. He started to sweat. "I swear I didn't touch her."

The hands whirled him around. Luis was now face-to-face with a large man with a gentle face. "Do you remember me?"

Luis struggled to recall. "You look familiar."

The man placed his hands on Luis' cheeks. "It's Pacheco."

His eyes searched Luis' eyes for a glimmer of recognition. Then it arrived. Luis opened his mouth. "Pacheco. *Pachecho!*"

The men embraced each other. It was an extended, crushing hug that never seemed to end. Ainsley could've baked a loaf of bread in the time the hug took.

They separated and Pacheco looked at him. "I knew you the second you walked in here."

Ainsley noticed that the two men kept their arms around each other. To her eyes, they looked as close as lovers.

Luis explained the relationship. "This little bastard grew up in my neighborhood."

Pacheco nodded. "Six houses down—"

"—and one block over. He lived next to—"

"—Yamile, what was her—"

"Fuentes, Yamile Fuentes—"

"That's right, Yamile Fuentes—"

Ainsley couldn't help but smile at their camaraderie. The two men were even finishing each other's sentences.

Pacheco leaned towards Ainsley. "I always told this little bastard that he would come back. But he wanted to leave so bad."

"I did," said Luis. "But that was a long time ago."

Then Pacheco paused, as though remembering something. "Do you remember the mailbox story?"

Luis shook his head, then turned away in an exaggerated display of self-pity.

Ainsley sensed a deliciously embarrassing anecdote. "What's the mailbox story?" she asked.

"No," said Luis, "don't tell it, please, no."

Pacheco drew himself up. He had the upper hand now. "This bastard was so desperate to get off the island that he figured out a special plan to get arrested and deported."

Luis had buried his face in his hands. Ainsley couldn't wipe the wicked smile off her face. "Tell me, please."

Pacheco continued. "Luis learned that if you go into a post office and smash a mailbox, in front of witnesses, it was a federal offense. Post office boxes are federal property."

"So?"

"At that time, a teenager would be tried in federal court and sentenced to federal reform school in ... where was it?"

"Ohio," said Luis. "Chillicothe, Ohio. Please stop talking."

But Pacheco continued. "And at the reform school you can get free food, free clothing, free education, learn good English, learn a trade. It was very tempting."

"Very," added Luis.

"We just joked about doing it, but this *cabron* actually went and did it. He goes into a post office with a big sledgehammer and destroys the place, swinging everywhere. I was there. He asked me to be a witness. He crushed *everything*."

Luis held up a dignified finger. "You forget, I wasn't the only one."

Pacheco was laughing. "Yes, that was the problem, remember? Other teenagers desperate to leave the island had already been pulling this trick too. So by this time, the judge had figured out the racket. There Luis is in court, the judge looks down on him, and sentences him to eight months." He jerked a thumb at Luis. "This idiot starts celebrating before the judge finishes talking."

Luis protested. "I didn't know—"

"Then the judge finishes, '—in *San Juan prison*!'"

Pacheco roared. Ainsley couldn't help laughing either. Luis, meanwhile, looked like he wanted to crawl under a rock. No wonder he had stayed away from Puerto Rico for so long. He'd probably become the laughingstock of the island.

He steered Luis towards a different group of people. "Follow me, I want to introduce you to my family."

As Ainsley watched the two old buddies disappear into the crowd, a realization dawned upon her.

She was going to have to find Roman Galarza on her own.

21

WITH HER LUNCH ON A PLATE in her hand, Ainsley left the buffet and circled the *lechonera* looking for an open seat at one of the folding tables on the cement floor.

This wasn't a casual decision to make. Anyone who's been to a dinner party knows the importance of having a friendly person next to you at the table. And in this case, she wasn't looking so much for friendliness as for a certain type of person.

Someone who would point out Roman Galarza.

She spotted an open chair beside a thin, blonde woman who was dressed primly and appeared somewhat uneasy in the surroundings. Part of Ainsley didn't blame her. Coming to this abandoned sugar mill felt a lot like finding an illegal rave in the warehouse district of her hometown, some-

110

thing she did a lot back in her early twenties. It hadn't felt too comfortable even back then.

Most importantly, Ainsley guessed that the woman was an American. She could tell by the need for personal space, which was most definitely not Puerto Rican. Her silence hinted at her discomfort with Spanish.

This woman might very well appreciate meeting someone like Ainsley.

She approached the woman and touched the open chair. "Excuse me," she said in English, "is anybody sitting there?"

The blonde woman looked up, startled. "Why, no, please, by all means."

Ainsley pulled out the chair, sat down, and used the plasticware to dig in. She started with the sides. The pigeon peas with rice were delicious, moist and buttery. She unwrapped the two *pasteles*, rich tamales made of mashed green bananas, purple *yautía*, and *calabaza* mixed with a pork filling. Those were even more impressive. She wondered where all this cooking was being done, exactly.

The blonde woman leaned over. "I'd skip that if I were you."

Her fork was pointing at a small sausage Ainsley had chosen on a whim.

"Why?"

"It's blood sausage. It's really gummy and doesn't have much flavor."

It sounded interesting, but she decided to play along. "Thank you for warning me. I'm Ainsley."

"Linda. Nice to meet you." They shook hands. Linda peered up at the corrugated roof far above them with a scrunched-up nose. "So how did you end up in this place?"

"I came with Luis."

"Half the men on this island are named Luis."

Ainsley had heard that already, and she pointed at her guide. "That Luis."

Linda followed her finger. "Oh, the one with Pacheco."

"You know Pacheco?"

"Sure, he's one of my husband's best workers."

"Who's your husband?"

"Him." She nodded towards a white middle-aged man, presumably American, who was standing around with a group of Puerto Ricans. They were hanging on his every word. "He's the plant manager."

That was top of the food chain. This woman was expecting Ainsley to seem impressed, so she did her best acting job. "He must be important here."

Linda nodded. She sat up a bit straighter. "How long have you been on the island?"

"Just a few days. What about you?"

"Ten years. We're getting ready to leave, though."

"Why?"

Linda huffed. "The pharmaceutical plant is closing." She gestured to the group. "Almost everyone here works for Pluvione."

Pluvione. Ainsley had heard that name before. It must've shown on her face, because Linda jumped in to explain. "It's one of the pharmaceutical giants. They all had plants here. But now they're all leaving."

Ainsley figured that betraying her ignorance wouldn't hurt her. "I didn't even know that pharmaceutical companies were here."

"Oh my, absolutely. Glaxo, Watson, Schering-Plough, Bristol-Myers Squibb—they've all had plants here for at least decade. Mostly in Arecibo. Puerto Rico is one of the world's top five producers."

"Why is that?"

Linda turned in her chair and explained the workings of her husband's business. It was, she said, a mere sixty-hour boat trip to the port in New York. There was no international paperwork to worry about. The manufacturers could write Made in the USA on the goods. The average worker expects four dollars less per hour than his mainland counterpart. And, until recently, the tax structure had been very tempting.

By now Ainsley had finished her food, and she decided to venture into the negative. "So what's the most frustrating part of this island?"

The words were barely out of her mouth when Linda answered: "Teaching my kids that yes doesn't mean yes here."

Ainsley cocked her head. "What do you mean?"

"Puerto Ricans hate confrontation, they hate saying no. So they say yes to everything. Once I was in a restaurant, and I asked if they had any coffee. The waiter said yes. So I asked him to bring me a cup. He said yes, they have coffee—but not that day."

"That would frustrate me."

"You have no idea." The woman chopped her hand onto the table. "Yes means yes. That's how I was raised. But not here. And the *mañana* culture is an issue too."

Ainsley could see that Linda was happy to find someone to vent to, and listened to her continue. "Puerto Ricans always say 'tomorrow, wait until tomorrow, we'll do it tomorrow'. Then it doesn't get done. It's been one of my husband's biggest problems at the plant."

She looked back her husband, the white man surrounded by darker men. Ainsley noticed that they were copying his stance, his mannerisms, even the brand of his clothing.

"Why does everybody come to an abandoned sugar mill?"

Linda let loose an exasperated sigh. "Nostalgia, mostly. It's been going on for a few months. I don't know how much longer they'll keep doing this. Tom comes becuase he says he wants to express solidarity with the workers, even to the end. They're losing their jobs, but we're just transferring back to Maryland."

Ainsley looked around. Many of these people were going to be unemployed shortly. And yet they were dancing, drinking, laughing, feasting on pork flesh. Her beautiful seatmate, Amaryllis, had been right. Nobody could party like Puerto Ricans.

Ainsley decided it was a good time to turn the conversation towards a more practical direction.

"Linda, can I ask you a question?"

"Of course."

"It's very sensitive."

The woman seemed alarmed but something flashed in her eyes, an excitement. "I'm discreet."

"I'm actually here to find somebody."

Linda allowed a smile to seep onto her lips. "You mean, *to date*?"

"No—"

"Because there's lots of *those*, if you want them."

Ainsley shook her head. "No, I'm looking for a missing person. Somebody told me that he likes to come here a lot."

"Well then, I've probably seen him. Tom and I come every Sunday."

"His name is Roman. Roman Galarza."

Linda mouthed the name to herself. "That's not familiar to me. But I can find out if anybody knows him."

"Would you mind?"

"Not at all. Let me talk to the women. I'll find you later."

As Linda stood up, she placed a friendly hand on Ainsley's arm. It was the first physical contact she had made.

22

When Ainsley found herself getting bitten by a monkey, she knew it was really time to stop drinking.

The afternoon inside the abandoned sugar mill had passed in a blur of rum, rain, and conversation.

While waiting for Linda, Ainsley circled through the factory, chatting with many of the partygoers. Near the roasted pig she found a group of men who were happy to explain the intricacies of *lechón* to her. How the pigs are never more than four months old. How the mainland ones are cheaper but inferior. How the pork cooks unevenly, even on a rotisserie. How the perfect *adobo*, or seasoning, contains salt, pepper, oregano, garlic, and local peppers called *ajicitos*—though even that sounded like it was up for debate.

But one thing was not up for debate, and that was the booze. It was flowing. After her third cup of a delicious concoction that coursed down her throat like liquid candy but made her eyesockets feel like glue, Ainsley had known she needed to stop drinking. When she found herself on the dance floor performing a terrible salsa dance, she had known she *really* needed to stop drinking.

Then a man had weaved through the party holding a small monkey. He looked vaguely homeless. The primate had been dressed in a small yellow polo shirt and had been holding a small can, on which had been written the words *Haga una donacíon al mono*.

She had understood. He had learned about this remote lechonera and was there to rattle his can.

Ainsley had pulled a dollar bill from her bag, and handed it to the small creature. The monkey had screeched and stuffed it into his own shirt. The owner had scolded the animal. So Ainsley had crouched down and stuffed her hands down its shirt. The monkey had screeched and sunk its teeth into her forearm.

The animal had been whisked away, Ainsley had been surrounded by concerned diners, and even more rum than usual had been poured into her cup. In Puerto Rico, she guessed, that was how you treat people who've been bitten by simians.

Now her wrist was being attended to by a kindly woman with a first-aid kit. It wasn't a serious bite. Ainsley listened to the rain drumming on the roof far above. The air was feeling moister. Glancing out a side door, she saw a thick veil of water pouring onto the ground from the overflowing rain gutters high above.

Outside, the tropical storm had returned with a vengeance.

"Ainsley, there you are," a voice said. It belonged to Linda, who was coming around the tables. "Was that you who was bitten by that stupid thing?"

"It was."

Linda sat down beside her. "So I couldn't find your man. Roman Galarza."

"Crap."

"I guess he didn't come today. None of the women knew who he was, but that doesn't really mean anything."

Ainsley understood the subtext. Linda was the boss man's wife. The women wanted to keep her happy. It seemed that Ainsley had made the right choice in sitting next to her.

"The good news is that one person did know him."

"Who?"

"Pacheco."

"Pacheco?" Ainsley looked over. He and Luis were pouring drinks into each other's cups, back and forth. It looked almost romantic. "That guy knows Roman Galarza?"

Ainsley watched Luis with distaste in her mouth. Her supposed guide was so hellbent on partying that he had completely forgotten the reason for their mission here.

She needed to remedy that.

Ainsley stalked across the dance floor and tugged on Pacheco's sleeve. The dancing had worked him into quite a state. His eyes were bulging and his skin was coated in a slick sheen of sweat.

"Beautiful," he shouted, "I don't know how this bastard managed to land you."

Ainsley played along. "It's a mystery to me too. Did this bastard bother to ask you about Roman?"

"Who?"

"Roman Galarza."

Pacheco held his cup out to Luis, who drunkenly swung a bottle of golden-colored rum towards his cup. "Roman. I know him. He's not here today. He must've stayed home."

The mixed drinks had done a number on Ainsley's sleuthing skills. She felt her mouth become more direct than usual. "Where does he live?"

But Pacheco drained his cup. He was drunk too. His eyes couldn't even find her own. "In my city. Mayagüez."

Then Luis lurched into both of them, singing awfully. A bottle of rum dangled from his hand. Ainsley suddenly had had enough. She placed her hand on Luis' chest and pushed him. He staggered backwards into an I-beam, then rubbed his head.

Then she turned to Pacheco. "Follow me."

23

SHE LED PACHECO AWAY FROM THE tables into a more remote portion of the factory. A spiderweb of rusted ironwork enveloped them. The shadows were deeper, the smells mustier. The salsa music was muted and distant.

Pacheco glanced around, unconcerned. "So what is the problem that you need to drag me away from the *lechón?*"

"We really need to find Roman Galarza."

"Luis too?"

Ainsley rolled her eyes. "Yes, Luis too."

His face brightened. "Of course. I can help you find him tomorrow."

"How?"

"We're having a *parranda*. Just drive over by eight pm. We'll stop at Roman's house near the beginning. Before it gets too crazy."

Ainsley felt thrilled. Then she thought about that term. *Parranda* translated to assault. She didn't want to attack anybody.

He seemed to read her mind. "Trust me, it's fun."

She wasn't sure about that. An assault sounded neither legal nor fun. "So where should I meet you?"

"At my house."

"I need your address."

"Luis knows where—"

Ainsley interrupted him. "Luis is drunker than anybody. Give *me* your address."

She fished a small notebook and pen from her purse. Pacheco leaned against the pillar and recited the street, number, and explicit directions to her.

She stowed the notebook away. "You're a prince, Pacheco."

"Then give me a hug."

"No, I'm Luis' property. Come on, let's go back."

He shrugged. They wended their way back through the machines. The *lechonera* was starting to empty out now. Pacheco was grabbed by a man with keys in his hand. He was starting to be steered towards the exit.

He broke free and came back to Ainsley. "It looks like I have to go. Where's that old shit-eater?"

They both spotted Luis at the same time. He was slumped at a table with his head in his arms. Pacheco went over and massaged Luis' shoulders.

"*Cabrón*, wake up. How are you getting home?"

There was no response. Pacheco looked at Ainsley. "You have quite a situation."

Ainsley nodded. Then she realized that Luis was the lesser of two problems.

The bigger problem was the fact that his little car had barely made it down the rutted road on the way into the Alondra ruins. The torrential downpour had probably rendered the road impassable now.

Panicking a little, Ainsley followed Pacheco to the front of the factory. At the doorway she looked out onto the parking lot. The previously packed dirt had now become an ocean of mud. The tires of Luis' car were already nearly halfway buried in slick reddish stuff. It appeared to be sinking into a swamp.

Short answer: There was no way that they were driving out of this place.

Pacheco waved goodbye and slipped into an SUV. She noticed for the first time that many of the other guests' vehicles, while old and dirty, were similarly high-clearance. They'd known what the rains would do to this area.

She ran back to the *lechonera*. The music had stopped now. The tables were being folded up. The cooks were loading the pig carcass into a large plastic bag. The meal had ended.

She and Luis were going to be closing down the place.

One of the cooks approached her. "Are you with him?"

He was pointing at Luis. The poet was crawling slowly across the factory floor. It looked as if he'd been poisoned.

Every cell in Ainsley's body wanted to deny it, but her mouth couldn't lie. "Yes, I am."

"So you're driving?"

"I would like to, but our car is stuck in the mud."

The cook was astonished. "But soon nobody will be left. You have to leave before it gets dark."

"Why?"

"There is no electricity without our generator. Do you want to stay here in the dark?"

Ainsley peered around. The machinery, the filaments of iron, the dank smells—it was already feeling creepier.

"I don't have a choice."

"Come with us."

He nodded to his friends. The other cooks, their gloves covered in pig grease, were leering at her. Then she looked back at Luis. He'd sprawled face-first on the floor of the factory. Passed out.

She sighed. "I'll stay here."

"Are you sure? Nobody's coming in the morning. This *lechonera* is closed until next weekend."

"I'll stay here anyways."

The cook went to the kitchen and returned with several ratty blankets. "Take these. You can leave them on the floor when you're done. We'll be back next weekend."

Ainsley thanked him. She watched the final guests stumble out to their truck. Then, a few minutes later, she watched the cooks pile into a van and roar down the road, spraying two roostertails of mud from the rear wheels.

She was alone now.

Ainsley stood in the front door, absorbing everything. The sounds of nature rose from the landscape. Raindrops smashing into the earth. Wet fronds brushing against one another. Bits of iron clanging in the breeze, like the tolling of a church bell.

She turned back to the interior of the empty factory. It'd grown nearly pitch black inside. Luis was still unconscious, but at least comfortably so. She'd rolled him onto the ratty blankets, made sure his head was supported, and left a large cup of water next to him.

Ainsley fought down the surge of panic that rose from her stomach. She needed to keep herself together.

The event was finished. She was alone, in an abandoned sugar factory, in a mild hurricane.

It was going to be a long night.

24

Ainsley had never been so grateful to see the dim light of morning, which was starting to creep beneath the crack of the factory door.

She had nodded off once, at about two o'clock. But a furtive rustle on the floor, followed by a light pressure on her leg, had woken her. She'd jerked awake to see the reddened eyes and sharp whiskers of a rat. A goddamned rat, sitting on her right leg, chewing on her pant leg.

The shriek had come from her very soul. A split second later, there'd been the bolt to her feet— and a panicked fifty-meter sprint outside, through the mud.

Standing in the pitch-dark driving rain had eventually driven Ainsley back into the factory. But she'd remained standing, leaning against a pole, flinching at every clink and thunk in the dark metallic jungle around her, listening to the rain showers pound the mud outside.

Then she'd spent the night going over in her mind why, exactly, she'd let herself get talked into this assignment.

Soon enough, the light had improved enough that she could make out the dim hulks of machinery around her. Her arms out, she felt her way back to the empty *lechonera*, towards Luis.

The blankets were still on the floor. But Luis was gone. She spun around. He couldn't have gone very far, not in his state.

Then, near the machinery, she saw the vague outline of a human.

It was Luis. He had rolled across the floor and been stopped by a giant iron gear, twice the size of a man. His head was fitted nicely between the cement floor and one of the gear's teeth. It didn't look at all comfortable, but Ainsley hadn't drunk her body weight in rum either.

Still, Ainsley could guess what had happened. At some point in the night, he'd probably woken up, still drunk and disoriented, and had stumbled around trying to find his way out.

She went over, her footsteps echoing in the industrial space, and crouched down next to him. She shook his shoulder.

"Luis."

He grunted. She shook him harder. "Luis. Wake up."

He blinked an eye open. His fingers felt the iron biting into the side of his face. The other half of his face was flattened by the concrete. "This isn't too bad."

"Do you know where you are?"

"No."

"We're still at the sugar mill."

"The *centrale?*" His eyes widened and darted around. Then he softened. "It's better than my apartment was in New York."

He tried to pull out his head from the gear. It wouldn't budge.

"I can't move my head," he said.

"Maybe it swelled up overnight." Then added: "More than it already is."

"I don't know. How do I look?"

"Awful."

He accepted that assessment. "I've been worse than that."

She was feeling impatient. "Listen, we need to go to Mayagüez. We'll find Roman Galarza there. Your friend Pacheco knows him."

"Pacheco," Luis said. "I *hate* him. He did this to me."

"You did this to *yourself.* Can we dig out the car? Can we make it down that road?"

"Whatever," he said, yawning. "I just want to sleep. Maybe I can slip out later."

Ainsley looked at the drunken poet with disgust. His eyes had closed again. She was damned if she was going to sit here all day watching him sleep off a hangover with his head wedged neatly between a gear and the concrete.

127

So she took the cup of water and threw it on his face. Luis spluttered and wiped it off.

"What?"

"I need to *leave*."

"Then *go*."

"How can I get to Mayagüez? Is there a bus?"

"No buses on Puerto Rico. Only *públicos*."

"What's a *público*?"

"A bus."

"You just said there were no buses."

"It's more like a van."

"Is there one near here?"

Luis rubbed his forehead. "In Yabucoa. It's just down the road."

"How far?"

"Maybe three kilometers. Down the main road." His finger swung in a wide circle.

"That's all?"

"Yes. You can walk there. Then you can wait in the plaza until the van arrives. Everybody uses them."

Ainsley felt a little pang of regret for ditching him. "What about you?"

"I'll drive home."

"No, come to Mayagüez. Pacheco wants you to come to the, what's it called..." She snapped her fingers, trying to remember. "An attack?"

Luis crinkled his forehead. "What do you mean?"

Ainsley remembered. "No, wait. He called it a *parranda*. We can meet Roman there."

Luis groaned and covered his face with his hand. "Oh God. A *parranda*. No, no, no. I need to recover first."

"What's a *parranda*?"

"You'll find out. Don't wait for me. Go take the *público*. I'll follow you later. Just let me sleep now."

"Are you sure?"

"Just go."

Ainsley shrugged and stood up. She watched him for a minute, until his mouth had sagged open and the sound of snoring emanated from within. Ainsley shook her head ruefully as she made her way through the machines.

She left the sugar mill and began walking through the morning rain.

25

As Ainsley made her way down the shoulder of the road towards Yabucoa, she began to appreciate how difficult life could be for rural people in poverty.

The gray skies were still dumping rain upon the ground. Her boots were caked with mud up to her ankle. She thanked her lucky stars that they were mid-calf height.

Two cars had passed her in the last half-hour, but she hadn't dared to ask for a ride from either of them. They hadn't stopped, either. Part of that made her sad. After being bitten by a monkey, and after spending a night alone in an abandoned sugar factory, she must look paranoid.

A road sign came into view: *Yabucoa, 14 km.* She cursed Luis under her breath. It was a lot further than he'd told her.

Nearly forty minutes later, her feet were already sore and her ankles were wobbly. Her stomach was grumbling. Ainsley guessed that she'd only walked a tiny fraction of that distance. She was beginning to feel cranky.

That's when a settlement came into view.

It was a cluster of no more than thirty ramshackle buildings, built a short distance off the road. At first glance, the homes looked abandoned, but soon she could hear dogs were barking. One shaky store even had its door open. In the middle of the settlement was a small plaza with a single dead palm tree. Ainsley guessed that this was where the sugar workers lived sixty, seventy years ago.

She could keep walking. Or she could stop here and ask for help.

A clap of thunder helped Ainsley make her decision. She stepped off the main road and walked past the decrepit homes. Their clapboard walls were shot through with holes. They looked like they hadn't seen a coat of paint since the height of the sugar era.

She closed her umbrella as she stepped into the small store. She wiped the rain water off her face.

The shop was literally as wide as her arms. A plump woman was nested into the tiny space behind the antique cash register. Her eyes were taking in Ainsley. "What happened to you?"

"You wouldn't believe where I spent the night."

Too late, Ainsley realized how that could be misinterpreted. The woman's belly jiggled with a giggle. "You go someplace else for lady pills," she said.

"I don't want lady pills."

"We don't have change either."

"I don't want that."

The woman tsk-tsked. "Look at you," she said. "Too much party. It's Monday morning."

Ainsley rolled her eyes. "Look, I just want to find the *publicó*. But I don't want to walk all the way to Yabuaco."

The woman said, "The *publicó* comes here."

"It does?"

"Oh yes."

"When?"

She shrugged. "In the morning sometime."

Ainsley looked at her watch. "It's eight o'clock right now. Should I wait?"

She shrugged again. "It's up to you."

"Can I wait here?"

"If you want."

This woman's eyes flicked towards the small television playing silently above the door. Ainsley realized that this was how she passed her life. Crammed into a small coop, eyes watching silent pictures on a screen, the hope of paying customers as long gone as the sugar refineries.

Ainsley paid her for a cup of drip coffee. As she took up residence on the stool, the woman watched her. "You come here for first time? To Puerto Rico?"

"Yes."

"Welcome to our island."

"Thank you."

The woman handed her a cup of coffee. "Cua-tros Sombras."

That translated as "four shades". That didn't make any sense. After one taste, however, she didn't care what the name meant, because it was phenomenally strong. Then again, if there was anyone in need of a strong cup of coffee at that moment, it was Ainsley.

She settled into her seat and sent her attention back to the television. It was a daytime game show. Ainsley tried to follow the action on the screen. It couldn't hold her interest.

More fascinating were the random collection of sundries offered for sale in this broom closet of a shop. Sponges, mops, cleaning agents, bags of *habichuelas*, boxes of cornmeal, sacks of rice, a rack of unfamiliar candies. These things were important out here.

When the program failed to keep her interest, Ainsley finished her coffee and just listened to the morning rain. She'd always found the rain soothing. Maybe the reason was instinctual. Maybe humans had evolved to be soothed by rain because it guaranteed the survival of the crops, and therefore the tribe.

An hour passed this way, until the shish of tires passed in front of the store. The sound of a door slam caused Ainsley to jerk awake. Given her sleepless night in the pitch-dark sugar mill, she was surprised she hadn't nodded off sooner.

She scuttled across the floor and peeked out the door. A battered white van, its exterior pockmarked with rusted dents, was parked a few meters away. A man was writing something on the windshield with an orange marker.

Caguas/Arecibo/Mayagüez.

That was her *publicó*. Excited, she headed back out into the rain and approached the driver. "I'm going to Mayagüez."

He nodded.

"How much is it?"

"Ten dollars."

Ainsley eagerly paid, then went back into the store. The driver followed her inside. "We're not leaving yet," he said.

"Why?"

"We have to wait for the others."

"How many others?"

He shrugged. "I don't know. Whoever wants to come."

Then the driver kissed the woman behind the register. She handed him a cup of coffee and he took Ainsley's seat on the stool. He took off his raincoat. They began a casual but involved conversation.

As Ainsley watched them, her nostrils flared. This *publicó* driver was going to leave whenever he damn well wanted to. She was more likely to find a sack of moon rocks than anybody with a sense of punctuality on this island.

Annoyed, she took her bag and umbrella and went out into the van to wait.

26

FOUR HOURS LATER, AS THE *PUBLICÓ* turned onto
the main road to begin its journey, Ainsley found
herself sharing a seat with a hen clucking inside a
wire cage.

The cage had been too large for the trunk space.
And its owner, a tiny middle-aged man, had insisted
that it couldn't be strapped to the roof. He'd explained that he was bringing the bird to his mother
in Arecibo for dinner that night.

Even without the chicken, the interior of the
van was as dirty and battered as the exterior. Ainsley shifted her weight and pinched her bottom
together, trying to sit lightly on the upholstery. She
kept her hands folded in her lap.

Behind her were two men, about Ainsley's own
age. Their hair was slick and they were passing a

bottle of rum back and forth. They had stumbled into the van just a few minutes earlier and seemed to be taking great advantage of the rainstorm.

As the van motored up into the storm cloud-cloaked hills of the Puerto Rican interior, Ainsley watched the rain slashing against the window. Even over the smooth sections of the road, the van rose and fell. The vehicle's suspension had seen better days.

The guys behind her were talking in Spanish. As she listened, she realized that they were talking about her.

"What do you think her name is?"

"Michelle."

"That's a stupid name."

"It's American."

"She's not American."

"Yes she is."

"Why don't you ask her?"

"*You* ask her."

"Idiot, you're the one who wants to know!"

"No, I don't care. It doesn't matter what her name is."

There was a pause. Then: "If she knows Spanish, we're both screwed."

Ainsley tried to hide her smile. There was already a chicken in a cage next to her. Now she had two even bigger chickens behind her. She decided that she would play dumb, since an introduction was imminent. She felt the men's eyes burning into the back of her head.

"I think she knows Spanish."

"No way. Give me the rum."

Ainsley heard a gulp. "Don Q has given me strength and courage. Now I'm going to ask her."

"You never know," said the other, "maybe she studies Spanish."

Ainsley felt a hand touch her shoulder. In English, the man said, "Excuse me, do you speak Spanish?"

"No, sorry," she lied.

"I want to say that you are very beautiful." The scent of his rum-soaked breath floated into her nostrils.

"That's sweet of you."

"Where are you going?"

"Mayagüez."

"To a resort? To meet your boyfriend?"

Ainsley decided to turn the tables, to see what she could learn from them. She turned sideways and laid her arm across the top of the seatback, earning herself a good look at her drunken suitors. They had harmless faces.

"No, I'm going to a *parranda*."

Both passengers burst out laughing. "But it's not Christmas," said one.

"It doesn't have to be Christmas," said the other.

"Of course it does—"

"No, not in some places, in the traditional places they do it anytime."

Ainsley held up a hand. "What's a *parranda*?"

"You don't know?"

She shook her head. It was the truth.

"You'll find out," one said. "We don't want to ruin the surprise."

They were toying with her now. Ainsley was feeling anxious. Had she been set up by Pacheco? Was she walking into a trap?

"So what are you doing on this island?" one said.

Ainsley knew that was coming and had already decided to reveal the mission. These guys, after all, were drunk enough to forget everything she said. "I'm looking for something."

"So you're a detective?"

"No. Just a stupid girl who doesn't speak the language." Ainsley smiled sweetly. "Can I ask you guys a question?"

"Absolutely not." Then he held out the rum. "I will not accept any more questions until you have a drink with us."

He held out the bottle. Ainsley pushed his arm away. "No thank you. Can I still ask my question?"

The guys shared another drink. "Okay."

"If you wanted to sell a piece of jewelry, where would you go to sell it?"

"The States," said one.

"Miami," echoed the second.

"What if you couldn't do that?"

The guys didn't say anything. Then they conferred with each other in rapid-fire Spanish. Ainsley assumed a stupid expression on her face, but she was listening closely.

"You tell her—"

"No, Omar said he's trying to stay low—"

"Why do you care about him? He's just a criminal pretending to be a *vejigante* artist. And his friends tried to fuck you up."

"I can't."

"You don't even know him that well."

"No, it's bad luck—"

"He's from Loíza. You don't even *go* there, *blanco*."

Ainsley was committing every term to her memory: *Omar. Vejigante artist. Loíza.*

Their conversation switched back to English. "No, we don't really know anywhere like that."

"Wish we could help you," said the other. "You sure you don't want some rum?"

The first one smacked his buddy on the back of the head. "You drink your own rum. Michelle is going to a *parranda*."

"A *parranda*," said the other, grinning. "Have fun."

To Ainsley's ears, that sounded ominous.

Five hours and even more stops later, the van arrived at Mayagüez. Her drunken suitors had passed out hours earlier. She stumbled out onto the street, her legs wobbly from the long ride, but ready to finish her mission. Ready to find out what a *parranda* was.

Ready to meet Roman Galarza.

Mayagüez

27

Ainsley was standing in Pacheco's living room trying to understand what exactly she was about to experience.

"It's like a snowball," the man was explaining, shaping his hands into a small snowball.

Another guy jumped in. "Close your mouth, *bobo*. We don't have snow in Puerto Rico." He looked for the words. "A *parranda* is just ... fun."

Ainsley was feeling confused. "I still don't understand."

A third guy stepped forward. "These idiots can't talk. It's just a party. A *parranda* is a big, long, rolling party. It gets bigger as it goes along. You understand now?"

"We go from house to house," added another.

"Are the people expecting the party?" said Ainsley.

The first man chuckled. "No, it's not like the mainland where you make an appointment to see your friends. You just show up. And they have to welcome you."

"We don't take no for an answer," said another.

Then a cry went up from the six men and two women gathered in the living room: "*Parrandero!*" They toasted each other, threw the liquor down their throats, and headed out the door. Ainsley found herself carried along in their wake.

They were in a hilly barrio of Mayagüez that, judging from the houses, had seen better days. But the trees were tall and arched. Ainsley knew nothing about this particular town except for what the guys on the *público* had told her: that Mayagüez was where all the drunken Americans docked their boats. She didn't think that they'd had much right to be pointing fingers.

The group walked several blocks in the darkness. It had stopped raining for the moment, but Ainsley smelled the dampness in the air, felt the drips from the tree branches hitting the top of her head.

Then the *parranda* turned up the driveway of a simple concrete-block house. It was painted aquamarine. A wire fence circled the modest yard, in which a bicycle was slowly rusting. A single light shone behind the metal slats over the living room window.

The revelers raised their voices as they approached the front door. Pacheco proudly banged on the door with his fist.

Ainsley stood at the back of the group. She didn't know their songs. She wasn't drinking their liquor. She wasn't anything to these people except a barnacle on the hull of their party boat.

The door opened. A man in a dirty white t-shirt appeared. His hair was as oily as a derrick, and his eyes were raised to half-mast. He had the resentful look of someone rudely awakened.

The *parranda* didn't even greet him. They just sang more loudly.

The homeowner leaned his head wearily against the doorframe. He held up a hand. "I have two sleeping children."

"There's no use resisting," said Pacheco. "They're going to wake up. It's just a fact. Let us in."

"*Ay bendito*," said the homeowner, but stepped aside anyways. The *parranda* pushed its way into the house, with Ainsley in the caboose.

The inside was as plain as the outside, simple rattan couch and a glass-top coffee table. From the back of the house appeared a husky woman in a t-shirt and shorts. A cotton sleepmask was pushed up on her forehead. She was squinting in the light.

"*Una parranda?*"

Her husband shrugged in a what-can-you-do manner. He hadn't asked for it either.

The woman sighed loudly and entered the kitchen. She came back out with a plate of plantain chips and a half-empty bottle of rum. She set both onto the coffee table and punched a hand onto her hip. "Who's first, bastards?"

A loud cheer went up. Plastic cups appeared, the bottle was emptied, and hearty hugs were delivered to the two homeowners. This was how a *parranda* worked.

Twenty minutes later, Ainsley found herself swimming behind the party boat again. This time, however, the assaulted couple was in the lead.

Ainsley sidled up to Pacheco. "Where are we going now?"

"Wherever they want. It's the way we do it here."

"We need to find Roman Galarza."

He nodded. "Don't worry, I'll make sure of that."

That next house was a slum. Ainsley saw the huge jagged cracks in the concrete block walls, the weeds overwhelming the front yard, the mound of garbage to the side. She heard the same songs, the same knocks, the same unlatching of the bolts.

The interior of the second house was unbear-ably dingy. Ainsley was grateful when Pacheco took the party into the tiny backyard patio.

This family reluctantly served rice and beans with the ubiquitous bottle of rum. Ainsley took the spoon and glopped some of the stuff onto her dish. She studied the food. The beans were red, not black the way the Cubans liked it, and served with bits of potatoes mixed in. She tasted the con-coction. This, the daily food for most of humanity, tasted pretty good.

Over the next hour, the *parranda* carried on, to a third, fourth, fifth home. By now the numbers had swollen to more than thirty. She'd seen ecstatic neighbors dashing out of their houses in flip-flops, carrying beers, to join the party brigade. But Ainsley was growing impatient. She was here on a mission.

"Pacheco," she said, tugging at his sleeve, "I hate to be a pest, but when will we get to Roman Galarza?"

"Luis asked me to wait until he arrives," he replied. "Are you having a good time?"

Ainsley looked around at the people jammed into the stranger's living room. "Sure, but I can't believe people just accept this. Right in their own homes."

He swigged from a bottle of beer. "In the bigger cities they don't, not anymore. There are too many gates, too much crime. Even for us, it's a special occasion."

"Which is?"

He grinned. "We celebrate the rainstorm. Nobody has to work this week."

Ainsley understood that. It was like a snow day back in elementary school. At the next house, she was inspecting a shelf of Catholic paraphernalia when she heard a roar. She turned around. Luis had arrived.

He didn't look too worse for wear. He was wearing a fresh shirt, and his hair was combed. But his eyes were bloodshot, and the pouches under his eyes looked more puffy than usual.

"You found the *público*," he said.

"It was easier than finding a bed last night."

He smirked. "So sleeping in the *centrale* didn't suit you."

"Who said I was sleeping?"

"It was an experience, huh?"

Ainsley felt her sharp tongue rearing up for the strike. "Sure, Luis. In fact, if room service hadn't undercooked my chicken cacciatore, then I might consider staying on the concrete again."

"It's my fault," he said. "Sometimes I just go too far with the drinking."

"We couldn't have left anyways. How did you dig your car out?"

"I called a friend with a winch. He towed the car back to the main road."

Ainsley sipped from her cup.

"What's in that?" he said.

"Soda."

"Have some rum."

Ainsley covered her cup. She was really getting fed up with the endless boozing. Plus she needed to be alert. "No, I really just want to get to Roman Galarza."

Luis nodded. "Oh yes, let me see about that."

She watched Luis move through the party, greeting people, smiling, kissing cheeks. He lived for socializing, would've been a great politician, with his cheerfulness, his evasions. She watched Luis confer with Pacheco, who nodded. Then she watched him thread his way back through the group.

Luis took Ainsley by the elbow and whispered into her ear. "Roman's house is next."

28

A FIVE-MINUTE WALK DOWN THE STREET, and Ainsley found herself looking at the front facade of Roman Galarza's house.

It was a bungalow too. The concrete block walls, so useful during hurricanes and insect invasions, were painted turquoise. The windows were still barred by steel slats.

But this house had a small satellite dish on the roof. Ainsley also noticed that a large sodium lamp shone a pool of yellowish light onto a side entrance. A guard dog barked madly as the group approached. All signs that something expensive was customarily kept inside.

Such as a crab-shaped pearl brooch.

Ainsley ran around to the front of the *parranda*, which numbered almost forty people by now.

She wanted to be at the front door when Pacheco knocked.

Pacheco unlatched the gate to the high fence that surrounded Roman Galarza's house. Inside the house, a light flicked on. A silhouette appeared in the window, then darted quickly out of sight.

Ainsley felt her heart speed up. That was her target. What she would do when the party knocked on the door, she wasn't sure yet. It wouldn't be too wise to accuse him of theft, not in the middle of the night, not after forty drunken people had just barged into his living room.

No, she would play it quiet, look around. No accusations. This was merely reconnaissance.

After one knock, a large middle-aged woman answered, her lips drawn tightly. "*Una parranda?*" she said. "*Esta noche?*"

Pacheco kissed her on the cheek. "Fifteen minutes. No more."

Her eyes scanned the group and landed upon Ainsley. "But Roman is sleeping."

"Wake him up," said Pacheco.

"Impossible. He sleeps like a dead person." A sense of acceptance came over her face. "Please stay in the yard. I'll join you."

She started to close the door, but Pacheco caught it. "Just bring out the rum. We know you have good stuff in there."

Roman's wife shut the door, then came out again a moment later with a new bottle. Ainsley saw the label: Don Q. The label featured an image of the famous windmill-tilter. It seemed to be the locals' favorite brand.

She unscrewed the top and began moving through the party, topping off everybody's cups. A hard look dominated her face. It seemed that the *parranda* wasn't being enjoyed by everybody.

When she came to Ainsley, the woman poured a shot into her cup. Ainsley didn't stop her.

"It must be difficult," said Ainsley, "having people demand a party from you."

The woman's eyes blazed with anger. "There's a reason nobody does these anymore. It's like hosting a party with a gun to your head."

"Would you mind if I asked one more thing from you?"

The woman grew wary. "What?"

"Do you think I could use your bathroom?"

She looked even more suspicious. "Just don't wake my husband."

"I won't."

Roman's wife moved on. Ainsley wasted no time. She threaded her way through the singing crowd and moved into the home.

The living room was decent. The warm wooden floors were slightly warped, from the humidity, but had been swept clean. An upholstered Queen Anne living room set had been placed at a perpendicular angle. A wide-screen television dominated the other side of the room.

Ainsley walked into the back hallway and found the bathroom. Then she saw another door, further along, closed tightly. A horizontal sliver of light shone from underneath the frame.

That was the bedroom. Where, supposedly, Roman Galarza was sleeping. With all the lights on.

Ainsley smelled something fishy. It seemed much more likely that he was awake. He probably just didn't want to be found by the *parranda*.

Ainsley bit her knuckles and looked back at the front door. Nobody had followed her inside yet. If she had the courage, she would push open the bedroom door, stick out her arm, and demand the pearl brooch. But that wasn't polite or even likely to work. The situation wasn't right. Ainsley was a stranger, and Roman could be in his underwear. It could be seen as possibly sexual and definitely rude.

Ainsley cursed under her breath. She was *so close*. She ground her teeth together in frustration.

Then the answer crashed upon her like a Caribbean wave onto a beach. She would do a leave-behind.

Ainsley smiled at the thought. It was the classic lady's move to ensure a second date. Years ago, before meeting the Legal Weasel, sometimes when Ainsley wanted to see a man again, she would "accidentally" forget something of hers in his home or car. Maybe a makeup item. Every woman knew this technique. It was a convenient, believable, and very useful trick.

She pawed around inside her purse. Her brow wrinkled. Mascara, no. Passport, definitely not. Birth control, no, unless she wanted to cause a divorce. No, the only item in her purse that she could plausibly forget here would be her mobile phone. She felt its heft in her hand. It would be hard to part with the phone, even for a few hours.

But she would return in the morning.

Ainsley scooted into the bathroom and laid the telephone on the toilet tank. It would look as though she'd laid it down to wash her hands, then absentmindedly forgotten it.

She flushed the toilet, in case anyone was listening, then washed her hands. Then she dried them on the hand towel, and left the bathroom. She stepped outside the front door and rejoined the party.

Pacheco and Luis stood on either side of the door, waiting for her to reappear. Luis cast a meaty arm across her shoulders. "We didn't see you go inside. Did you find Roman?"

"He's asleep," she replied. "Supposedly. But the lights are on."

"Did you knock on his door?"

"No, please. It's the middle of the night. I'll come back tomorrow."

Luis nodded. "That's a good plan."

Ainsley felt a yawn take possession of her. She checked her watch. It was three o'clock in the morning. "How long will the *parranda* go on?"

"Until it stops," said Pacheco. "It's a force of nature. Like a hurricane."

He and Luis toasted one another, and soon they were leading the charge out of Roman Galarza's front yard, onto the next house.

29

SEVEN O'CLOCK AM.

Ainsley was limping on foot back towards Roman Galarza's house, feeling like a piece of reanimated roadkill.

The soles of her boots had started to collapse. Her hair was plastered to her scalp with rain and sweat. Her skin felt sticky and dirty. An unexplained cut on her forearm had smeared blood on the sleeve of her shirt.

They'd underestimated the momentum of the *parranda*. Roman Galarza's house hadn't even signified the halfway point. The group had kept rolling through the night, gathering force, until the numbers had swollen to nearly eighty.

Then, just after dawn, it had finally burst, pricked by a bolt of lightning that announced an honest-to-God thunderstorm. The final stop had been a house only a few blocks away from Pacheco's house, where it had started.

By the end, she'd noticed, the hosts had switched to pouring black coffee and serving chicken soup. But caffeine and soup couldn't perk up Ainsley. Almost nothing would. The red spiderweb of burst capillaries in her eyeballs would only be repaired by an uninterrupted twelve-hour date with a pillow.

She knew where to go for that. Luis had found two rooms in a cheap motel nearby and given her the address and the key. He was surely asleep by now. She didn't know how he could go like this, quaffing liters of rum at the *lechonera*, passing out in a rat-infested sugar factory, then speeding across the island in a rainstorm before joining a party the next evening, and drinking even more rum at twenty-three different houses (by her count). Ainsley herself had barely survived this gauntlet, and she wasn't even yet thirty years old.

But sleep would have to wait. She squinted and looked around the street for landmarks. She recognized the stand of magnolia trees. This was Roman's street, for sure.

She found the house. The same fenced yard, the same satellite dish. Its edges looked somehow sharper in the grayness of the rainy morning, its paint somehow brighter.

Ainsley tried to run her fingers through her hair, to look presentable. They wouldn't enter. It was too tangled.

She strode to the front door of the Galarza residence and knocked boldly.

Roman's wife answered. A small smile decorated her face. "I think I know why you're here."

"I forgot my phone."

"It's right where you left it." She gestured to enter.

Ainsley stepped inside and beelined for the bathroom. The phone was still on the tank, untouched. She stowed it in her purse. Then she looked up at the shelf of toiletries.

The man's sundries were gone. Half the shelf was empty. Someone had cleared out.

Roman Galarza was gone.

Ainsley chewed on her lip. She was feeling something weird stirring in the background of this wild manhunt.

She exited the bathroom and quickly glanced at the bedroom. The door was open and the room was empty. Some male belongings—shorts, socks—had been scattered across the bed. As though they'd been rejected by someone who'd packed in a hurry.

Ainsley walked into the living room. Roman's wife was looking at a small notepad. As she drew closer, Ainsley could see that on the paper was a telephone number, beneath which was scrawled what appeared, even from her perspective, to be an address.

Roman's wife saw Ainsley and quickly tore the paper from the pad and stuffed it into the front pocket of her jeans. She tossed the pad onto the kitchen table, well away from her visitor.

There was a four-alarm fire of suspicion blazing inside Ainsley now. She peered at the woman.

"Where is your husband?"

"He had to leave."

Ainsley had figured that. "It's too bad. I was hoping to meet him."

Roman's wife shrugged.

"Where did he go?"

"I don't know. But he said he would be back in a few days. You know, his job takes him all over the island."

Ainsley nodded. Her eyes glanced at the empty notepad on the table. "Could I ask a small favor?"

"Okay."

"I feel really dehydrated. Could you get me a bottle of water? To take on the road?"

"Of course," said the wife. "You need to drink water during a *parranda*."

She turned away and moved across the kitchen towards the refrigerator. Ainsley seized the opportunity. She quickly grabbed the empty notepad and slipped it into her purse.

The woman returned with a can of Diet Coke. "It's all I have right now."

"That'll be great."

Ainsley really disliked diet sodas. But she thanked the woman and attempted a bit more awkward small talk. There wasn't much there.

A minute later, she had said goodbye and was exiting Roman Galarza's house.

A minute after that, Ainsley looked back. Even at a distance, in the doorway of the house, his wife was watching her intently.

30

IN HER ATTEMPT TO DECIPHER THE handwriting impression on the top of the pad, Ainsley had broken the motel room's only lamp.

With difficulty had she found this fleabag joint near the highway. It had been Luis' choice. It featured the kind of cell-block ambience that only a failed poet could occupy. The concrete block walls were festooned with dusty oil paintings. The television was crowned by the last surviving pair of rabbit-ear antennae in the western world. The mattress was thin. A dead brown cockroach lay in the corner like a chewed-out stub of a cigar.

If she lifted the pad horizontally to her eyes, with a light source behind it, Ainsley could make out the minute depressions left by Roman's wife's pen. The problem lay in the light source. It wasn't high enough, and Ainsley sure as hell wasn't sitting on the floor of this room.

That's when she'd gotten the bright idea to hoist the lamp higher by looping its electrical cord through an exposed pipe overhead.

At first, it had worked, transforming the room into a deranged vision of a pirate ship's hold. She'd been able to make out a couple letters.

But then the electrical cord had popped out of the base. The lamp had dropped and shattered on the linoleum.

Before she could clean it up, there was a knock on the door. She opened it. It was Luis. She was amazed to see him walking upright.

"What's going on? I heard something crash."

"I broke the lamp."

He peered around the room. "I don't know why you're bothering. This room won't ever be pretty."

"I was trying to read something."

Then she noticed his appearance. Luis was showered, shaved, and dressed in a fresh shirt. "What's up with you? I thought you'd be sleeping all day."

"Doña Pilar called," he said. "She needs me to go back."

Ainsley felt a small stab in her heart. Luis, despite his obvious shortcomings, had been an invaluable guide. He seemed to know everybody everywhere.

"So you aren't going to help me anymore?"

Luis shrugged. "Doña Pilar is a difficult woman. She likes to change her mind."

"Roman Galarza left his house early this morning."

"Really?"

"Yes. He went somewhere. But I don't know where." She pointed to the pad of paper. "I think the address was written on the paper, but I can't figure it out."

He held up his hands in a sign of mercy. "Don't ask me to help. I'm terrible at that kind of detective stuff."

"Okay."

He sucked on the inside of his cheek. "Ainsley, can I ask you a question?"

"Maybe."

"How much is Doña Pilar paying you?"

"Nothing. But there's a three-thousand dollar reward from the museum. And Pilar promised to get me off this island as soon as possible."

Luis seemed genuinely surprised. "How is that?"

"She said she knows somebody. A pilot."

"What's his name?"

Ainsley struggled to recall the man's name. So much had happened in the last three days that her memory felt dull. Then it came to her.

"She said his name was Ivan Torregrosa."

Luis looked even more surprised. "Ivan? She told you that Ivan would fly you somewhere?"

"Yeah. To Miami."

He shook his head. "I know Ivan. He lost his pilot's license years ago. I saw his sister last month. She can't find him since he got out of prison." He gazed at her sadly. "Ivan isn't flying you anywhere."

Ainsley sat down on the thin bed, which squeaked beneath her. She felt deflated. Then she began to feel angry, furious, even enraged at every-thing—at the bed, the lamp, the room, Luis, Doña Pilar, Tomás, Amaryllis, this assignment, and, most of all, herself.

Nobody had forced her to commit to three days of insane careening around Puerto Rico. She'd chosen it, out of pity for the old woman, out of boredom, but mostly out of an intense desire to get home.

Now the curtain had been yanked away, reveal-ing the lie beneath. The reward had been a sham. Doña Pilar had no way to help her get home. She was the wizard behind the curtain.

Ainsley felt malaise creeping up her legs, like the filthy black waters of a rising flood, threatening to fill her very soul. There was no escaping the reality that, until the airport drained its runways, she was stuck on this island.

"Thank you for that information," she mut-tered, "thank you very much."

His face was full of concern. "Look, Puerto Rico isn't an easy place to live. I left for almost forty years, remember?"

Ainsley did remember. But she was hunched over her knees, her head dropped between her elbows.

"My advice," he said, "is to forget about the crab brooch. It's lost. Doña Pilar isn't going to see it again."

"I wish you'd told me that three days ago."

"You wouldn't have listened to me."

There didn't seem to be anything more to say. The wind had been taken out of Ainsley's sails. She was adrift.

"Call me if you need anything," said Luis. "I already paid for the room."

"Thank you," she said, "but that was unnecessary."

"Why?"

Ainsley stood up. Her eyes were aflame. "Because I am going to a resort, like a goddamned ordinary tourist. I'll stay there until the airport reopens. It's what I should have done all along."

She tossed the notepad into her bag, zipped it up, and stalked out of the room.

31

THE NEXT MORNING, THE SUNSHINE HAD finally broken through the cloud cover.

Ainsley was luxuriating in the ultraviolet rays. At this moment, she didn't care whether they were UVA or UVB. Or C, D, or Z. She didn't care what they were doing to her skin. She just liked feeling warm and dry for the first time in a long while.

She was reclining in a chaise lounge alongside an enormous pool. A man was performing a lazy freestyle, the ripples rolling across its tranquil surface. A glass of pineapple juice stood beside Ainsley. Beads of condensation had run down the sides of the glass and soaked a ring into the wooden table.

This was the Casa del Mar, a two-hundred unit luxury resort, owned by a gigantic global hotel chain. It offered every distraction that a modern tourist has been trained to desire. There were wind-surfing lessons, snorkeling expeditions, volleyball, shuffleboard, three different bars, four different pools. The wait staff wore white polo shirts and even more dazzlingly white smiles.

It'd been recommended by the taxi driver who'd picked up Ainsley. After sleeping upright on the floor of an abandoned sugar refinery, she was willing to give just about anything a shot.

Except Amaryllis' family. If she were going to give up on Doña Pilar, she couldn't face those people.

So Ainsley had passed out on the bed, not even bothering to climb inside the high thread-count sheets. At midnight she'd ordered room service, showered, then fallen back asleep again.

Now it was eight o'clock the next morning, and Ainsley finally felt human again. She sipped her juice. It had just the right balance of sweetness and tang. She settled back into her chair and faced the sun again.

The sound of feet padding across the deck opened her eyes. She craned her head. A retired couple had arrived and chosen two chaise lounges nearby. They seemed hale and hearty people, the lucky ones who'd maintained full health into their sixties.

"That girl's got the right idea," said the wife, pointing at Ainsley.

"Do you think it's safe to swim?" replied her husband. He had peeled off his shirt and was peering through the glass railing towards the beach.

"I don't know."

Ainsley turned her head. "There's no swimming anywhere in the ocean yet."

"Really?" he answered.

"The waiter told me the beach is closed."

The man nodded. "The runoff. I should've known."

"Puerto Rico is no paradise," said his wife. "It's actually quite filthy. Have you left the resort yet?"

Ainsley smiled to herself. "Yeah."

"Not us. We're staying right here. What's your name?"

"Ainsley."

"I'm Steven and this is Kate. We're from Boston."

"Nice to meet you."

"Are you here with someone?" said Steven.

"Just me."

"Vacation?"

"Rerouted flight. I've been here four days."

"Oh my," said Kate, "that hurricane. It's destroyed our trip too. This is the first sun we've seen."

"If we'd known," said Steven, "we could've just rescheduled. We're retired now. We're flexible."

"Nothing to do," his wife replied.

"Nothing at all."

They sat back in the chaise lounges, basking in their uselessness. Ainsley supposed it probably felt good after a lifetime of practicality.

"But there's something to be said," Steven announced, "for having a purpose."

"My purpose," said his wife, "is to sit in the sun and eat whatever I want."

But Steven was serious now. "I mean, I wake up in the morning and wonder, what am I doing today? Is my day headed somewhere?" He looked at Ainsley. "You probably don't know what I'm talking about. You're too young yet."

Ainsley flipped her sunglasses back down over her eyes. She didn't want to reveal the truth that he'd managed to distill her entire identity crisis into just a few sentences.

True, she wanted to get home. But to what? There was very little left there for her. Her husband, the Legal Weasel, had upped and disappeared months earlier. Her regular career had been laughable, a series of dead-end jobs. Her friends were busy raising families of their own.

All she really had was this budding career as an international gemstone detective. Yes, it had fallen into her lap. Yes, it was slightly ludicrous. Yes, it was extremely unstable, and she had no idea how to perpetuate it, or advertise herself.

But she couldn't simply toss it away, either.

"I do understand," she said.

"Good," he replied, "but my wife doesn't. My God, I'd give anything to have a purpose again. That's what I miss most about my job. Not the money. The sense of *mission*."

Steven noticed a resort waiter circling around the pool. "Hey, what's the word on the airport?"

"Still closed," said the waiter.

"For how long?"

The waiter picked up Ainsley's empty glass and placed it on his tray. "The last I heard, at least three more days. They're pumping water off the runways. Isla Verde always floods badly when it rains."

Ainsley willed herself to feel happy by the news. Three more days with nothing to do in a tropical paradise. She felt a slight chill pass across her body. She glanced up. A cloud had passed across the sun.

She stood up and adjusted her top. Her new bikini, a floral number purchased in a shop inside the resort, wasn't fitting right. She walked to the railing and looked out over the peaked waves of the ocean.

This was an inner crisis. And the answer was making itself clear.

As long as she was marooned in Puerto Rico, Ainsley had to keep searching for this crab-shaped pearl brooch. Not for Amaryllis, not for Doña Pilar, not for Luis, not even for the three thousand dollar reward from the museum.

But for *herself.*

Then Ainsley thought about the drunk guys sitting behind her on the *público*, the ones who'd been talking about her in Spanish. They'd mentioned someone, a well-known fence. Ainsley looked down and pounded the heel of her hand on the railing as she scraped her memory banks.

Then it returned to her. *Omar. Vejigante artist. Loíza.*

She picked up her towel and her purse. The retired couple looked over.

"Hope we didn't scare you away," said Steven.

"Not at all," said Ainsley. "I just have something to take care of."

32

FROM THE MOMENT SHE STEPPED OUT of the taxi-cab in shabby downtown Loíza, the prickly feeling at the back of Ainsley's neck told her that there were many eyes watching her.

Maybe it was the music. From several doorways she could hear the loud echoes of reggaeton, the saucy Spanish rhymes galloping over the thumping party beat, a dollop of horns sprinkled around the edges. She had remembered hearing it in clubs.

Or maybe it was the unemployed men gathered outside the liquor stores. They looked no different from the unemployed men hanging out at corner liquor stores in countries all over the world.

Ainsley felt herself clutching her purse more tightly under her arm. Years of exploring seedy neighborhoods back home had conditioned her this

167

way. She walked quickly, head high, as though she knew exactly where she was headed. Of course, this marked her as even more of an outsider, since few people in the Caribbean ever walked quickly anywhere.

Her purposefulness was a fiction anyways. She hadn't the faintest clue where to find this Omar, or how she would broach the topic of the crab brooch if she found him. But first she had to pass the liquor store.

She felt the men's eyes tracking her up and down. She knew what was going through their besotted minds. Too tall, too skinny, not Puerto Rican. She knew this because they let her walk by without shouting a single come-on. That was a relief.

On the next block, she saw a teenage boy perched on a tall concrete wall alongside a gas station. It made him look like a puppet. A pair of flip-flops dangled from his ashy feet.

He didn't waste time. When his eyes landed on her, he said, "You need something?"

"Yeah," said Ainsley, "I'm looking for some-body."

"Who?"

"Omar."

"My cousin is named Omar."

"Does he make *vejigante* masks?"

She didn't yet know what that word meant, but faking it was a part of every successful woman's arsenal.

He brightened up. "Oh, *that* Omar. His shop is over there. You know how to get there?"

Ainsley shook her head. "No, but I'll figure it out. That way?"

The teenage boy leaped down from the wall. He wore a white tank top and long basketball shorts that went down below his knees. "I'll take you."

She protested. "No, that's not really—"

"Please," he said. "This neighborhood isn't for tourists."

"I'm not a tourist."

The teenager smirked. "Trust me, you're a tourist."

Ainsley felt indignant. It seemed that the power of definition wasn't in her hands.

A wailing police siren announced itself. Seconds later, a squad car sped by. Her guide's eyes followed the vehicle until it turned out of sight. Ainsley suspected that it paid to know who the police were bothering.

"This way," he said.

They moved down the sidewalk, past an open doorway. Inside she glimpsed a small shrine, several tambor drums, and a man wearing a white cap. The smell of incense assailed her nostrils. Ainsley recognized all this paraphernalia. It meant that *santería*, the famous Afro-Caribbean religion, was practiced here.

Her guide didn't seem to notice. She followed him two more blocks, then around a corner. Off the main drag, she felt even more eyes watching her from doorways, windows, automobiles.

"Loíza isn't safe after dark," he said, "and it's hard to get taxicabs."

"For tourists?"

169

"For anybody. There's too much violence."

His eyes glanced at her. Ainsley continued to follow but began to doubt herself. She felt damp heat growing inside her clothing. The day was overcast, but humidity had returned to the island with a vengeance.

Then they came upon a small shop. An intricate sign above the crooked door read *Artesanías Omar*. A hand-scrawled sign declared the opening hours to be whenever.

"You've been very helpful," she said.

"It's my pleasure," said the teenager. "Just tell Omar I helped you."

"What's your name?"

He shook his head. "Point at me. He knows me."

This kid had some kind of agenda. Ainsley was at least streetwise enough to sense that. It wasn't her business. She pushed open the door of the artisan shop and stepped inside.

33

AINSLEY STOOD THERE, GAPING, UTTERLY TAKEN aback.

The walls of the shop were covered in masks. Not flimsy plastic ones, or tiny dainty ones—but *large* masks, intricately carved, with enormous papier-mâché horns branching out like deer antlers.

These, she guessed, were *vejigante* masks.

An older black man looked up from behind a desk. He was tall, long-limbed, and moved like sludgy molasses. A conspicuously heavy door behind him had been deadbolted shut. The rest of the shop was so ratty that a handicapped child could break into it, but that door was something different. Ainsley knew she needed to get into it.

"*Bienvenida*," he said.

"Omar?" she asked.

"Yes."

She pointed out the window, to the teenager who was loitering outside on the sidewalk. "That was my guide. He wants you to know that he helped me find your shop."

Omar craned his neck, looking outside. "Benny. That little *comemierda*." He made an abrupt hand gesture.

Ainsley also knew that *comemierda* meant "shit eater". She glanced outside. The teenager was making some aggressive hand gestures in return. She didn't know what to make of this antagonism. After all, Benny had been perfectly helpful to her. She felt currents swirling deep below the surface.

She said, "I heard you're the best at making these masks."

"It's true," he replied. "At least since Castor Ayala passed away. He was the master."

"Can you tell me about them?"

Omar silently pointed to a placard on the wall. It was titled *Historia de Vejigante*. Ainsley walked over obediently. She really didn't care about the masks. What she really wanted to know about was this man's sideline.

Fencing gemstones.

Nonetheless, her eyes scanned the text. The placard explained that *vejigante* masks had originated in Spain, where they were designed to represent the Muslim enemy during the fifteenth-century Spanish Crusades. In Puerto Rico, they have somehow become a recognizable symbol of merriment and mischief. They're still seen in Loíza on July 25 each year, at a huge festival in honor of St. James, one of the original apostles, whose image was used by Spaniards as a symbol of Christian might against the Muslim infidels.

Ainsley tapped her toe. That was all well and good, but she had a mission. Being seen as a tourist from the mainland wouldn't lead anywhere. She needed to reframe this conversation. It would require a bit of force.

"How many do you sell each month?"

His eyes crinkled. "Why do you care?"

She glanced at his wrist. He was wearing an expensive watch with an enormous face. It looked like a Bulgari. "Enough to afford that?"

He smiled. "This was a gift from a client."

Ainsley sighed. She spread her hands on the counter, then leaned forward over them. "Omar, I have to tell you something. I'm not here to see your masks."

The man grew very still. His face grew watchful. He leaned forward and clicked off the television. Then he leaned back in his chair and laid his long brown hand against the side of his face.

"So why are you here?" he said.

"You can guess why."

"No, I can't. I'm just a simple *vejigante* artisan."

Ainsley decided to show her card. "I'm looking for a piece of jewelry. A special one."

"Why would I have something like that?"

Now Ainsley was getting frustrated. She'd never had patience to break through the people who played dumb. But Omar was doing exactly that, and doing it well.

"Because you sell jewelry."

To her surprise, he blinked. His stone face had cracked. "Who told you that?" he said.

"I found a note at the bottom of a bottle of rum."

A smile began to spread across his mouth, and she noticed his teeth. They were clean, white, and large, planted in his mouth like two rows of white picket fencing.

Omar betrayed nothing more. "What do you want to know?"

"We're going to talk here?"

"It's possible."

"I thought you were going to ask me to step into the back."

His eyes narrowed. "Who *are* you?"

Ainsley realized she had overstepped her bounds. She started to feel hot flashes of panic. She willed herself to remain calm.

She tapped her fingers on the glass case. "An investigator. Not the law."

He nodded, as though he'd been thinking that. "My belly is telling me it's time to have lunch. Maybe we can talk tomorrow."

Omar took out his keys and came around the counter. They made a jangling sound. Ainsley noticed his bare feet.

He walked past her and stepped outside. Ainsley was left alone with his *vejigante* masks. She realized that her directness was making him uncomfortable.

He was standing outside the door, keys in hand. Waiting for her to leave.

She joined him outside the door. Omar locked the door behind her without a word. Then he walked down the street, his ashy brown feet hitting the pavement. He didn't show any sign of discomfort going barefoot. He'd probably grown up without shoes.

Ainsley realized that he really didn't want to address her problem. His avoidance mechanism was strong, and if she pursued it, she might wind up with a gun pressed to her temple.

But she didn't have days, weeks, months, years to gradually cultivate a relationship with this double-dealer. She needed answers now. She couldn't let him leave.

Ainsley sprinted until she was caught up to Omar. He was lighting a cigarette. He glanced sideways at her but didn't break stride.

"I can't wait until tomorrow," she said.

"There's no hurry," he said, puffing.

"No, I'm in a hurry, Omar. I've been hired to find a piece of jewelry."

"Lunch," he said. "It's a good day to eat, huh?"

Ainsley was stupefied. He was deflecting her mainlander's directness. This was the *mañana* culture. She didn't like it.

She swallowed her impatience and followed him for another block. The salty smell of ocean water grew stronger, and soon a large canal came into view. To the right, Ainsley could see that the mouth of the waterway was only a few hundred meters away. Beyond that lay the dull gray matte surface of the open Caribbean.

Omar shuffled down to the canal's edge, then found a grated metal door that opened onto a ramshackle dock. He pulled out his keys and unlocked it.

"Is this where you get lunch?" said Ainsley.

Omar nodded. "I go fishing."

Ainsley had to make a decision. She couldn't let him leave. If she allowed him to get on his boat alone, he might motor to the other side of Puerto Rico, or elsewhere. He might not come back for several days. He seemed that skittish.

"Do you mind if I join you?"

Omar bent over, his shoulders loose, his whole body quivering. At first Ainsley thought he'd had a heart attack. Then she realized that he was laughing.

He straightened up. "This isn't a public fishing expedition, young lady."

"I know."

"You really like this sport?"

Ainsley had never so much as held a fishing pole. It seemed to be the pastime of creaky old men and was indistinguishable from sitting in a boat like an idiot. This would be the biggest whopper she'd ever told.

Drawing a deep breath, she plastered her winningest fake smile onto her face. "Growing up, I did it every weekend. Out there on the lake with dad. I can't live without wrapping my hands around a rod."

Omar was looking at her with a skeptical eye. "*Señorita*," he said, "you are a terrible liar."

He turned his back on her. Ainsley was forced

to resort to her least favorite method of extracting cooperation.

"Here, Omar, take this," she said. She opened her bag and removed a fifty-dollar bill and pushed it into his hand.

The old artist looked confused. "What is this?"

"It's a bribe. I need to know everything you know."

He looked disgusted by the bill in his hand. Too late Ainsley remembered that he was wearing a Bulgari on his wrist.

A smile spread over his face. "You are so desperate, that it makes me laugh. Okay, come with me. But you might not get any answers."

Ainsley breathed a sigh of relief as he unlocked the gate. Maybe all it took was a little grease to prove to him that she wasn't an uppity girl. Maybe she had just needed to prove that she was willing to get into the mud.

Whatever the reason, she followed him onto the rickety dock.

34

As Ainsley looked at the brownish ocean water, she knew it was the cause of her queasiness.

She had followed Omar into his small aluminum boat with an outboard motor. He'd yanked the engine to life, then quickly left the canal and headed out into the open ocean. But the disgusting sludge water in the canal hadn't cleared up. The stink still clung to Ainsley's nostrils.

"That's from the rain," said Omar. "It's not always this bad."

"But the ocean here never looks clean."

"It's usually better than this," he replied. "But yes, it's true. You have to go out to Vieques to find the best water now."

Vieques. That was at least the third time she'd heard of that place. She was thinking about that as

Omar accelerated with a twist of the handle, and the boat followed the coast for a few minutes. The brown spray that kicked up into the air soon turned bluer.

Suddenly the *vejigante* artist cranked the rudder to the right, and the boat jetted out into the open water. He went about half a kilometer. Then he stopped the boat and killed the engine.

Soon there was no sound but the gentle lapping of waves against the hull of the craft. A lazy tern circled overhead.

He was prepping his fishing pole. "Back in the eighties," said Omar, "Colombians used to drop huge loads of cocaine into the water right here. We would pull them out at night and smuggle them to the mainland inside the suitcases of white tourists."

"Really," said Ainsley.

He smiled. "Those were the good old days."

Hunched over near the bow, Ainsley suddenly felt nervous. She had finagled her way into floating on an open boat with a complete stranger who was a borderline criminal. She wondered just where the hell this little creature known as her better judgment went when it deserted her.

Omar was reaching for his tackle box. "What kind of lure do you want?"

"I'm not picky," she said.

"Neither am I," he replied. "Tell me what kind you want."

She just stared at him. Worms were the only kind of bait she knew, mostly from cartoons, but Ainsley suspected that real fishermen never even glanced at worms. They probably used some

179

new-fangled synthetic contraption that cost nine-ty-five dollars.

Omar smiled. "You really don't know how to fish, do you?"

"No."

He nodded. "Just watch me. My people have been doing it for hundreds of years."

Ainsley dutifully watched him for a while, how his fingers tied the lure onto the line, how he repaired the knots in the line, how he cast with a tiny flick of the wrist. Then she felt herself getting bored. Her eyes wandered back towards the shore. The beach looked orange, with a horizontal back-drop of green pine trees. It was beautiful.

"That's Piñones," said Omar. "I grew up run-ning on those dunes when it used to be a pineapple farm. Now it's a public beach."

While his hands slowly reeled in the line, Omar continued talking about Loíza. How it had the island's oldest church. How two-thirds of the town was black, ever since the Spanish king had issued a decree in the 1600s that runaway slaves from the surrounding British colonies were to be placed there. How this area had been chosen by the crown because it was the weakest flank of defense of the island, and how the Spanish hoped that the freed slaves would help defend the island against British invaders.

Ainsley saw her opportunity to interrupt. "So you must know the story of Olayinka?"

Omar nodded. "Of course. She is like rice and beans."

"She was a real pirate?"

"Oh yes. She stole her master's boat from Martinique and sailed the ocean, robbing other ships. But the people on those ships were criminals too." He laughed. "Everybody was stealing in those days."

"I'm looking for a piece of jewelry that she'd once owned. It was stolen from its owner last week."

Omar finished reeling in the fishing line. Then he changed the lure and cast it again. "I don't know anything about it," he said.

That was bad news, but Ainsley still grew excited. He'd finally opened the door to a conversation about his real occupation. "It's a pearl brooch," she said. "Shaped like a crab."

Omar shook his head. "Nobody has contacted me about it."

"I can buy it from you."

"It's not possible—"

"I'll pay more," Ainsley insisted. "Tell me what other people are offering."

Omar looked at her. There was seriousness in his eyes. "Listen to me. *I don't have it.*"

Ainsley frowned. "But they told me that loose jewelry finds its way into your hands."

His face remained neutral. Then he shrugged. "I usually hear about some things, sooner or later. This time, they want to keep it a secret. Who knows why?"

"It belonged to Señora Pilar."

His eyes grew wide. "In Caguas?"

"Yes."

"You're working for that old *blanquita*?"

Ainsley grew alarmed. "Yes. Why?"

Omar was so surprised that he dropped the fishing rod. He fumbled for it in the boat. "Listen to me. Don't mention her name in Loíza. She has a bad reputation with my people."

Ainsley thought back to Doña Pilar instructing her, if she got into any trouble with the *prietos*, to use her name. There couldn't possibly have been worse advice. The old lady was utterly out of touch.

She started to feel crestfallen. This impromptu fishing trip, this visit to Loíza, had been a total bust. She would return to square one.

Then Omar spoke up.

"Olayinka," he said. He was musing. "Do you know that she left buried treasure on Vieques?"

Ainsley's ears perked up. There was that name again: Vieques. "Buried treasure? Really?"

His line jerked. Omar spoke distractedly while he began reeling it in. "It was in the nineteen-fifties. Some very old documents turned up in a house somewhere, I don't remember where. They said that Olayinka buried her treasure on Vieques before she was killed."

Ainsley felt a tingle go down her body. There was real buried treasure somewhere on Vieques, which was nearby. "So who found it?"

He shook his head. "Nobody has."

"Where are the papers?"

Omar gave a mysterious smile. "They're in an archive."

"Who owns it?"

He reeled in the line and busied himself with replacing the lure. "I don't want to answer any more questions."

Ainsley smelled a new thread opening up, one worthy of investigation. The person who stole the pearl brooch presumably had a strong interest in Olayinka. And the presence of an archive indicated that maybe there was more information about the pearl brooch. It was worth Ainsley's while to follow this lead.

The *vejigante* artist stood up and cast the line far out into the water. He slowly lowered his butt to the seat, his eyes fixed on the water. Ainsley sensed that he truly was finished talking.

"Omar," she said, "I'd really like to see this archive."

Suddenly the line jerked, quite hard. Omar stood up in the boat. "This is a big one," he said. The fence bit his lip as he grunted and pulled in the lure.

A short battle later, he lifted a glorious fish the size of Ainsley's forearm. It kicked and twisted on the line. He dropped it on the floor of the boat. Then he picked up a small mallet and smacked it once on the head. The fish immediately lay still.

"A red snapper." He looked up at Ainsley. "It's going to be a good lunch."

35

THE ALUMINUM BOAT ARRIVED BACK AT the ramshackle dock. Ainsley stepped off first, relieved to be back on dry land. After tying up the boat, Omar followed, carrying the bucket with the fish.

"About this archive—" said Ainsley.

Omar shook his head. "I think we're done talking about that."

She persisted. "I don't care about the buried treasure. I just want to know more about Olayinka."

"No, I shouldn't have said anything."

He trudged back towards his *vejigante* shop. Ainsley followed, moodily inspecting her cuticles. She didn't want to resort to begging. There was no dignity in that. But she didn't see any crack in this particular wall, short of even more massive bribery.

And she didn't want to spend that much of her own money on such a lark.

Omar turned the corner to his shop. Then Ainsley heard him shout, once, hoarsely. He dropped the fish and took off running, as fast as a man of his age could.

This wasn't good.

Ainsley huffed up to the corner and turned. There was Omar, in front of his very own shop, grappling with a teenager. The kid had cornrows and white athletic shoes. He broke free of the older man and took off running in the opposite direction.

Omar whirled towards his door, cursing in Spanish. "Another one! ¡Cágate en tu madre!"

He picked up a wooden two-by-four from the sidewalk—and charged like an angry hippo into his own shop.

Ainsley felt her heart thumping double time. They'd just interrupted a robbery in progress, presumably by neighborhood kids who knew about Omar's real occupation. They'd been lured by the valuables that she guessed were kept behind the heavy door in the back of the store.

She circled around the door, careful to leave a wide berth in case it spilled outside. She couldn't see anything yet, but she could hear the confrontation. Violent cries. Smashing sounds. Heavy thuds.

Then, through the windows she spotted Omar. He was swinging the wooden weapon into another figure, who fell to the ground.

Then there was silence. Nobody came running out of the shop. Ainsley waited for something to happen. A small crowd had started to gather.

A minute later, she decided to hazard a look.

Ainsley moved warily along the sidewalk and tiptoed into the artisan shop. Standing in the middle of the room was Omar, holding the two-by-four in his hand. He was breathing heavily. Behind the counter, the heavy door had been attacked, presumably with a gun, maybe with small explosives.

On the floor were shattered pieces of several *vejigante* masks, the shards of red-and-blue painted coconut, the polka-dotted papier-mâché horns, the white teeth. And in the middle of this riot of color and texture lay something else.

A person.

He wasn't moving. Ainsley quickly approached the prostrate figure to get a better look. It was a teenager, dressed in a white wifebeater and long basketball shorts. A pair of flip-flops dangled off his feet.

It was Benny, the kid who'd been sitting on the wall at the gas station. The teenager who'd led her to this shop.

Omar was still breathing hard. "I knew," he gasped, "this ... was coming. He's ... been watching my operation ... for a long time. I wouldn't let him into it."

Ainsley crouched down. "Did you hit him in the head?"

"He was robbing me."

"Is he even alive?"

Omar spat into his handkerchief, then stuffed it into his shirt. "I don't know. You can check."

Ainsley took a mirror from her purse and held it in front of his nose. It slowly misted.

They stood there, looking at the kid. "Do you think we should turn him over?" she said.

Omar shook his head. "Leave him just the way he is. So the police can see."

Of the people gathering outside, nobody was offering to help, or even enter. Ainsley felt revolted by the situation, by crime, by the human condition. But the little hamster in her head began spinning. It was reminding her that with every crisis comes an opportunity.

"Omar," she said, "how are you going to prove to the police that this was provoked? They must know your reputation. They might not trust your word."

He didn't say anything. Then he pointed behind the counter. "They were trying to get into that room."

"The room with all the jewelry? You don't need the police asking about what's behind that door."

Ainsley moistened her lips. She had to put this delicately. "Listen, right now, I'm the only person who can vouch for whatever story you tell them. I am your only witness. And they'll be here soon, judging from that crowd, so you'd better make up your mind."

He was listening. "Go on."

Ainsley pressed him further. "I'll tell the police that I was a tourist looking at your *vejigante* masks when this boy came in to rob the store. When he started to attack me, you came out swinging. They'll like the fact that you were protecting the innocent tourist."

"And?"

"In return, you tell me who has this archive, the one with the documents about Olayinka."

He was glaring at Ainsley. She'd delivered the message: this was blackmail. The sweetest, most well-intentioned kind, but she needed to get some mileage out of this too.

"No," he said.

"I'm on your side. It's no skin off my nose."

Omar had listened, she knew, because he had dropped the two-by-four and circled around the counter and dialed the telephone. She hadn't known that he could move this quickly. He said something in urgent Spanish, then hung up.

He looked at Ainsley. "His name is Orlando le Grand. You can find him in Old Town above La Isla Bonita."

"This is the man with the archive?"

Omar nodded. "He used to be a professor."

Orlando le Grand. That was quite a name. Ainsley wrote down the address information in her small notebook while Omar disappeared into the backroom. She could hear the sounds of jewelry scraping, of silver, gold, platinum, the bracelets, necklaces, earrings—all dumped into an expensive tangle of precious metals.

She leaned against the wall, her hands hidden demurely behind her. The teenager still lay facefirst on the floor. He was out cold—or even worse.

A heavyset woman came running into the shop, shouting Omar's name. He came out from the back room and thrust two bags into her hands. They looked heavy. Ainsley heard the clinking of metals inside. The woman sprinted out without a word.

"Okay," said Omar, reaching for the phone, "now we call the police."

Two hours later, the street had been blocked off by police tape, the authorities had descended, and a crowd of nearly a hundred had grown. Ainsley had offered her testimony to the police officer, who had listened closely and taken notes. She'd painted herself as a traveller (true) trapped on the island because of the weather (true) who was interested in *vejigante* masks (not so much). The police officer copied down her driver's license, address, and mobile phone number. He said that someone would call to follow up.

As she slipped into the taxicab that the police had called, she was thinking about her experiences thus far—hurricanes, poverty, desperation. None of it exactly matched the popular image of sunny Puerto Rico, the vacation paradise.

But that was the purpose of travelling. Not to be pampered, not to become helpless, but to expand the frame of mind and heart. To learn and appreciate how other people live their lives. To discover truth.

And to uncover lies.

She was still thinking about all these things as she sped towards Old San Juan.

San Juan

36

An hour later, the taxi driver's singing was starting to fray Ainsley's last nerve.

He was happily scatting a tune, drumming his fingers on the wheel. Ainsley looked at him with envy. He hadn't embroiled himself in a wild goose chase thousands of miles from home. All he was thinking was whether to get into the passing lane or not.

Then the scatting stopped. His eyes caught hers in the rearview. "You see that crime happen back there?"

Ainsley wondered if she should answer that question. Maybe the taxi driver knew the teenage gangbanger. Maybe he would attempt to influence her testimony. Maybe he would drug her and toss her into the ocean.

Then again, the police had called this particular, so this guy had to be trustworthy. Ainsley threw caution to the wind. "I did," she said.

"The crime is getting very bad. More murders than the mainland." He looked back at her. "Maybe that boy today will die too."

Ainsley really didn't want to think about that. She leaned forward to see the damage that was going to be done to her wallet. The meter was turned off. "Why isn't that meter on?"

The driver shrugged. "It's never been on."

"Never?"

"We don't use them here."

That made perfect sense, Ainsley thought sarcastically—installing a device only to ignore it. "How much is this going to cost?"

"I forgot where you said you want to go."

"Old Town San Juan."

"Forty dollars."

That seemed more than fair. Ainsley stared out the window until the taxi pulled off the freeway. She was deep in the busy, congested heart of San Juan, not too far from Santurce, where Luisa and Tomás lived. The few hours she'd spent with them had occurred only four days ago, but it felt like a lifetime ago. When you live intensely, she reflected, time seems to telescope.

The taxicab zoomed down a slim isthmus of land, heading west, towards the end of the peninsula. She knew that she had entered Old Town when the buildings turned colonial. The street turned to cobblestones and began torturing the tires of the vehicle.

"Where are you going?" said the driver.

"I don't know. Is there a hotel somewhere?"

He looked at her in the rearview mirror. "One point four million visitors pass through every year. Yes, my dear, there are hotels here."

"I don't know where any particular one is."

"This is your first time in Puerto Rico, isn't it?"

She wasn't in the mood to be pinned down by strangers any more. Her uncomfortable grilling by the police that afternoon had given her enough of that. "Yes," she snapped, "I was shipwrecked and washed up on shore like a mermaid."

The driver was staring at her. "You know, I'm just going to stop here. El Morro."

Ainsley didn't argue. She paid the forty dollars, added ten more for a tip, and stepped out of the taxi. The driver lowered his window. "Okay, Ariel, listen. Old Town is only eight blocks by ten blocks. Walk any further and you fall back into the ocean. You can't get lost."

"Thank you."

"And don't go into La Perla." He pointed backwards. "You can see it down there, next to the cemetery."

"Is it dangerous?"

He nodded. "Don't go there. Ever."

The taxi drove away. She listened to the growl of its tire treads on the cobblestones before it disappeared down a nearby one-lane street.

Ainsley spun around. Behind her was the postcard view, the one that everyone brings home from Puerto Rico.

El Morro.

The fortress was a brownish slash of rock against the gunmetal gray of the sky. Its wide green lawn, the *esplanade*, normally covered with picnickers and kite-flyers, was empty. It looked sodden. The storms must have driven everyone off.

Ainsley liked having the historical site all to herself. She kicked off her shoes and walked across the grass. Her heels sunk slightly into the muddy turf with each step. It felt cool on skin of her feet.

At the wall, she scrambled onto the thick ramparts and sat cross-legged, gazing out across the vista.

From this angle, she could see her first *garita* jutting out from the vertex of two of El Morro's many defensive walls. It was a hexagonal turret with a roof that looked like the helmet of a *conquistador*, and she recognized it as the symbol of the island. It was incredibly romantic today.

Below her spread a cemetery, a maze of gray tombs and stone mausoleums. Just beyond that was huddled a motley collection of red, blue, yellow, brown, and black shacks. They looked like scraps of dirty confetti flung against the hillside by an indifferent deity. That, she guessed, was La Perla. Above those shacks lay the rest of Old Town. To the left, the ocean crashed endlessly against the island.

Ainsley enjoyed the trade winds caressing her face. These were the same breezes that had propelled the most avaricious and adventurous of sailors across this very ocean, to these very shores. She luxuriated, for a while, in history. Moments like these didn't come often, given the breakneck pace of her adventures. Being a gemstone sleuth wasn't suited for the slow, the stupid, or the elderly. Ainsley was always on high alert.

A seagull wheeled overhead. Waves crashed against the side of the fortress.

Nearly half an hour passed. Ainsley's shoulders had slumped forward and her eyes glazed over. She'd fallen into a short trance.

She was having an important revelation. Ainsley understood that she didn't need a spa treatment or a golf course to feel rejuvenated. She didn't need the ideal tropical vacation that had been sold to the public. She didn't need to meet a new man. She didn't even need a cocktail.

It was simple. All she needed was a stone wall and a nice view.

A child's happy squeal snapped Ainsley out of her reverie. Behind her, a blonde family had arrived.

Ainsley jumped off the wall and wiped off the seat of her pants. The tension that had been building in her body for days was gone. Her mind was now clear. As she slipped her shoes back on and turned to the narrow streets of Old Town San Juan, she refocused on the mission.

She was going to find Orlando le Grand. And ask to see his archive.

37

An hour later, Ainsley was standing on Calle San Sebastián. Beneath her shoes were the famous blue cobblestones. They'd been baked in Spain in the nineteenth century and used as ballast in the holds of ships crossing the Atlantic.

She was looking at the front of the Isla Bonita. It was narrow, consisting of one double-wide doorway, which was open to the street. This way, the bar could admit thirsty customers, cool breezes, and vermin all at the same time.

Ainsley studied the layout. Perched over the bar, on the second floor, was an apartment with a narrow balcony. A wooden bucket had been slung by a rope over the wrought-iron railing. Next to the slatted balcony doors was a black flag, on which was the image of a skull and crossbones.

Ainsley nodded to herself. This was the place. Orlando le Grand couldn't have advertised himself any more clearly.

Finding his front door, though, would be a different matter. Ainsley squinted. There didn't seem to be a way inside. She circled the block, looking for an entrance. Maybe a small Spanish foyer. Or even a discreet mailbox.

She found nothing but a store selling *guayaberas*, a dusty church, and several semi-abandoned buildings. By the time she'd circled back to the Isla Bonita, Ainsley was thoroughly puzzled.

There seemed to be no way into this second-floor apartment. Maybe Orlando le Grand ran along the roofs, leaping from one to another, and swung himself down onto the balcony. Or maybe he entered through an elaborate system of tunnels, the remnants of colonial-era smugglers.

Ainsley stopped herself. Her imagination was sometimes too strong. A better answer was staring at her right in the face.

Maybe Orlando le Grand entered his home through the bar itself.

It wasn't that outlandish an idea. She'd seen weirder living arrangements. In fact, back in college, Ainsley herself had been briefly homeless, and had spent three weeks sleeping on a couch in the student government office. She'd showered at the university gymnasium every afternoon and cooked dinner for herself every night using a plug-in hot plate.

That had been over a decade ago, and now she was starting to feel like a nomad again. She glanced at Isla Bonita. It was worth an attempt. She tucked her bag beneath her arm, inhaled deeply, and stepped inside.

The establishment was dimly lit. That was the best way to hide filth. A long bar counter made of dark wood formed a right angle. The bartender was rubbing circles on the counter with a rag while his eyes watched a basketball game on television. A sad drunkard sat on the other side with his hand crooked around a glass filled with brown rum. His eyes were fixed on the rag as though the bartender were uncovering hidden messages in the wood.

Ainsley tossed her bag onto the bar top, pulled out a stool, and threw her shoulders back.

She cleared her throat. "Do you have any happy hour drink specials?"

The bartender's hand stopped rubbing slow circles into the counter. He slid the drinks menu towards her. The page was laminated and felt sticky. She really didn't feel like having any alcohol, but she needed to break the ice somehow.

She scanned the listings. "I don't know what to order."

"What do you like?"

"Something strong." She was trying to get his attention and his respect.

The bartender's eyes finally left the television screen and found her. His name badge read Jaime. "Can I give you some advice?"

"Sure, Jaime."

He looked at her very seriously. "Don't call the devil if you aren't prepared to dance with him."

Ainsley smiled. She knew she had his attention now. "Oh, I'm ready to dance."

Jaime nodded. His hands began to assemble a drink. She watched them flit expertly across the bottles, picking certain ones, pouring, shaking the cobbler, then finally straining it into a tall glass.

He laid a paper napkin on the countertop, then gently placed the glass on top. It was a milky brown liquid. He garnished it with a sprig of mint.

"What's it called?"

"Just taste it."

She lifted the glass to her lips and drank. It was sweet yet bitter. There were notes of sugar, spice, citrus, cream, and other flavors she couldn't identify.

"Unbelievable," she said.

"As usual," he replied.

"You've practiced a lot."

"Ever since college," he said. "Can you believe I went to college? Most bartenders on this island would chew their arms off to get a college degree. Me, I went backwards." He shook his head, feeling immensely sorry for himself.

Ainsley didn't answer the poor-me routine. She had Jaime's attention, and that couldn't be wasted. "Tell me," she said, "I was just admiring this building. Who lives above this place?"

Jaime was washing glasses now. "A very disturbed individual."

"I saw the black flag."

"Did you see the bucket?"

"Yeah."

"That's for beer."

"Really?"

199

Jaime nodded. "He refuses to come downstairs to get his drinks. He just shouts and throws the bucket over. I put the beer in the bucket. Then he lifts it up."

Ainsley found herself smiling. "So when does he pay?"

"He doesn't like to. Sometimes the owner threatens to evict him. Then we get some money."

"What a character." Ainsley looked around as innocently as she could. "So how does he get into his house?"

Jaime pointed to the back hallway. "Past the bathrooms, there's a small staircase. But he doesn't like anybody to come up. That's why he uses the bucket."

And that's when she heard it. From the second floor came a loud shout, followed by a loud clunk.

"Look," said Jaime, "there."

The bartender pointed outside. Ainsley saw a wooden bucket, attached by a rope, crash onto the sidewalk. It clattered loudly.

"He's thirsty today. That's the fourth bucket this afternoon."

Ainsley thought quickly. "Can I put the beer in the bucket for you?"

Jaime frowned. "That's weird. But yes, if you really want to."

He yanked three cold Medallas out of the ice and slid them across the countertop. Ainsley slung her bag under her arm. Then she found a circular serving platter and loaded the beers onto it. She hoisted it onto her hand easily. She remembered the skill from working as a server years earlier.

Instead of going outside to the sidewalk, she walked down the dark passageway, towards the staircase.

Jaime watched her. "You should use the bucket. He doesn't like when I knock on his door."

"That," said Ainsley, "is because you're not a girl."

38

Ainsley brushed her hair in the bathroom, re-applied lipstick, and examined herself in the mirror.

She wasn't Miss Universe material, never would be, but with a few tosses of the hair, she could probably get a few whistles from a construction site.

What mattered, however, was getting Orlando le Grand to let her in his front door. She knew that her big mouth and her improvisational skills would guide her from there. They always did.

She hoisted the tray of beers and left the bathroom, moving further down the dark passage-way. Behind her, the sound of the television grew smaller and disappeared. The dank smell of trop-ical earth filled her nostrils. Colonial iron fixtures hanging at regular intervals cast circles of light.

At the end of the dark passage, a flight of steps

rose towards the second floor. Squinting her eyes, Ainsley could see the yellow-and-blue geometric tilework on the risers. It was very Spanish.

She slowly ascended the staircase, balancing the serving platter on the palm of her hand. This exercise was starting to feel a bit desperate. She felt as though she were bringing light refreshments to a political prisoner locked in a tower in Madrid.

At the top of the staircase stood a carved door with a heavy brass knocker. Another skull and crossbones, this time with a knife between its teeth, had been carved into the door. A thick layer of dirt had settled onto the edges of the design.

Ainsley was taken aback. This was all feeling a little Disney. She knocked on the door anyways.

"Go away," a loud male voice boomed.

"I have your beer," she said.

The door was quickly flung open. An enormously overweight man wearing a white fleecy shirt and breeches answered. His heavy black beard had been groomed to a sharp point. There was a hint of lunacy behind his eyes.

This was Orlando le Grand.

"Serving wench," he said, "I have arranged for the convenience of a bucket for such transactions."

Ainsley was momentarily speechless. He seemed to be talking in pirate. Then she regained her senses and decided to play along.

"The convenience," she replied, "is yours alone. For I've been sent to deliver Orlando le Grand his barley refreshment ... in the flesh."

She allowed him to scan her from head to toe. He licked his lips. "In the flesh ye very well may,

203

lass. But this may be the last sight your poor eyes ever do see. Countless scurvy lads have been keel-hauled for committing lesser offense."

The fat pirate delivered these lines with practiced seriousness, as though he'd been rehearsing them all afternoon. Ainsley tried to stifle her laughter. She had known theatrical personalities before, people for whom all the world's a stage. They were usually a lot of fun.

They were also usually hiding a very deep pain.

"This serving wench has been on her feet much too long," she said, pushing her way inside. "She needs a beverage."

Orlando le Grand stepped aside, welcoming her. She was happy that he was tubby. It would be easier to outrun him, if necessary.

She set the beers down and glanced around. His home looked as though a meeting of bachelor pirate enthusiasts had just concluded. In the corner, a parrot squawked from its perch inside a cage. A brace of swords was hung above the sofa. A bookshelf contained at least a hundred books on Caribbean pirate lore. And at her feet lay an open treasure chest filled with bottle caps.

Ainsley opened a beer, tossed the cap into the treasure chest, and turned to him. "So when's the raid?"

"I'd expect a wench to serve first and leave second," he said.

She threw him a bottle. "And I'd expect a salty dog like you to drink something stronger than Medalla."

"Aye, but the doctor won't allow it," said Orlando. His face became very sad. Then he took a deep breath, and issued an enormous cough. It was loud enough to shake the floorboards.

When the fit had passed, he settled down into a large recliner. "So what's the purpose of ye visit? Aside from the upcoming tumble in the bunk, of course. Which is quite mandatory."

She ignored the come-on. "Omar recommended you."

He paused. The name seemed familiar to him. "The artist from Loíza. An honest soul."

Ainsley sincerely doubted that, but it was time to cut to the chase. "I'm here to learn about the pirate Olayinka."

"Ah," he said. His fingers drummed on his belly as his eyes scanned the ceiling and he began to recite his knowledge. "Olayinka. A personal favorite from the roster of female buccaneers. A lusty fighter with a legendary cutlass. A terrible scourge who threatens to knock out the brains of any man who speaks contrary to her. Inspires dread in all who cross her. More profligate than Anne Bonny, less sentimental than Mary Read." He paused and explained for his listener. "Mary has been saved from the gallows by a pregnancy."

Ainsley blinked. Orlando le Grand had it down, even the present tense verbs. He was either an excellent actor or clinically insane.

"I was told that Olayinka was a black woman."

He nodded. "Aye, it's the truth. An escaped slave from Martinique. She wreaked havoc upon this island for almost ten years."

"Do you know how she died?"

He fell silent for a moment. Then he said, "There is some debate. 'Twould find my answer best in between my bedsheets." He winked.

"Stop it," said Ainsley. Then she remembered Doña Pilar's story. "I was told that she was pursued and killed by a *centrale* mill owner for stealing his wife's pearl brooch."

He looked confused. It was enough to drop the pirate talk. "No, that's not how it happened. Who told you that?"

"You wouldn't know her."

"Challenge me. I know everybody."

Ainsley debated the wisdom of revealing the elderly woman's name, then decided that there was little to lose. She hadn't held her tongue with anyone else. "Doña Pilar. In Caguas."

Orlando le Grand shook his head. The pirate language reappeared. "That viper is known to me. She's as foul as you are fair. Listen to her forked tongue, and you're likely to become convinced that the earth is flat."

Ainsley leaned against a tall writing desk. A quill fell out of its inkwell. She put it back. "That old lady has hired me to find this pearl brooch," she explained. "It's been stolen."

The fat pirate scholar was studying her closely. "So the visitor is an investigator." His face grew sadder. "I have sad tidings for ye. I possess no information about the missing brooch."

"None?"

He shook his head again. "But I do have news about Olayinka." He leaned forward with a glimmer in his eye. "Would ye be desiring of my assistance?"

Ainsley nodded. "That's why I was referred to you, Orlando."

He grinned. Then he glanced at the period clock on his wall. "Oh look. Four pm. It's time for supper. Or perhaps another libation."

"On one condition."

"What be your condition?"

She fixed him in the eye with a stare. "Drop the accent."

"Can't be done, lassie. 'Twould be easier to separate my flesh from bone."

"Then we're finished here." Ainsley turned to leave.

Orlando le Grand lunged forward and tried to catch her by the arm. "Sorry, I get carried away. Please. I'll tell you everything I know about Olayinka. It's quite a lot."

His eyes were pleading with her. There was pain in them.

"You seem lonely," she said.

A vulnerable look came into his wide eyes. "Aye, that I am, dear—"

She sent him a sharp look, and he stopped. "Sorry. I meant yes." He lowered his head. "It's been a very long time since a woman brought me beer."

Ainsley smiled. "Then show me a place where a pirate might relax."

He pulled himself to his feet. "It would be a pleasure. The life of a pirate scholar gets very dull."

39

"The problem with studying pirates," the fat scholar was saying, "is that most people don't know the real stories."

Ainsley was facing Orlando le Grand over a simple dinner table. As promised, he'd dropped the pirate accent, and this time it had stayed away. He spoke in perfectly fluent English, better than most full Americans. It betrayed his years of scholarship.

They were at El Picoteo, a restaurant overlooking the inner courtyard of the Hotel El Convento, a luxury property that had been a nunnery centuries earlier. Candles flickered in the old religious hollows of the walls. Ainsley thought that a pirate probably would've cut off his nose before entering such a place, but she wasn't going to say anything. It was gorgeous.

Orlando had decided to offer a crash course in Puerto Rican cuisine. Sampler plate after sampler plate had been brought to the table. First were *sorrullos*, or fried corn sticks, served with mayoketchup. Then came *yuca* fries. Next was *mofongo*, a mashed plantain with oil and garlic. Ainsley was convinced that Puerto Ricans had never met a starch they didn't like.

Ainsley thought that they'd reached the end of the meal when the waiter delivered the entreé—an enormous deep-fried slab of pork chop, overlapping the edges of the plate. It was called *chuleta kan-kan*. It looked to like a heart attack on a plate. Ainsley doubted that she could even eat a fraction of the meat.

"I certainly don't know the real stories," she said.

"Here's an example," said the scholar, his hands sawing the crispy pork into bites. "Walking the plank. You know it, I know it. We've seen the movies. We assumed it was a fact. But actually, nobody was made to walk the plank. It's fiction."

"Interesting."

"And there are misconceptions about the time period too. People today don't realize that, by the seventeen-twenties, the entire pirate era was finished. The royal patrols had driven pirates out of their lairs, then hanged them in huge groups. The party was over, just like that." He shrugged. "These waters haven't seen a pirate hull in three hundred years."

"It seems that—" Ainsley began.

But Orlando wasn't finished yet. "And something else. We imagine there was a clear line between sailor and pirate. You know, white hats versus black hats. But that's not true at all. There were thousands of ordinary ships carrying special letters from their royal power—Spain, France, Netherlands, England, wherever. They were called *letters of marque*. They gave the ordinary ships permission to attack any enemy ship, on behalf of the royal crown."

"Why?"

"So that the monarchs didn't have to build navies. It was cheaper for them just to give their merchants some guns and official permission to raid."

Ainsley had to admit that made financial sense.

"These letters were abused, of course. They became licenses to steal. Ordinary merchant ships attacked other ordinary merchant ships, just because they hailed from different nations. Sometimes even the real pirates would sometimes show up in the midst of a merchant fight to blackmail everybody."

Ainsley chewed on her pork. It was tough. "So you're saying it was a mess."

The fat scholar pounded the table. "There were two thousand unlicensed pirates and even more of these royally licensed ones. It was *anarchy* on the seas. *That* is the world that Olayinka entered. Doña Pilar can't point fingers. In fact, you might even give Olayinka some credit. She escaped slavery *and* learned to play the pirate game."

Ainsley corrected him. "Actually, I think Doña Pilar doesn't like Olayinka because she stole her family's favorite pearl brooch."

"We'll see about that," he said.

Ainsley thought about Olayinka. What had she looked like? She tried to picture a black female pirate from three hundred years earlier. There would be handkerchiefs. Ripped pantaloons. Maybe a knife between the teeth. Certainly a head full of dreadlocks. Come to think of it, Olayinka had probably looked much like other pirates—frightening and repulsive.

Then Orlando was seized by another coughing fit. Ainsley sat patiently, grateful for the hospitality of the Puerto Rican people. Here she was, an utter stranger, and this pirate scholar was happily entertaining her at a terrific, lively restaurant.

There could be many explanations for this. Maybe he was lonely. Maybe he liked having a friendly ear to listen to his enormous reserve of historical minutiae. Maybe he had romantic designs on her. Or maybe he owed Omar a debt of some kind, and entertaining Ainsley was his method of paying it off.

In any case, she hoped that she could pay back the favor somehow.

After the coughing had subsided, he drank some water. "It's good that I like to be the center of attention."

"With a cough like that, there's no avoiding it."

"For sure."

She crossed her silverware on her plate and steered the conversation back to the mission at hand. "So Omar told me that you have some sort of archive."

"I do."

"And it has information about Olayinka?"

He nodded. "Yes, quite a lot."

"I would love to see it—if you're not too busy."

"Maybe if you're nice to me, and let me eat dessert without telling my doctor." He signaled for the waiter.

Then another coughing fit attacked his body. This attack was by far the worst. It was so bad that the other diners stopped eating to watch the fat man bent over in his seat.

"Do you want me to call for help?"

Orlando shook his hand at her. Then he reached into his pocket and popped a plastic inhaler into his mouth. He sucked deeply on the mouthpiece. Ainsley guessed that it was opening his airways.

When he'd recovered, he slumped tiredly in his chair and held his hand against his forehead. "I wish somebody would've taken away those cigarettes when I was younger."

"It doesn't sound good."

"It'll never be good," he replied. "It's chronic bronchitis." He issued a final violent cough, then wiped his mouth clean and stood up. "You know what? Forget dessert. Let's go to my archive."

40

As they stepped out of the old convent, Ainsley stopped to admire the plaza.

Night had fallen onto the darkened streets. Pigeons cooed in the stone walls. Down the Caleta de San Juan was the old colonial gate, the most ceremonial entrance of the five surviving entrances, the one that visiting dignitaries would use when they arrived at the city.

A singer with a guitar strolled the shiny wet cobblestones, crooning a love song beneath the dripping branches. Above him something in the trees issued three distinct notes. It sounded like *koh-koh-KEE*.

She recognized the melody. Orlando had described it, saying it was emitted by tiny frogs called *coquís*.

He'd explained that the famous call consists of (in musical terms) a first, first, and seventh, which is unique in nature.

It would be easy to fall in love here in Old Town. But she wasn't going to do that. She was with an overweight pirate scholar suffering from chronic bronchitis.

She spun around, looking for him. She spotted Orlando le Grand trudging uphill, past the cathedral. His left leg was deformed, causing him to walk with a rocking gait. He was leaning on a tough bamboo cane.

Ainsley hurried alongside him. "I thought you were trying to lose me."

"No," he said sadly, "I was just getting a head start."

"You're taking me to the archive now?"

He nodded.

"Can I ask you another question?"

"Sure."

"You've lived in San Juan all your life?"

"Yes, I'm one of the lucky ones who never left."

She followed him past the international retail chains that had crammed themselves into centuries-old buildings. The tourist shops, closed for the night, selling postcards and trinkets.

She decided to hazard another personal question. "Can I ask you something else?"

"You can try."

"What do you do for a living?"

He was wheezing by now, but his answer came quickly. "I give onboard lectures to cruise ship passengers. But I used to be a professor." He paused.

"I lost my job because of department politics. Universities can be so petty."

"What was the problem?"

He became agitated. "I wouldn't do field research. Look at me. How do you travel with this body? I'm trapped."

"Then they shouldn't have demanded that from you."

"Oh, you don't have to tell me. But it's okay. I got them back."

"How?"

"A friend in the department tipped me off the night before they fired me. So I went to the library with a couple of students and took back all the documents that I was storing there. Eighty-nine boxes of primary source materials."

"Your archive," said Ainsley.

"The university wants it back. But they're not getting it. *Never.* I will run ten marathons before those bastards get my papers."

"Does anybody else want it?"

He shrugged. "I talked to the Ponce Museum of Art once, but they turned me down flat. So I keep it here, in a very safe place."

Ainsley could commiserate. She'd been turned down by that museum too.

"I'm flattered," said Ainsley, "that you trust me enough to show me the archive."

"Oh, whether I trust you or not doesn't matter," he replied.

Ainsley cocked her head. That was an odd response.

"Orlando," she said, "we don't know each other. You're showing me your archive to a total stranger. I could be from the university for all you know."

He smiled mysteriously. "It doesn't matter."

"Why?"

"I'll show you."

They had climbed back to Calle Norzagaray and were standing on a small strip of grass, just to the east of El Morro. Before them was a pile of black garbage bags piled against the edge of the battlement that ran the length of this street.

Next to the garbage bags was the top of a staircase. A young man with a spiderweb of tattoos on his arms and neck had planted himself near the top step. His arms were crossed behind him. He looked like a gangbanger but was positioned like a guard. He was pretending not to watch them.

Orlando le Grand moved across the grass towards the staircase. As they drew closer, Ainsley peered over the edge of the battlement. Below was a jumble of red, blue, yellow, brown, and black shacks.

She recognized them. These were the scraps of colorful but dirty confetti that had been flung against the hillside. The small *barrio* that the taxi driver had warned her about. And this was the staircase that led into its very heart.

This was La Perla.

"We're going down there?"

Orlando grinned. "You know this neighborhood?"

"I was warned about La Perla," she replied. "It's supposed to be really dangerous."

He waved off her concern. "It's safe if you're with the right people. And I am the right people." He patted his stomach. "The size of two."

He nodded at the tattooed gang member, who nodded back and stepped aside. Ainsley felt the kid's eyes staring at her as they passed.

The progress down the staircase was painfully slow. Ainsley stood behind Orlando as he lowered first one foot, then the other, then paused to rest. She summoned all her patience. He didn't have to be helping her.

At last, Orlando lowered himself off the final step onto a dirty lane. Ainsley quickly glanced around. They were in the heart of La Perla, and the shacks appeared even more decrepit up close. Colorful stucco walls were pocked with holes. Roofs had blown off or collapsed. The eyes of feral cats followed her from windows, doors, interior ruins.

Ainsley felt something different in the air here. The Old Town above carried a breezy and romantic atmosphere. But here, just a hundred meters down the hill, the people felt harder, tougher, more desperate.

She felt a hand on her shoulder. It was Orlando. "Stay next to me," he ordered.

They began walking, and she obeyed. Men with silver cans of beer leered outside a seedy neighborhood bar. Orlando greeted them in Spanish, but they didn't say a word. They seemed to be holding their tongues for a lady.

"So I have another question?" she said.

"Can I guess what it is?"

"Try."

"You want to know why my archive is in such a dangerous place."

Ainsley nodded. "And inconvenient for you." She pointed at his leg.

Orlando sighed and nodded. "It's all true. But the answer is easy—this is the last place anyone would look." He fixed her with a serious glance. "I have amassed one of the Caribbean's most sought-after historical treasure troves. And this is the only place it's truly safe."

"Who's guarding it?"

He lowered his voice. "The drug gangs. I pay them for protection."

"That's all?"

He looked at her like she was crazy. "That's all? Of course that's all. Police don't come in here. Normal citizens don't either. Once in a while, maybe, a new commissioner pretends to clear out the slum, but it's all for show. Both sides know that the island needs the revenue too badly."

Then Orlando pointed straight ahead. "And here we are."

41

ORLANDO LE GRAND WAS POINTING TO a house at the farthest end of a dead-end street. It looked like it was about to buckle in on itself.

Granted, the solitary streetlight wasn't doing it any favors, but Ainsley could see that the house had lost its shine long ago. The ochre paint had peeled off the walls. The balustrade that ringed the second-floor balcony was missing half its balusters, many of which lay in the grass below. A few milk crates lay scattered on the porch.

She could understand how it had once aspired to beauty, but now had resigned itself to rot and decay.

"I keep the place like this on purpose," Orlando said. "When it looks like this, nobody has any suspicions."

The fat pirate scholar stepped onto the porch. Its boards sagged beneath his weight. He found his keychain and unlocked the front door.

Ainsley was dumbfounded. "That's all you have for protection? One bolt?"

His finger twirled in the air. "The real protection is all around us, remember?"

He opened the door. The interior of the house was pitch black. He stepped into the darkness and flicked on a light switch. Nothing happened.

"I thought that had been fixed," he said. "Please, one minute."

Ainsley stood on the porch alone, hanging onto her bag as though it were a life preserver. She glanced around the neighborhood. Despite Orlando's reassurances, she imagined eyes monitoring her every step, waiting for a chance to leap.

She was relieved when his footsteps grew louder, and the fat pirate scholar reappeared in the doorway. He was holding a hurricane lamp, the wick casting a yellow glow. "Tonight, we will study the old-fashioned way. Please enter."

She followed him into the dark house. It smelled musty and dank, like a sea captain's locker. Orlando closed the door behind her and locked it. She wasn't worried about being alone with him in the dark. Ainsley felt that she could trust him.

Orlando walked ahead, the lamp swinging from side to side. Its light revealed a room packed with rows of cabinets, shelves sagging under leather-bound books. She glimpsed stacks of documents on the floor, yellowing pages curling out.

"You don't come here much anymore, do you?" she said.

"No," he replied, "it's too damp. But where can I find a drier facility? It's always raining on this island. And it rains more every year."

Then he noticed that Ainsley had wrapped her arms tightly around herself. "Stupid me. You're scared and I'm talking too much. Let's find Olayinka's papers. Can you hold this please?"

Ainsley took the hurricane lamp from him and waited while he crouched on the floor and sifted through the papers of a soaked cardboard box.

She peered over Orlando's shoulder. There was greenish mold growing at the corners of the papers. On the floor, around the box, were tiny black pellets that could only be rat droppings. Ainsley scrunched up her nose. She'd already had a close encounter with one of those creatures on this island.

"No, no, no," he was muttering, "these must be the sixteen-sixties, because that is the Belvis bequeathment. And those over there were the second half of the Lopez papers. Where on earth? Ah. Here. The Cardoso papers were in drawer twenty-seven. Ainsley, help me up."

He reached for her arm and attempted to stand. His bad leg buckled, and Ainsley caught him. Orlando was heavier than a sack of cannonballs.

She followed as he maneuvered his way through the boxes and shelving to a filing cabinet on the far side of the room. It had three drawers. He pulled open the middle one. It'd been marked '27'.

Ainsley expected to see hanging files with clearly labeled tabs. This was the way that she organized her life. But this was not how Orlando le Grand preferred to live. Inside was a scramble of old envelopes, pamphlets, slim books, and loose papers.

"You might save time if you organized this place," she said.

"This is on purpose," he replied. "If somebody wants something in this archive, they have to come to *me*."

"So you love control."

His eyes popped out. "This archive is the only thing I *do* control. Look at me." He gestured to his rolls of fat, his twisted leg. "You think I control any of *this*?"

Ainsley nodded. "So what are we looking at?"

"The Cardoso papers. Let me explain."

He spoke as he rustled through the contents of the cabinet. "The Cardoso family was from a small town on the east side of the island, near Fajardo. Twenty years ago I heard rumors about a trove of papers that they were holding onto, and they wanted to clean it out. So I visited them.

"Their family had been the unofficial notary public of the village for more than a hundred and fifty years. They had accumulated many public documents. Some of the documents had been brought across the water from Vieques."

Ainsley's ears perked up. That word again. "I've heard about this Vieques so much," she said. "What is it?"

"Vieques is an island, seven miles off the east coast of Puerto Rico," said Orlando. "Five thousand people live there. The U.S. Navy occupied the island until 2003. Now it's free."

"Is it nice?"

"It's *beautiful*. You should go. They say it feels like the old-fashioned Caribbean. No resorts. Clean beaches. Clean water."

"You haven't been there?"

"No, no." He looked at his shoes. "I don't travel."

Ainsley understood his hesitation. She'd seen his trouble walking down the long flight of stairs. But she was of the opinion that travel was too important to ignore, and that where there was a will, there was a way.

"Anyways," he continued, "when I finally got the trove from them, I remember looking through the letters. There was one in particular about Olay-inka."

"What did it say?"

"It had been written by a man who'd been on Vieques doing some research. I forgot his name, but he wrote it to his fiancée."

His voice trailed off. He lifted a yellowed letter out of the drawer. It had been folded twice, so that it was in quarters.

"And here it is."

42

ORLANDO GINGERLY UNFOLDED THE LETTER. IT looked incredibly delicate. Ainsley clenched her jaw, afraid that the document was going to fall apart at the seams.

She edged in closer, holding the hurricane lamp closer to the paper. The handwriting was spidery and loopy, full of blots, in that peculiar nineteenth-century way.

"It's difficult to decipher," said Orlando, "but I will try to translate."

His eyes flicked back and forth across the page. His lips moved silently on his face. Ainsley could sense the great powers of concentration.

Then Orlando began to read in English.

"October, 1843. My love, I have been studying the history of this island that we grew up looking at across

the water. One of the old men, eight years retired from the centrale, *has spoken to me at great length about our favorite character, the Negro pirate Olayinka who was based in Vieques. This old man knows the location of her personal belongings, which he said that Olayinka herself buried before her capture and transport back to San Juan. He couldn't offer any suggestion about the contents, except that certain people may value them highly. I go to sleep every night waiting for the day when I may have the opportunity to search for it."*

Ainsley felt a tingle race into her tummy. That was a piece of real history in his hands. "Wow," she said.

"There's more." He cleared his throat and continued:

"In the event that I cannot achieve this dream, I want you to know what he told me. The location of Olayinka's treasure is just south of the crest of Mt Pirata, inside a circle of stones planted by the original inhabitants, the Taíno. I am planning an excursion next week and will report what I find. Your betrothed, Tomás de la Guerra."

"So do you know what he found?" asked Ainsley.

He shook his head sadly and carefully closed the letter. "He never found anything." Orlando reached into the drawer, rummaged, and pulled out another letter. "This was written by the local authority to his fiancée. It says that Tomás de la Guerra had caught yellow fever and died the very next week."

Ainsley felt a stab of sadness for this person whose ink smudges were all that remained, a century and a half later. It was a reminder of how short life could be, especially in those days, for even the most healthy.

"Poor guy," she said.

"But it's very good news for you."

"Why?"

"Because his fiancée didn't find Olayinka's treasure either." He produced a third letter from the drawer. "She wrote this letter in her old age. She says that she never left her village."

"Sounds familiar," said Ainsley.

The pirate scholar shook his head. "True. I'm living in the wrong time."

Ainsley thought about whether or not this letter changed her situation. According to this long-dead correspondent, there was actual pirate treasure, buried in a remote portion of a nearby island, a treasure that had been unseen for centuries. It had been personally placed there by the pirate who'd stolen Doña Pilar's ancestor's brooch. And Ainsley could be the first to discover it.

That was immensely tempting.

But digging around for buried treasure wasn't her mission, despite the connection with Olayinka. Ainsley was goal-oriented, after all, and she wanted to stay on the case of the missing pearl brooch. She'd promised the old woman, and she didn't like to renege on anybody.

"Do you know if anybody else has seen this letter?" she asked.

"Certainly not in the last twenty years. Before that ... who knows?"

Then a suspicion clouded Ainsley's mind. How could Orlando le Grand have sat upon this information for so long without acting upon it? If she'd owned this archive, she would have taken off after that treasure the moment she'd read the letter from the too-soon-departed Tomás de la Guerra.

Orlando seemed to guess her thoughts. "I would love to have hunted for this treasure. But I didn't, because this part of Vieques, the west end, has been closed to civilians for decades. It was the Navy munitions storage ground. And trespassing on Navy property meant an automatic prison term."

"But you said the base closed in 2003."

He shrugged. "Honestly, by then, I'd forgotten about this letter. I'd forgotten about it until this very afternoon, when you visited me." A smile came across his face. "Olayinka is only a minor pirate. They pay me to lecture about the big names."

Then he coughed deeply once again, as if to remind her of other factors limiting his adventurousness. Ainsley felt sorry for him. She guessed that the challenges accompanying a bum leg and chronic pulmonary disease could discourage even the best of us.

Orlando was eyeing her. "Why don't *you* go?"

"I can't," she replied. "I'm supposed to be finding a guy named Roman Galarza."

"I don't know him. Do you have any leads?"

"Only this."

From her purse, she produced the pad of paper that she'd filched from Galarza's wife. "He's staying at an address that I think was written on the page above this one. It made an impression on the paper. But it's too faint. I can't read it."

Crinkling his brow, Orlando removed the pad from Ainsley's hands. He held it up to the hurricane lamp at an oblique angle. "May I?"

Ainsley nodded. Textual analysis, after all, was his area of expertise.

The obese scholar rummaged around in a desk until he found a piece of thin, nearly translucent rubbing paper. Then he produced a broad, flat piece of lead from one of his many coat pockets. He laid the thin tissue paper over the pad and proceeded to rub the lead sideways across the page.

Ainsley wanted to smack herself. He was basically doing a crayon rubbing. How could she have forgotten that? She had done them as a child once, on a class field trip to a nearby cemetery.

Slowly, the writing revealed itself on the tissue paper:

Casa de Bohio, Esperanza, Vieques

Ainsley sucked in her breath and held it. She read the words again.

Casa de Bohio.

Esperanza.

Vieques.

43

"So he's in Vieques too," said the pirate scholar.

"That's quite a coincidence."

He corrected her. "There's no such thing as coincidence. This is a sign from heaven. You need to go there."

Ainsley stepped back and thought about her situation. Hundreds of years ago, Olayinka had buried something valuable on Vieques. And just yesterday, Roman Galarza had fled to Vieques.

Orlando was right. Ainsley had two ironclad reasons to go there.

She blew air out of her mouth. Despite the dampness in the room, she was starting to feeling overheated. "Orlando, I have to ask you something else."

"What is it?"

"Will you come with me?"

"I would love to find that treasure and get rich," he said. "It would solve many of my problems. But it's not possible. Look at me. The leg, the lungs, the fat." He shook his head sadly.

"Please," she urged, "you can go, if you want to badly enough." Ainsley crouched down before him, putting her hands together as if in prayer. "Orlando, you're an expert. Plus I could use you as backup when I find Roman Galarza's hideout."

The fat pirate scholar lowered his head. Then he lifted his face. "I haven't left the city in nearly twenty years. I feel like it's just too late for me. San Juan is my home."

He turned his head away. The pain was evident on his face, the embarrassment. Ainsley was disappointed too. She stood up and brushed off the dirt from her pants. Maybe a hard sell approach would work. Maybe he just needed some pressure, a ticking clock.

"You have ten seconds to change your mind."

The obese scholar turned his face away. He didn't speak. Fifteen, then twenty seconds passed.

"Fine," she said. "If that's your decision, so be it. I'll go there alone. I'm used to doing that anyways."

He pointed to the east. "There's a ferry that leaves from Fajardo. You'll have to take a *público* to get there. Do you know them?"

"Unfortunately, yes."

"On the island you'll have to find a guide, someone with specific knowledge of the Mount Pirata area. You can't find the treasure alone."

She was aware of how difficult this would be. "Is there anything I can do to repay you?"

Orlando le Grand struggled to his feet. "It's too soon for goodbyes. You still need me to get out of La Perla."

Ainsley stopped. She'd forgotten about that.

On the porch, she waited for Orlando to lock the door. She stayed close to his side as they passed out of the dangerous neighborhood. She helped him up the long staircase, along which he stopped to breathe several times. At the top, he nodded at the guard with the spiderweb tattoo.

Ainsley accompanied him back to the Isla Bonita, his balcony overlooking the street from above. In the street, she shook his hand formally. "Can I say goodbye now?"

"Yes." But the scholar looked like he wanted to say something more.

"What is it?"

Orlando had that hungry dog look. The expression that men get when they want something from you. Usually it's followed by an awkward kiss, a too-rough grope, and other fumbling attempts at foreplay.

"There is something you can do to repay me," he said.

She flinched. Ainsley'd thought that he above that sort of thing. Disgust clogged her throat. She imagined Orlando's naked, corpulent body on a bedsheet, awaiting her. She pictured him wearing an eyepatch. A pirate hat. None of that was going to happen. She began to formulate a diplomatic response.

When it came, his answer surprised her. "When you find Olayinka's treasure," he said, "bring it to me first, before anybody else."

She breathed a sigh of relief. He was great company, but she would sooner have sprinted naked, drunk, and blindfolded through a cactus garden than have sex with him.

"Absolutely," she said.

"Enjoy yourself. I have often dreamed of visiting the island. It's supposed to be beautiful." The obese scholar smiled ruefully. Then he turned and wordlessly left her. Ainsley watched him rock sideways on his twisted leg.

A moment later, the lights in his apartment flicked on. The black flag with the skull-and-cross-bones looked somehow smaller now, like a sports banner hoisted by a man who has no hope of joining the team. She felt a wave of melancholy wash over her body.

Then Ainsley shook off the feeling. Tomorrow morning, she was onto the next stage of her adventure.

Vieques

44

THE NEXT DAY, THE SUN HAD burst through the clouds like a linebacker through a paper banner.

Riding the upper deck of the ferry towards Vieques, Ainsley rooted around in her bag for her sunglasses. This was the first time all week they'd been necessary.

She looked around at the boat. It was more than eighty meters long and was totally full. She had been turned away from the first two boats, and was lucky to have squeezed her way onto the third. The seats were in great demand after nearly a week of rough weather.

Most mesmerizing, though, was the bright blue chop of the Caribbean. From the upper deck, Ainsley could see the hull cutting a clean line through the waves like scissors through a shag carpet.

And that line led directly into the heart of Vieques.

She gazed at the island in awe. It was wide, stretching thirty kilometers across, the bony hump of green mountains rising out of the middle of the landmass. As the ferry drew closer, she could see the port, Isabel Segunda, approaching. It was a small grid of dense streets and colorful structures, all huddled inside the protective arm of a harbor.

Ainsley felt her body shifting into action mode. After all, she had made no plans here, was flying by the seat of her dirtied pants. It demanded that she be on high alert.

Then her eyes landed upon something that made her heart skip a beat.

One of the passengers was on the wrong side of the railing. It was a full-grown man, rangy and thin, with stringy blonde hair. His feet were planted on the lip of the deck, his hands were gripping the metal bar—but his entire body was hanging out over the water.

The only things keeping him from becoming shark food were the tensile strength of his palms and the soles of his rubber flip-flops.

Ainsley blinked in amazement. He was bouncing, up and down, like a hyperactive child on a playscape. A huge idiotic smile spread his face as he noticed her watching him.

She had seen that fool's grin before. It was the sign of poor impulse control. Maybe he had some sort of attention deficit. Maybe he'd fried the most important processing centers of his brain with recreational drugs.

Maybe he was acting out for attention. Or maybe it was all of the above.

Ainsley had a choice. She could watch this man-child accidentally kill himself as soon as his palms began to sweat. Or she could try to talk him back onto the human side of the railing.

Her motherly instinct won out, and she casually sauntered down the deck. The blond idiot was really showing off now, doing one-handed moves. The fall was just a matter of time.

Ainsley adopted an amused tone. "My my, you *are* an energetic little monkey, aren't you?"

The rangy blond man laughed. "This is *fun!*"

"I bet you like to play on railings at home."

"Yeah."

"What's your girlfriend say about that?"

"She moved out, so now I can do whatever I want."

Ainsley understood immediately why that woman had left this man. "Do you know that we're almost at shore?"

"Are we?"

"If they see you hanging off the railing, they might not let you get off the boat."

"No way?"

"Really." She cocked an eyebrow to indicate her seriousness.

The dirty blond man hoisted himself back onto the deck in one clean move. "That would *suck*. I guess I'll be a good boy." He pouted for a moment.

Then he looked at Ainsley as though he'd just had a brilliant idea. "Hey, do you want to come see my motorcycle downstairs? It's *heavy*."

His rotten luck: Ainsley hated motorcycles. Besides, she knew that attempting any kind of relationship with this guy would be like strapping a stick of dynamite to her body and inviting people to throw burning matches at her. It could only end in a disastrous explosion.

"That's okay," she said, "just don't jump overboard again."

Ainsley turned away before he could reply. She could practically hear him moping. Then she hazarded a backwards glance. The dirty blond had wandered off, presumably below deck.

The ferry arrived at the harbor. Ainsley stood at the railing, watching the mountains loom larger before her, blotting out the sun. She listened to the churning of the ferry's massive engine as it sidled along the dock. She watched the dockhands wind the ferry's ropes around the metal cleats. She heard the automobiles roaring to life below.

They let the motorized vehicles off first. First out of the gate was a large yellow motorcycle with fat tires. Stringy blonde hair flowed out from beneath the rider's helmet.

She recognized him immediately. The guy on the railing.

As the bike rolled down the dock, he held his fist into the air. There was no reason for it, except to gain attention.

Ainsley smiled to herself. Deep down, she admired people who lived their lives with energy and passion. Even if they did act like blooming morons.

45

She waited patiently until the gate was opened. The other passengers were ushered off the boat. She moved onto the dock, feeling the waves slap against the wooden pilings beneath her feet.

There she stopped and scanned her surroundings. A single two-lane street led the others towards the commercial district, which was visible a few blocks away. In the other direction was a square lighthouse on a small bluff, overlooking the harbor.

A man was talking in pidgin English behind her. She ignored him at first, then listened.

"Bio bay tour?" he was saying. "A tour of the bio bay? Almost beautiful as you! Bio bay tour?"

She turned around. His t-shirt and shorts were dirty and threadbare. He carried a black three-ring binder that he seemed very eager to show her.

"No thanks," she said, walking past him.

"Where are you staying?"

"I don't know."

Ainsley tried to walk faster, but the tout kept at her heels, nearly trotting now. He was desperate.

"I can get hotel for you," he said.

"Really."

"Oh yes. Do you have a car?"

"Not yet."

"I can get you a car too. It's hard to get one in Vieques." He pointed up. "The sun is already going low."

"No thank you."

"Tonight is last chance to see the bio bay," he said. "You make decision fast."

That made zero sense to Ainsley. You could artificially reduce the supply of toothpaste, currency, even sexy men ... but not bays. They were creations of wind and water, sculpted by God. They were always there.

She stopped walking and faced her tormentor. The man had a silly grin on his face. "High-pressure sales tactics won't work on me," she said. "Nobody can close a bay."

"They do," he said, touching her arm. He was clearly thrilled to have Ainsley's attention. "When moon is big, bio bay is closed. The moon light makes so you cannot see nothing in the water."

"Really."

He nodded vigorously. "This is last night to see bio bay for a week."

Ainsley stared at him for a moment, processing this. She couldn't refute it; he made perfect sense.

But she didn't want to give him the satisfaction. "I don't know," she said.

"You stay here one week?" he said.

"Not if I can help it."

"Then tonight is the one time chance. I can help. Please. You alone."

"I need to think about it."

Ainsley turned forward and kept walking, with no goal in mind. She could hear his footsteps behind her on the concrete. Ahead was the Isabel Segunda fish market. She crossed the street and headed inside. Here she would collect herself, admire the fresh snapper, tilapia, crabs. She would figure out what to do.

Inside, Ainsley found several rows of empty stalls. The heavy smell of fish that hung in the air was the only sign of ocean's bounty. This market was closed. The only person there was one janitor who was using a rubber hose to clean out a case of half-melted ice. He nodded hello. Ainsley nodded back.

She realized her foolishness. Across the world, fish markets were strictly morning activities. It was already four in the afternoon.

On cue, she heard the door swing shut behind her. She turned. The tout with the three-ring binder had followed her inside. "Fish market closed," he said.

"I know."

"You like fish? I can get good fish dinner for you."

Ainsley sighed. He was a persistent little sucker. She ran over the pluses and minuses in her mind.

The tout was offering her a ride, lodging, dinner, and a tour of something called the bio bay.

Try as she might, she couldn't really think of any glaring dangers here. The worst-case scenario was that she would ditch him somewhere. In fact, he might even be able to help her with the mission.

"Okay," she said, "you win."

The tout looked surprised. "Really?"

"Yes."

He grinned like the ugly guy who'd just successfully asked out the hottest girl in his class. He slapped the binder against his thigh. "How much?"

Ainsley sighed. Asking the client how much she wanted to pay was the sign of a total newbie. "Let's talk about that outside."

The tout bounced out the door, ecstatic about his salesmanship. Ainsley followed him, waving goodbye to the janitor. He waved back.

Outside, as she moved down the sidewalk, the sinking sun drew a long, sinister shadow on the ground behind her.

46

TWO HOURS LATER, AS THE SUN drowned below the waves, Ainsley stood on a beach holding a kayak upright in the sand.

Ainsley had travelled to the other side of the island, having bounced across the mountains in her tout's military-issue jeep. His name was Edwin. It sounded vaguely nerdy, which wasn't totally inaccurate. His nervous darting eyes betrayed his discomfort with the tall *gringa* client.

Ainsley, meanwhile, felt equally uncomfortable. One reason was the new floral bikini that she was wearing. It didn't feel right to be wearing this little at night, even though the soft Caribbean breeze was sliding around her hips and purring at her.

In her left hand, the edge of the fiberglass kayak felt hard and unforgiving. Its nose was buried deep in the sand. She ran her fingers along its ribbed footwells, its sleek bottle nose.

Before her lay the calm surface of Mosquito Bay.

The name was deceptive. Maybe there were mosquitoes, but a quick flip through Edwin's three-ring binder had told her this bay was famous for a different type of tiny creature: a tiny dinoflagellate. When it was agitated, it emitted a blue glow. This was called bioluminescence. And this was why this bay had become one of Puerto Rico's main tourist draws.

Tonight, though, the lagoon was empty. Edwin stood next to Ainsley, holding his kayak. "Very beautiful. We launch soon."

"When?"

He glanced over his shoulder. "One more coming. We have to wait."

Ainsley stood patiently and watched darkness blot out the last streaks of light until a black dome had fallen atop the island.

Then Edwin perked up. "He comes now."

She turned. A large musclehead had come down from the palms that fringed the beach. He was carrying the kayak on his shoulder as casually as a small duffel bag. Ainsley hadn't even been able to lift hers.

He drew closer. The orange tip of a lit cigarette dangled menacingly from his lips. His eyes were a pair of knife-slits in his face.

"You ready?" said Edwin.

The musclehead grunted, then effortlessly tossed the kayak into the water. It made a gigantic splash, ripples moving across the water.

This was Ainsley's kayaking partner? She tried to catch his eye, but he wouldn't look at her. This tour was feeling more than a little weird. Lunk-heads like him didn't usually make special nighttime trips to splash in sparkly water.

Edwin turned to Ainsley. "Let's go."

"I'm ready," she said. Then she spotted anoth-er person, much further down the beach, a heavy figure. He was coming their way. "Who's that?"

Edwin turned and looked. His eyes narrowed. "Looks like a bandit."

"A bandit?"

He nodded. "Vieques has many beach ban-dits. We have to go." He pointed at Ainsley's bag. "Don't leave nothing. Keep that in your kayak."

Ainsley didn't argue. She would dive to the bottom of the bay to retrieve it, if necessary.

Edwin helped her lower the kayak into the water. Then Ainsley slipped the life vest around her neck, buckled it, and hopped into the seat. He handed her the purse, which she stowed between her feet, then gave her the double-ended paddle.

The group of three began moving out to the center of Mosquito Bay. Ainsley hadn't ever kay-aked before, but she took to it easily. The motion was even easier than walking, especially on such a tranquil night.

The waxing moon rose above the horizon, casting white shimmers on the black surface of the water.

244

Ainsley dipped her oars into and out of the water, watching it cascade off the flat blade. "So how do the little things work? The dinoflagellates?"

"I don't know," Edwin said.

"What about the tides? Do they affect the bioluminescence?"

"I don't know."

Ainsley crinkled her forehead. "I thought you were supposed to be a tour guide."

He shrugged. "I just paddle."

So much for conversation. The musclehead behind them hadn't spoken either. She wondered if he had had his mouth sewn shut. Ainsley was feeling as though she'd let herself be carried into a bad situation.

"Here," said Edwin, dipping a paddle, "look."

His paddle was glowing blue. Ainsley trailed a finger in the water. It felt unbelievably warm and clean, but even more surprisingly, it glowed. A sheath of purple luminescence surrounded her finger and left a trail in the water as she glided by.

Her mouth dropped open. "That's beautiful."

"We'll go further out, so you can swim," said Edwin. "It's against the rules, but who cares, huh?"

In her peripheral vision, Ainsley glimpsed a figure. It was a dark figure in a kayak, paddling towards them.

The heavy bandit.

"Look," she whispered.

Edwin glanced their pursuer and frowned. "He make trouble, we have problem. Go faster."

He doubled his pace, and Ainsley followed. The leisurely paddle had become a pursuit. The sounds of splashing echoed across the surface of the bay. Her shoulders began to ache. She wondered where on earth Edwin could possibly be leading her.

She twisted around. She could hear the furious dipping of the bandit's paddle behind them. What would he do if he caught up to them? Pull out a gun? Strap a knife on the end of his paddle? Ainsley had heard of carjacking, but she'd never heard of kayakjacking.

"He's fast," said Edwin.

"What should we do?"

Edwin's arms stopped moving. He drifted to a halt and put his paddle across his lap. "We fight him."

Ainsley stopped paddling. The musclehead came up alongside the other side of Edwin. They exchanged a few low words. She assumed they were planning the defense.

Ainsley watched them uneasily. She wished that she had never entered this situation. What was supposed to have been a dreamy excursion into an aquatic wonderland was about to become a low-tech robbery.

She turned the kayak around. The bandit was approaching quickly. She could see a swirling puddle of glowing blue with each dip of his paddle, left, right, left, right.

"What should I do?" she said.

Edwin's eyelids had lowered oddly. "You don't have to do anything."

That was a strange answer. Then she heard the bandit shout something at them. She listened. He had a deep voice. It sounded familiar.

He was shouting her name.

Ainsley peered across the water. The waxing moon, while not yet full, was strong enough to illuminate faces. And as the bandit came closer, she saw the outline of a heavy man.

The stranger shouted her name again.

She glanced at Edwin. A strange reptilian look had fallen across his face. She realized that the musclehead had disappeared.

Then she felt something crush into the back of her head with enormous force. A sheet of white light blinked across her field of vision.

The last thing Ainsley remembered was pitching over the side of her kayak into the water.

47

WHEN SHE CAME BACK TO CONSCIOUSNESS, Ainsley
felt as though she was floating in a warm bath.

She moved her tongue around. The taste of
salt water was in her mouth. Then her eyes blinked
open. Above her were thousands of points of
white light, punctures in the black sky. Those were
stars.

She was in the bioluminscent bay. Her life vest
was still wrapped around her chest. Ainsley suddenly understood why these were mandatory. She
would've been dead without it.

Ainsley concentrated on the other sensations.
The gentle current swirling past her arms and legs.
The gentle bite of a rope in each of her armpits.
The rhythmic dip of a paddle.

That's when she realized that she wasn't floating alone. She was being dragged through the bioluminescent bay. By a rope.

Ainsley tried to twist her head around to identify her abductor, but a pain knifed through the back of her head. It was so severe that she nearly blacked out again.

She looked at the overhead sky again. The sound of water swirling past her ears was soothing, like a water fountain in the corner of a yoga studio. Her body was encased in the bioluminescent blue glow. Except for the head wound, this experience was actually quite pleasant. People would pay for this type of treatment at a day spa.

Then she heard the soft sound of her abductor's kayak running aground. She heard small waves crashing around her. A small whitecap crested and splashed onto her face, sending salt water down her nose. Ainsley gagged and sputtered. This must be the break zone.

Then she felt hands hooking under her armpits and dragging her out of the water onto the sand. She closed her eyes and pretended to go limp. She felt her abductor's heavy footsteps in the sand. She heard his labored breathing.

He set her down gently on the sand. Then he spoke.

"Ainsley," he said.

It was the same familiar voice. She opened her eyes.

Above her was the friendly face of Orlando le Grand. The pirate scholar was dripping with sweat.

"You're ..." she said, then found herself at a loss for words.

"Here, yes," he finished. "On Vieques."

He handed her something white and leather. It took a moment for her to realize that it was her Marc Jacobs bag.

"I'm sorry, but it got a little wet." He paused. "So I tried to catch those guys, but they were too fast for me."

"How did you get here?"

"I followed you on the next ferry." He paused. "Don't you check out tour guides before you follow them into lonely bays at night?"

She struggled to sit up. Her head was throbbing. "I don't know. That guy seemed okay."

"That guy was a criminal. A bandit."

She blinked. "He said that *you* were a bandit. That's why we were paddling away from you."

Orlando laughed. "You fell for that? I thought you were smart."

Suddenly Ainsley realized how naive she'd been. She felt gypped, exploited. She could've been robbed, maimed, raped, or killed—and she had nobody to blame except herself.

The realization went straight to her stomach. Nausea swelled up her esophagus and into her mouth. She leaned over and retched onto the sand. Nothing but salt water came out. She was surprised it wasn't glowing blue.

When she was finished, Orlando le Grand handed her his handkerchief. She wiped her mouth and lips. She felt a little better.

"How did you find me?"

"I asked around. It wasn't hard. Isabel Segunda is small. People watch and listen. The janitor at the fish market remembered you because you went off with the bandit. He knew the guy's reputation." He seemed to relax. "Vieques is full of people like him."

"But you've never been here before."

"It doesn't matter. You don't have to be from a place to know about it." He looked at her head. "I'd really like to get you some medical attention."

Ainsley nodded. Her entire head was throbbing. Her fingers went around to the base of her skull and touched the wound gingerly. Another wave of pain knifed through her.

"Where can we go?"

He shrugged. "There's no hospital here, but I booked a small suite at a *casa* here in Esperanza. Maybe the owner can help us."

There was something in his voice that radiated authority and confidence. Ainsley looked at her portly rescuer. Something or someone had lit a fire underneath the pants of this semi-alcoholic pirate scholar with a severe limp and pulmonary disease. She didn't think that he'd had it in him.

"Orlando," she stammered, "this is a huge surprise. What made you change your mind to come to Vieques?"

He sighed. "I just couldn't be a failure anymore."

Orlando lifted Ainsley to her feet. Her knees buckled. She leaned on him for support, and they began trudging across the sand towards the small lights of Esperanza down the road.

"I don't think you're a failure," she replied. Her head was throbbing hard now. "You have the archive. And you're smart."

He waved off the compliments. "I'm tired of the archive. It's a chain around my neck. Paying those gangs isn't cheap."

Ainsley clung to him as they staggered together into the brush that fringed the beach. "God, I feel like hell."

"We'll get you better. Tomorrow's going to be a busy day."

"Why?"

"Last night I made some phone calls. I found someone who's going to help us find Olayinka's buried treasure. We're meeting him at seven am."

"Can't we postpone it?"

"I already put down a deposit for the both of us."

"Then I'll have to get better."

They stumbled out of the brush onto the dirt road and headed towards the small lights of the town of Esperanza.

48

At six-thirty the next morning, Ainsley sat
on a stone picnic bench on the esplanade, watching
the orange sunrise across the blue bay.

It was going to be a hot day. She could already
feel the heat on her arms.

There was even more heat coming from the cup
of coffee in her hand. Next to her lay an empty
cup that had held yogurt, fruit, and granola. Ainsley
rummaged inside her purse for her medicine bottle.
She dumped an industrial-strength ibuprofen tablet
onto her hand, put it on her tongue, and washed it
down with the coffee.

The *casa* had been serviceably good. The owner
was a generous woman who cleaned the salt water
and blood from Ainsley's hair. She'd said that the
wound actually hadn't been as bad as it could've

been. The musclehead assailant had only smacked Ainsley with the flat side of the paddle. If he'd used the sharp edge, she would've needed a hospital.

She'd slept in the bedroom of the suite while Orlando had snored on the couch in the main room. His stentorian snorts had been loud enough to crack crab shells. But she hadn't heard any of it. She'd passed out before her head had hit the pillow.

Now, in the early morning, she was waiting for Orlando to arrive with their guide.

She watched the ocean. She listened to the sounds of the street. It was the only street in Esperanza, and at this hour, nothing was moving. A rooster crowed somewhere in the distance.

Then a different sound caught Ainsley's ear. It was a snuffling, followed by an unmistakable neigh.

She gingerly turned her head. A horse was walking down the street, all alone. It was a chestnut brown mare. There wasn't a human anywhere in sight.

Ainsley rubbed her eyes. The animal's legs moved with an odd little shuffling gait that seemed both dainty and affected.

Unattended, it moseyed into someone's yard and began eating mangoes from a tree. Ainsley chuckled.

She faced the Caribbean again and sighed. She wasn't too excited about this little excursion. After all, she had a thick bandage across the base of her skull. Picking her way across through the scrublands of Vieques wasn't going to help it feel any better.

Mostly, she just wanted to knock on the door of the Casa de Bohio, which was somewhere in or near this little town. Behind that door would be the object of her search. Roman Galarza, the man with the crab brooch.

But Orlando's hired guide was only available on this one day, and Ainsley hadn't had the strength to argue. She would help look for the treasure today. Roman Galarza could wait a few more hours. She hoped that she wouldn't miss him entirely.

She heard male voices coming from the other direction. She twisted her body around.

Orlando le Grand was lurching down the street. He was wearing a broad-brimmed straw hat. That was probably a good idea today.

With him was a raw-boned white man in his early fifties. He had muscular arms and a square jawline. His hair was shorn into a flattop. He walked with precision. It didn't take a genius to see that this man was military.

"Ainsley," said Orlando, "meet our guide, Jim Sherman."

She rose up and greeted him. "Nice to meet you. I'm Ainsley Walker."

His hand pumped hers roughly. It felt calloused. "Jim Sherman, retired U.S. Navy," he said. Then added: "It's a pleasure, miss."

Ainsley nodded. She appreciated his manners.

"He's a munitions expert," said Orlando.

"At the base?"

Sherman agreed. "I was posted here fourteen years. Helped shut down the base, actually. I liked the island so much I just stayed."

"Thank God we won't be worrying about munitions today," she said, then laughed.

Ainsley noticed both men were staring at her. As though she'd just suggested that a nursery didn't need diapers.

"She doesn't know?" said Sherman.

Orlando shook his head. "No."

"What don't I know?" Ainsley said.

Orlando broke the news gently. "Sherman says that Olayinka's treasure is located in what is now a restricted area."

She remembered. "Yes, the circle of stones was just south of the crest of Mt. Pirata."

"Correct," said Sherman. "Mt. Pirata is on the far western tip of the island. It was the ammunition depot for the navy base. Eight thousand acres."

Ainsley didn't like where this conversation was headed. "But the navy is gone, right?"

"The navy is gone," said Orlando, "but all the munitions aren't."

"*What?*"

Fixing his eyes on the horizon, Jim Sherman widened his stance. "There is unexploded ordnance in the vicinity of the location."

She could practically see the calm exuding from his pores. It took a moment for his words to sink in. "So you're saying that the military didn't get everything."

"Affirmative."

"So there are *bombs* just laying around?"

"Not bombs. Anti-personnel devices."

"What are those?"

256

Orlando cut in. "Land mines. They're all over the forest floor."

Land mines. Ainsley finally understood the real reason for its designation as a restricted area. "But you know where they are, right? That's why we're paying you?"

"Of course," said Sherman. "Finding them and detonating them was my job for years. We'll be fine. Just keep the nose of your horse to the tail of mine, and we shouldn't have any—"

Ainsley whipped off her sunglasses. "*Horses*? Who said anything about *horses*? I thought we would be driving."

He looked at her with infinite patience. "Unfortunately cars can't access this location. We may not even be able to take the horses all the way."

Ainsley felt her stomach drop to the soles of her shoes. If there was any form of transportation she loathed, it was horses. They had held zero romance for her, ever since she'd been bucked at summer camp in middle school and fractured her left arm.

"But I hate horses," she said.

He ignored her protest. "They're an optimal form of transport on this terrain."

"We're giving you the best one," said Orlando. "In fact, she's right over there."

He pointed down the street towards the horse in the nearby yard. Ainsley turned. It was the mango-stealer.

"I'm riding that thing?"

"She's well trained. And she really likes beginners."

Ainsley felt miserable. She'd suffered a mild head injury last night. She was being asked to ride a horse through a field of land mines. And all she really wanted to do was to find Roman Galarza.

"Are you ready?" Orlando held out his hand. "The treasure of Olayinka awaits."

Ainsley reluctantly took his arm and stood up.

49

As the trio of horses moved down the beach, the fact that she was in a tropical paradise was completely lost on Ainsley.

They were trotting just beyond the break of the waves on the beach. The water was insanely clear. Even from the shore, Ainsley could clearly see fish circling a reef, which was thirty meters away underwater. The smell of brine floated across the air.

Ainsley, though, couldn't forget that she was sitting with her legs splayed on top of a mammal that could get spooked by something as frightening as a bottle cap glinting in the sun.

But she could admit that the weird shuffle, the four-beat ambling of the *paso fino*, made for a smooth ride. And her steed was very tame. It followed Orlando's horse without any extra urging.

259

To her right spread a small pond the color of a tea stain. Green sea grasses grew in tufts out of the middle of the water. On the other side a stray cow grazed in the brush.

Sherman slowed down alongside Ainsley. "These are the best trail horses in the world. They're actually trained here, in the shallows." He pointed at the water.

"Great," she replied, trying to look calm.

He studied her riding posture. "Try to loosen your hands."

Ainsley looked down. Her fingers were nearly white from the death-grip on the reins. She tried to unclench them.

"Thank you. What's in the bag?"

Sherman had tied a large duffel bag across the rear of his mount. "Oh., the usual kit. Metal detector, tools, food, water. Orlando's oxygen tank."

Ainsley felt relieved to hear that. She hadn't been relishing the prospect of dragging the fat pirate scholar out of the wilderness on a gurney if his chronic bronchitis had decided to really act up.

He pointed ahead. "We're going to go up to that curve, then cut inland." Then he breathed out happily, looking around. "Do you see why I stayed here?"

"You're a lucky man to live here."

He took that as a cue to begin talking about Vieques. Ainsley didn't mind. It kept her mind off the horses.

Beginning in the 1940s, he said, the U.S. Navy had purchased land at the eastern end of the island. The military had used the land for live training exercises, ship-to-shore gunfire, air-to-ground bombing, and amphibious landing practice. It'd been bombed two hundred days a year for several decades. Within that area was a nine-hundred acre Live Impact Area (LIA) used for targeting live ordnance.

That meant blowing shit up.

This morning's destination, however, was on the opposite end of the island, the western end. It had served as the weapons storehouse. Because of this, said Sherman, it was still littered with mercury, lead, copper, magnesium, lithium, napalm, depleted uranium, and unexploded ordnance.

"That's terrible," said Ainsley.

The civilians, Sherman said, had been uncomfortable with the navy presence for decades. Then, in April 1999, the protests had really begun, when a bombing accident on the island accidentally killed a Puerto Rican security guard. A pair of five-hundred-pounds bombs fell on his guard shack during an F-18 training sequence. Puerto Ricans simply walked onto the base in protest. They were charged with trespassing. The case began to get some notice in the press. Celebrities had begun showing up to lend their support. Soon even President Clinton was listening, and he established a review team to make a recommendation.

Two years later, the new president, George W. Bush, announced that the U.S. military would leave Vieques by May 2003. Some had doubted this, but the Navy kept its word, departing that very month. It was a mildly violent reoccupation. Local civilians swarmed the base, using drop hammers to destroy buildings, lighting fires to leftover jeeps.

But the Navy, on its way out, went even further than requested. It also closed the much-larger Roosevelt Roads base on the main island. This, Sherman said, dealt a huge blow to the local economy. Puerto Rico immediately lost six thousand jobs and two hundred and fifty million dollars per year.

Since then, he explained, the Environmental Protection Agency has been assisting the Navy with clean-up issues on Vieques. However, the thick growth has prevented testing for contaminants. And it's nearly impossible to remove the growth, because of the unexploded landmines littering the forest floor.

It was a catch-22.

Meanwhile, these environmental hazards prompted the new Puerto Rican governor, Sila Calderón, to call for the former bombing range to be placed on the Superfund National Priorities list of most hazardous waste sites. In 2005, the EPA took this step, and both parties eventually struck a compromise.

The land was designated a wildlife refuge, meaning humans aren't technically allowed to set foot in those places. This, Sherman said, allows the Navy to avoid the expense of cleaning up the site.

In her saddle, Ainsley reflected upon that. So many public battles end up in such a stalemate, stuck in a legal limbo in which organizations are satisfied, but the public somehow loses. In this case, it was the people of Vieques. It left a bad taste in her mouth.

Sherman finished talking and jerked his horse to the right. They'd reached the end of the beach.

Ainsley followed him as he led them across the sand and up to the vegetation. They formed a single-file line and plunged into the greenery.

The trail was singletrack, made of sand, with large gray rocks that lay like sleeping dogs in the middle of the trail. Soft, rounded, shiny leaves swept against Ainsley's arms as she was carried into the interior of the island.

The horses walked like this for half an hour, splashing across the occasional creek, slipping on the rocks beneath the sand. They disturbed a brown pelican from its nest beneath a low palm tree. It flapped away in the air.

Eventually the beach scrub disappeared. Underfoot, the loose sand turned to hard dirt. Ainsley twisted around in her saddle. The ocean was already a kilometer behind them.

The sun had become brutally hot. Ainsley thought fondly of the cool rains of the last week. But she still didn't dare to let go of the reins to reach for her water bottle. Instead, she focused on keeping her mare's shaggy mane pointed directly at the rear end of Orlando's horse.

In the distance, a bird of prey issued a scream.

Ainsley heard the motorcycle long before she could see it. It sounded like the deep-throated purr of a cat, even at a distance. But it wasn't like any motorcycle she'd heard before. It didn't have the ear-splitting blats of a Harley-Davidson. Neither did it resemble the revved-up whine of a Kamasaki threatening to redline on a crowded freeway. This bike sounded like it was equipped with a heavy engine.

Sherman halted the horses. They circled in a small clearing bordered on one side by a chain link fence with razor wire. Next to Ainsley was posted a sign that read:

No entrance. By orders of U.S. Fish and Wildlife Service.

It went on to say that trespassers would be prosecuted. She noticed that no further explanation for the closure was given.

Beyond the sign, someone had used wirecutters to peel back a piece of the fence. The resulting hole was wide enough to admit a person, a horse, or a motorcycle.

"We're going in there?" she said.

"We are," said Sherman, "after we say hello to the other visitor."

The sound of the engine was nearly ear-splitting now, and no sooner had he finished the sentence than a heavy motorcycle broke out of the under-brush into the clearing. The sides were painted yellow, the tires grotesquely fat and studded with knobs.

Ainsley knew that motorcycle. She looked up at the driver. It was the stringy blond guy from the ferry.

50

THE YELLOW MOTORCYCLE WAS HEADED DIRECTLY towards Ainsley. "Whoa whoa whoa *whoa—*" the rider shouted. She could see him wrestling with the handlebars, trying to turn it aside, to brake.

Ainsley didn't have to move her horse out of the way. It suddenly turned and bolted along the fence all by itself.

There was no time to react. It all happened in the swish of a tail. She watched her right knee dragging along the fence. She saw the fabric of her pants rip, then the skin of her knee shredding. Then the blood began to spread.

Jesus Christ, she thought. This horse was going to abrade her knee right down to the bone. She glanced backward. There was a horizontal line of red drawn along the fence.

Ainsley yanked back on the reins. The horse didn't slow. Then she yanked the horse's head down and to the left. It didn't obey that either. It was panicking, beyond instruction.

Summoning all her energy, Ainsley gave the reins several more strong yanks, and finally the animal turned off the path and dashed into the foliage. Branches and leaves whipped Ainsley's face. She held a forearm up. She felt them whapping against her skin.

The mad dash felt like it would never end. Finally, the *paso fino* slowed down to a mere trot. Ainsley could finally catch her breath. A minute later, she stopped the animal and quickly dismounted. When her feet hit the ground, she felt the jolt in her knee. It was wrecked.

On foot now, she took the reins and walked the horse back into the clearing. The blond guy's yellow motorcycle had been turned off and was laying sideways in the dirt. He had taken off his helmet and was standing over it while Sherman was crouched down, examining the bike.

Orlando looked down on Ainsley from his saddle. "I didn't know horses could run that fast."

She played it casual. "Oh, I couldn't tell. My eyes were closed."

He jerked a thumb at the interruption. "So this guy says he knows you."

The motorcyclist looked up. "Hey. That was pretty gnarly, huh?"

"We were on the ferry together yesterday," said Ainsley.

Then the blond guy saw her knee. "Whoa, that's *sick*. What happened?"

Ainsley was annoyed with him. "I got in a fight with the fence."

"That's crazy. You should get that checked out by a doctor or something."

With his hands buried in the guy's motorcycle, Sherman looked up at the rider. "So how long have you had this bike?"

"I just got it, man," said the blond. "Dude, I barely know how to ride. All I know is that it goes *way* too slow."

Sherman stood up. "That's because it's a Rokon Trailbreaker."

"A what?"

Sherman kept his patience. He had a lot of that. "Your motorcycle only has six horsepower. This vehicle is built for off-roading. Look, see here? The shafts and gear boxes are connected to both wheels."

"Far out."

"Which, by the way, are hollow. You can fill them with water or gasoline for really long trips." He gazed at the machine admiringly. "We used to keep a few of these on base back in the day."

But the rider was hopping around, excited. "I have hollow *tires*? That's *sick*!" Ainsley laughed. This blonde guy was an unrepentant adrenaline junkie. They usually didn't live long.

"Top speed of only twenty miles an hour," said Sherman, "but there's no terrain it can't conquer. You really should learn more about your bike."

"Righteous fuckin-A," said the rider. He crouched down and lifted the bike by the handle-bars. When it was upright, he threw his leg across the saddle. "This boy is ready to rock."

"Where are you headed?" said Sherman.

He pointed towards the gap in the fence. "In there."

Sherman crossed his arms. "I would highly recommend avoiding that area."

The blonde-haired idiot jumped on the start-er, and the motorcycle's engine roared to life. He wasn't listening.

Sherman repeated himself. "Listen to me. That's a *restricted* area."

"Why?" said the motorcyclist. "So the birdies' little nests don't get disturbed? Hell no bro. This land is *our* land, from California, to the Puerto Rican iiiii-slands."

The rider pounded his chest with his fist, then made a sideways peace sign. He popped the bike into gear and rode through the gap in the fence. He was quickly swallowed by the foliage.

Ainsley shook her head. So he was selfish too. It shouldn't have been a surprise. That trait usually came preinstalled along with the other parts of his personality package.

Ainsley listened to the Rokon engine until the sound was lost amongst the foliage. She looked at Sherman. He was shaking his head.

"He won't get far," said the military man, "not even on that bike. Beyond the fence it gets treach-erous."

Then he paused. He was looking at Ainsley's leg. "Hey, bring that knee over here. I've got a medical kit that can do wonders for that."

Ainsley obeyed, and Sherman disinfected and bandaged her knee in less than three minutes. She drank from her water bottle, then stowed it back in her bag.

If the land beyond the fence really was treacherous, she was about to find out for herself.

51

Using a handkerchief, Ainsley wiped the
sweat from her face and peered around at the tangled mess that was the wildlife preserve.

The fence was half an hour behind them. Her
horse had been carrying her on a gentle uphill
course through the brush, through a maze of tur-
pentine trees that were twisted like corkscrews. The
soft touch of ferns brushed her legs like lovers.

Then the trees had grown taller, more arched,
their red leaves spraying from branches overhead.
The trail slipped away from them like a guest from a
party that had gone on too long.

Now Ainsley found herself picking her way
across the floor of a tropical jungle. Dappled
sunlight and shadow played on the ground, on the
foliage, on her hands. It was almost noon. This

was the time of day, and the type of climate, to make Ainsley want to take a nap.

She had almost nodded off in the saddle when a quick, furtive movement in her peripheral vision startled her. She turned her head. A long, scaly tail was disappearing into the underbrush.

"What was that?" she said, alarmed.

"An iguana," said Sherman.

"It was huge."

"They grow really big on the island. They have no natural enemies. Look—there's another one."

He was pointing towards a small boulder. Lying atop the rock, baking its knobby green skin in the sun, was another specimen, at least a meter and a half long. Its merciless eyes seemed to be looking at her from a prehistoric era.

Ainsley was intrigued. She'd never seen such a creature in the wilderness before. She turned the horse off the single-file line and approached the boulder.

Sherman turned around in his saddle and saw her. "*Stop right there*," he ordered.

Something in his voice told Ainsley that he wasn't kidding. She yanked on the reins. Her horse stopped walking.

"What's wrong?" she said.

"We are entering an area with unexploded ordnance. Turn your mount around and rejoin the formation. Retrace your steps exactly."

Her heart beating, Ainsley tugged her horse one hundred eighty degrees and walked it back to Orlando the same way she'd come.

Sherman drank from his canteen, then screwed the cap back on. "This area is extremely hazardous. I've scouted much of it. Follow me, and I'll show you why." He paused. "And *stay in formation*."

He sounded like a military field guide, but Ainsley did as ordered. Ten minutes later, he suddenly stopped his horse and held up a hand. She and Orlando stopped too. "There."

He was pointing at the ground. Ainsley scanned the area. It looked like sun-dappled forest floor. Rocks, dirt, leaves, sprouts of weeds.

"Do you see it?"

"What?"

"Right there. Stay in formation."

Ainsley scanned the ground again. Then she glimpsed it. No more than ten meters away, the sun glinted briefly off something metallic. She squinted her eyes and looked harder.

Rising out of the ground was a long, thin, silvery antenna. Her heart wanted to believe that it was a simple piece of trash. A radio antenna from a long-gone navy vehicle. But her mind knew that it wasn't that simple.

"That," said Sherman, "is an antipersonnel device."

"Can you put that in ordinary English?" said Ainsley.

Orlando looked back at her. "It's a land mine."

"We need to dismount now," said Sherman. "Walking is the only option at this point."

She wasn't going to argue that. Ainsley swung her leg around the saddle and lowered herself from her horse.

Her feet landed on the ground as lightly as possible, her eyes fixed upon that antenna.

She helped Orlando dismount, which was a fairly tricky task. As they drank some water, Sherman explained.

"In the remediation community," he explained, "we call them UXOs. Unexploded ordnance. I spent the last three years of my life searching this island for them."

"Why didn't you take this one out?"

Sherman looked pained. "This little monster was the last one I discovered before the program was shut down. We didn't have time to get to it." He pointed back the way they'd come. "But I personally cleared everything up to this point."

"Why did they shut down the program?"

"It's expensive. It costs a thousand dollars to demolish every UXO on site. Trust me, you can't do it for less."

He was excited now. Hands on his hips, Sherman went on to categorize everything involved in detonating a landmine. Surveying and mapping. Removing vegetation from the site. Transportation of personnel. Occasionally, he said, they resorted to digital geophysics detection using land and airborne systems.

Soon Ainsley stopped listening. She was gazing at the latticed branches, dreaming about how this island must've looked to the pirates who'd camped out here three hundred years ago. How the pirate Olayinka had survived here, probably living like a queen on these very slopes, plotting her next raid.

Sherman's voice brought her back into the present.

"And that," he was saying, pointing to the antenna, "is a tilt-rod fuze. It's a type of anti-handling device."

"How does it work?" said Orlando.

"Simple really. You stumble into the tilt-rod fuze, and it detonates. But there are many other types."

"So we can thank the U.S. Navy for this lovely gift?" said Ainsley.

Sherman ignored the gibe. "You *can* thank the navy for many things," he said, "such as a development-free island." He spun around, his arms outstretched. "Did you notice how there are almost no ugly resorts here? That was the military's doing."

Ainsley had to admit that he had a point. No matter how many chemicals the bombs had released into Vieques' environment, no matter how high the resultant rate of childhood cancer, no matter how many UXOs were strewn around wildlife sanctuaries ... the military had at least kept the real-estate speculators off the island.

"So where do we go now?" she said.

"We tie the horses nearby, then walk," he said. "Your circle of rocks is about a hundred meters further."

52

MONSTER MOVIES HAD BEEN GETTING IT all wrong, Ainsley decided. The world's worst antagonists weren't scaly reptilian brutes, drooling green saliva in the faces of their victims.

The scariest things you couldn't see, such as microbes, bacteria, viruses.

And mosquitoes.

She looked down at her arms. They were starting to look like a Seurat painting. They were damned near polka-dotted. She wasn't even bothering to squish the little bastards anymore. She'd become a bug buffet. That's the way it would have to be.

They'd tethered the horses to a lemon tree further back, then began plodding uphill again, past the deadly silver antenna, past the end of the trail.

Now they were slogging through thick foliage, which had slowed them down considerably. After some practice, however, they'd figured out a good process.

First, Orlando passed the metal detector across the brush. No beeps. Then Sherman stepped forward with a machete, swinging athletically, clearing a large part of the heavy brush. Then Ainsley replaced him for the last few strokes, clearing the lower brush, and pushing all the massacred clippings aside. Then the three of them stepped into the new clearing and repeated the process.

They were advancing at about a meter a minute. Standing there, her face slick with sweat and her chest reddened with exertion, Ainsley understood why so many pirates had hidden on Vieques. It was impenetrable. Olayinka had been nobody's fool.

She looked over at Orlando. He wasn't faring much better. He was panting through his open mouth, and dark rings of sweat soaked his black t-shirt.

"How are you doing?" she said.

He sucked on his inhaler. "Not as bad as I'd thought. But I don't know how much longer I can last."

Sherman dropped the machete. "Thank God." He'd broken through the last of the foliage. Ahead was a lane of open ground.

"I think this is it," said Orlando. "Fat men first."

The scholar led the way across the threshold, rocking on his deformed leg, swinging the metal detector back and forth over the ground. Behind him, Sherman kept up a steady patter about the topography.

Ainsley wasn't listening to him. She was looking up the hill to her right. A few meters above them lay the peak of Mount Pirata, but she noted that it wasn't a peak at all. It was a rounded hilltop blanketed in more of the same heavy foliage.

She walked slowly, feeling twigs and thorns flaying her skin. They felt like the fingers of dead pirates clawing at her, keeping her from their treasure.

"Ah *ha*," said Orlando. He was pointing to a small clearing on the right.

There, a circle of gray rocks, twelve in all, had been laid in the back of the clearing. It looked manmade.

"Is that it?" she said.

"There aren't any perfect shapes in nature," said Sherman. "This is your target location."

Ainsley agreed. This looked like the work of humans. A wall of green brush had grown behind the circle of stones. It looked like a beautiful grotto.

And inside that circle of stones was buried the secret of Olayinka, the Caribbean's only known black female pirate.

Orlando stepped into the clearing with the metal detector. Ainsley watched the flat head of the device sweep across the weeds. Nothing. He took another step forward. Nothing. Two more steps, and the flat head was swinging close to the rock circle.

Then it beeped.

Sherman stood with his hands on his hips. Ainsley saw his pupils darting back and forth. "Swing it again."

Orlando obeyed. Every time the flat head approached the stones, it beeped. Orlando stretched out and held the device directly over the center of the circle. A long stream of agitated beeps sounded from the device.

"That's enough," said Sherman. "Back away."

Orlando backed out of the clearing, then tossed the metal detector onto the ground next to Sherman. "Goddamn it," he said. "Why here? *Why?*"

The heat was slowing Ainsley's brain, but soon she realized what was happening. If Olayinka's treasure really was buried inside this circle of stones, it was possible that some moron had placed a live land mine directly on top of it.

Sherman wasn't talking. Both she and Orlando looked at him. Taking care of such situations, after all, had been his job for years.

"What are you thinking?" said Orlando.

"I'm trying to guess what type of anti-handling device it might have."

Orlando looked perturbed. "How many kinds are there?"

The former military man ticked them off on his fingers. "A pull fuze. Light-triggered. Anti-lifting—those were popular in Vietnam. If it's a newer electronic one, then we're really screwed. Those could be seismic, thermal, light-sensitive, infra-red, motion-sensitive, or—"

Suddenly Sherman interrupted himself. He tilted his head. "Do you hear that?"

Ainsley held herself very still. Ainsley could hear the breeze brushing the leaves of the trees above them. Somewhere a pair of birds was jabbering.

Then she heard it. A low *blat-blat-blat-blat*. It sounded familiar.

"Oh Jesus," said Orlando. "It's your friend on his motorcycle."

"He's *not* my friend," Ainsley said.

"Do you think he's following us?"

Sherman had fixed his eyes back down the trail. "There'd be nothing stopping him. We cut a trail."

They listened to the distant sound. Then Orlando spit on the ground. "What if it's not a landmine, Sherman? What if it's just coins in there? Olayinka was one of the richer pirates on the historical record. I could take that shovel and just start digging, you know?"

The munitions man looked at Orlando. There was cool detachment in his voice. "I don't think it's *just coins*."

"Well, I do."

"Do really you want to take that chance?"

The pirate scholar didn't answer. Ainsley chewed her fingernail and thought about the situation. "Can we get someone up here to find out for sure?"

Sherman answered. "My team could've, but we were disbanded last year. I'm not even supposed to be here on site anymore, much less guiding you two." He shook his head. "No, I don't see a happy ending to this story. We should just go back."

The trio stood in the shade of the lane, sweating and feeling defeated. Ainsley heard the motorcycle engine growing louder in volume and higher in pitch. He was drawing closer.

"What about that guy? What should we do about him?" said Ainsley.

"Your friend?" cracked Orlando.

"Knock it off. He's *not* my friend."

"We can't do anything," said Sherman. "He wouldn't listen to me back at the fence."

The sound of the engine pitched even higher. Ainsley turned her head just in time to see the fat tires breaking out of the cleared section of trail. There was the yellow Rokon, the leather gloves, the streaming blond hair, the fool's grin beneath the helmet.

The lane was only about twenty meters long, and the bike was headed towards her again.

Ainsley stepped out in front of the others and held up her hands, like a traffic cop. *Stop*, she mouthed. But the motorcycle barreled towards her.

There wasn't any stopping him. He was a man in charge of his own destiny.

Ainsley stepped aside as the heavy yellow motorcycle chugged by. The blond idiot saluted her.

"*Turn around!*" she yelled, mere inches from his ear.

But the helmet was too thick, his engine was too loud, for the rider to hear her. He turned his motorcycle into the small clearing. With horror Ainsley saw that his front tire was pointed directly at the circle of stones.

He was heading directly into the land mine.

The rider saw the circle, then quickly turned his handlebars to the left, sliding his bike sideways. The motorcycle stopped a hand's width away from the circle of stones.

Ainsley exhaled in relief. This idiot had almost blown himself up.

He cut the engine and took off his helmet. He looked back at his audience.

"Dude, this hill is *gnarly*. Did you know there are, like, land m—"

But the rider never got to finish his sentence, because the earth suddenly exploded behind him.

54

AINSLEY DIDN'T HEAR ANY NOISE—BUT she did feel a great force pick her up and fling her backwards into the air.

She was wreathed in a cloud of dirt and black powder. She instinctively threw her arms up over her face. The debris floated around her flimsy defense and into her open mouth and nostrils.

An eternity later, she landed on her heels, stumbled backwards, then tumbled down a short ravine. She came to a rough stop against a bush. There she lay, coughing up dirt, as even more dirt rained down around her.

She started as something heavy hit the ground next to her. It was a piece of torn yellow metal. It was part of the motorcycle.

For a moment, she ran a finger around the inside of her mouth, cleaning the dirt out from beneath her tongue. Land mines had been misnamed. They should have been called dirt mines.

Ainsley waited a minute to be sure that all was clear, then pulled herself back up the short ravine. She rolled over the lip of the ravine, onto her belly, and took in the scene.

Her ears were ringing, but she could hear the tiny sound of hissing metal. The smell of explosive powder was strong in the air.

Then she saw Orlando le Grand. He was laying backwards on the ground less than a meter from where he'd been standing. Too heavy to take flight, his body had been blown over like a bungalow in a twister.

He opened his eyes as Ainsley approached. His face was covered in a fine spray of black powder. "Sherman was right," he said. "Those weren't coins."

Ainsley chuckled in spite of herself. "Are you injured?"

"No, I don't think so. Where's our military man?"

She helped the pirate scholar sit up. They both looked around. She saw Jim Sherman a few meters away, leaning against a tree trunk. He'd been blown backwards too.

Sherman staggered to his feet and brushed off his face and shirt. "Goddamn, it's been at least seven years since one blew on me like that. Holy smokes. Is anybody hurt?"

Ainsley brushed the dirt out of Orlando's hair. "We're fine," she said.

"It was an acoustic trigger," said Sherman. "I knew it too, don't ask me how. But that Rokon engine, it's loud, like a snowmobile."

Orlando said, "So what about the idiot?"

That was the question nobody had dared to ask. The motorcycle had been blown apart. Ainsley saw pieces of the motorcycle everywhere. A strip of rubber tire here, a twisted piston rod there. A cracked rearview mirror.

"There's the gear box near the blast site," said Sherman. "That didn't go too far."

Then Ainsley saw a scrap of clothing a few feet away. It was a leather glove. She bent down and picked it up. There was a hand still inside of it.

She screamed, threw it onto the ground, and danced away. She felt Orlando touch her shoulder. "Hey, you tried to stop him."

"I don't know," she protested. "I could've jumped in front of his motorcycle or something."

"You did enough," said Sherman. "Something was going to get him, sooner or later."

Ainsley watched him approach the blast site. He lifted the heaviest parts of the motorcycle and looked down onto the ground. His eyes went wide. "Oh boy. That's a bad one."

"Tell us," said Orlando.

"It took off the entire back of his skull and drove his face about a foot into the ground."

"I don't want to see," said Ainsley.

"No, you don't." Sherman stood up, walked over to his duffel bag, and pulled out a small blue tarp that had been folded down. "I'm going to cover him up. It'll slow down the wildlife."

Ainsley watched him fix the plastic sheet over the remains. He weighed down the corners using pieces of the exploded motorcycle. "Thanks for doing this," she said.

He wiped his hands on a towel. "In a way, I'm relieved. If this had been a military accident, I'd have had four months of paperwork and meetings." He studied her, a queer expression on his face. "This isn't exactly what you had in mind for today, is it?"

"No," she replied.

"But there is a silver lining," said Orlando. He was looking at the blast site.

"What?"

"That mine did a lot of digging for us."

Ainsley looked at the ring of stones. It was totally gone. A small crater had been blasted into the earth where it had once stood.

Sherman nodded. He pulled the collapsible shovel from his duffel bag and held it out to the pirate scholar. "Here you go." He glanced at the sun. "We have maybe an hour at most before the birds get here. Let's make it quick."

Orlando stood there, holding the shovel. "Really, I've always wanted to do fieldwork. This is going to be fun." Then he doubled over, wracked by an enormous coughing fit.

Ainsley listened to the pulmonary disaster. When he straightened up, his face was slightly gray. His shirt was completely soaked in sweat. It was a miracle that he'd made it this far.

"I can dig," he said.

She took the shovel away from him. "No, definitely not. I can't stomach two deaths in one day."

"Let me try," he said. "I can do it. Just give me a ..."

His face had turned gray. Ainsley realized he was gasping for breath. He looked a few seconds away from collapse.

Ainsley helped lower him to the ground, then darted over to Sherman's bag and pulled out the oxygen tank. It was devilishly heavy. She dragged it across the dirt next to him. He fumbled for the mask, so she helped to strap it around his face.

As she watched Orlando take huge gasps of oxygen, Ainsley realized that the digging would be up to her—by default.

That was fine. She could handle that. She took the collapsible shovel and walked back to the blast site. She steered a wide circle around the blue tarp and the human remains beneath.

She stood at the edge of the small crater and looked down. It was about a meter and a half deep. She covered her nostrils with the top of her t-shirt, crouched down, then leaped into the pit.

Her feet sank into the dirt. It felt warm here. The acrid smell of explosive powder singed her nostrils.

Ainsley telescoped the shovel, locked it into place, and began digging. She'd never shied away from physical labor. This would be easy, actually, compared to some of the retail jobs she'd worked. At least she didn't have to wear heels.

As her arms worked themselves, she began thinking, once again, about how she'd managed to embroil herself in this ludicrous assignment. Why had she accepted it? She didn't even care about Olayinka. She had only wanted to find Roman Galarza, take back the pearl brooch, and claim her reward from the museum in Ponce. End of story. Running this gauntlet to find a pirate's buried treasure was exciting—maybe even lucrative—but tangential to her real purpose. The treasure had probably been discovered decades ago anyways.

Thunk.

Ainsley stopped. The tip of her shovel had just hit something very solid beneath the dirt. Her heart leaped. She willed herself to stay calm. Maybe it was just a stone.

She crouched down and cleared away the loose dirt with her fingers. It wasn't a stone. It was a thick piece of wood, smooth and coffered. Her fingers cleared away more dirt until she found its edges. There was a corner.

This felt like an old chest.

"Orlando," she said, trying to sound calm, "I found something."

55

Ainsley waited, chest deep in the pit. Sweat and dirt had caked her skin. She ran her fingers along the calluses that were forming on the insides of her thumbs.

The pirate scholar hobbled to the edge of the pit and peered down. His face had regained a healthy reddish color, and an ecstatic grin danced across his face. "That you did," he said.

"Don't even think about helping," she said.

Then the navy munitions expert appeared at the lip of the pit and looked down. He sucked on a tooth. "That's going to be hard to remove," he said.

"Can you help?"

Sherman hemmed and hawed. It was the first real emotion she'd seen the navy officer betray.

"Look," he said, "I only signed on to be a guide. This would be breaking protocol."

"Break it, please," said Ainsley.

Sherman sighed loudly. Then he leapt down into the pit, took the shovel, and began excavating the chest. Ainsley climbed out and watched him work. He was like a terrier. He'd had a lot of practice digging objects out of the earth.

Soon the munitions expert had separated the dirt from the edges of the trunk, and excavated part of it as well. Now the chest sat there, half uncovered at the bottom of the pit.

Ainsley had to pinch herself. They had literally found a pirate's buried treasure. She looked over at Orlando le Grand. His eyes were shining, his teeth gleaming. He looked invigorated.

At last Sherman straightened up and tossed the shovel back to Ainsley. "There, free of charge. You two can do the rest."

He climbed out of the pit and went to a nearby tree and sat down. Ainsley thought it was curious that he didn't care about the contents of the trunk. He didn't seem to have a greedy bone in his body.

"I guess you're going to finish the job," said Orlando.

Ainsley shook her head. "No way. I'm just going to open it right now."

Orlando disagreed. "No, we should remove the whole thing, and take it to my archive before we open it."

Ainsley mentally traced all the steps that would require. After digging the chest out of the earth, they'd have to haul it out of the pit, transport it down the trail by hand to the horses, lift it onto one of the horses, walk it back to Esperanza, load it into a car, drive it across the island to Isabel Segunda, then dolly it onto the ferry, then dolly it off the ferry in Fajardo, then lift it into another car, then drive it to Old Town San Juan, then drive it into that dangerous neighborhood, La Perla, then unload it and carry it into his weathered old house.

That was way too much effort. Ainsley jumped into the pit again.

"What are you doing?" he said.

"Opening it here."

"But—"

Ainsley fixed Orlando with her best dirty look. "You don't have any authority here. This is your first time in the field."

Something in her voice made the pirate scholar back down. "As you wish."

Ainsley positioned the tip of the shovel on the ancient brass latch at the front of the trunk. Then she positioned the heel of her shoe on the back of the spade. She drew a deep breath—then drove her foot into the shovel, and the flat of her palm into the handle.

It was a good attempt. But the tip of the shovel slipped, slid sideways across the chest, and buried itself in the wall of the pit.

It was a fail. As she wiped the sweat off her face, she heard Orlando laughing. He was holding his enormous gut.

"You know, I can just leave right now, and you'll never get your treasure," she said.

"No, no," he protested, "keep trying, please. I was laughing at something else."

She frowned. "Right."

Ainsley turned back to the chest. The last time, her diagonal position had allowed the slip. This time, she squared herself to the treasure chest. The shovel couldn't slip sideways if she were at a perpendicular angle.

She repeated the same foot and hand positions, took a deep breath, and pushed with all her might.

This time, the shovel slipped upwards and skittered across the top of the chest. Off balance, Ainsley stumbled and fell forward. Her face hit into the loose soil. The handle of the shovel drove into her gut.

She came up spluttering. There was dirt everywhere on her face—in her hair, on her scalp, in her ears, in her nostrils, in her eyelashes.

This time, Orlando didn't try to hide his laughter. Even Sherman had a smile on his lips.

"Ainsley," the military man said.

"*What*," she hissed, wiping her face dry. "I'm *trying* to open the goddamned *chest*."

"Come up here."

"Why?"

"Just come here."

Ainsley climbed out of the pit. Sherman immediately jumped in again. He crouched down and peered at the treasure chest latch. He felt around his back pocket until his fingers found a small tool. He popped open a long, delicate protuberance and slid it into the latch. With the precision of a surgeon, he worked the tool.

There was a small click. Ainsley craned her head. The latch had sprung open.

Sherman looked up. "That's why."

He climbed out of the pit. "It's all yours. Unless it's bullion. Then you guys were *my* guides."

He grinned and slapped Ainsley across the back. She was struggling with embarrassment and frustration. But it was soon replaced by giddy excitement. After all, the treasure chest was ready to be opened.

Orlando handed her a fresh handkerchief. "Put this around your face. Who knows what's inside."

Ainsley knotted the cloth around the back of her scalp. Her nose and mouth were safely covered. Then she climbed down into the pit for the third time.

She kneeled in the dirt, put the tips of her fingers at the seam where the lid met the chest, and began to open the treasure of the pirate Olayinka.

56

ONE OF THE CURSES OF HAVING high expectations is constant disappointment, and Ainsley Walker knew this better than anybody. After all, once upon a time, she'd expected a top-notch career, a sky-high bank account, a grade-A husband.

She'd gotten none of those things.

So, here in the dirt hole on the island of Vieques, she was managing her expectations about what lay inside the three-hundred-year-old treasure chest. It was probably worthless. A pile of stones. An old shoe. Maybe Olayinka's favorite scabbard, at best.

Still, a small part of Ainsley hoped to see a gleaming stash of gemstones—rubies, emeralds, silver, gold, rings, bracelets, necklaces. The accumulated booty of a hundred different raids.

The lid resisted at first, but with a grunt, she cracked it open. A line of cold air seeped out. So she jammed her fingertips into the seam and lifted even further. The resistance was stiffer than she'd thought. With effort she got the lid up to a thirty degree angle. It wouldn't go any further.

Ainsley sat back and exhaled. That's what three centuries of being buried in dirt will do to hinges.

"Open it all the way," said Orlando.

"I can't," she replied.

"Then try to see what's inside."

Ainsley tilted her head, trying in vain, but the angle was too sharp for daylight to reach.

"It's too dark to tell," she said. "Do you have a light?"

Orlando shook his head. "Sherman, do you?"

The munitions expert snapped his fingers. "Negative. Battery just died." Ainsley was surprised. He seemed to be the most prepared man alive.

Orlando shrugged. "You know what you have to do."

"What?"

"Put your hands inside."

That kicked Ainsley's imagination into hyper-drive. She pictured snakes sinking their fangs into her hand. Dead iguanas. A human skull with a pair of soupy eyeballs.

"I don't know if I can do that," she said.

"You can't quit now," he pleaded. "This is the very last step."

Orlando was right. And this was like ripping off a bandage: it was better not to overthink it.

Ainsley inhaled deeply, held her breath, then thrust her hands quickly into the darkness of the treasure chest.

Her eyes went wide. She was touching coarse fabric. It was a bit of letdown, truth be told. She felt around the edges of the material. It was wrapped around something squarish and soft. She gripped the package with both hands and carefully withdrew it from the chest.

In her hands was a burlap sack. The buried treasure of Olayinka.

Orlando was on his knees at the edge of the pit, his arms outstretched. "Hand it here," he said, "quickly."

She obeyed. It was fairly light. His hands took the burlap package and quickly set it on the ground on a sheet of white plastic that he'd unrolled. Ainsley clambered out of the pit and wiped her hands on her pants. They were ripped, dirtied, bloodied, and smelled like horse sweat. They'd have to be burned before she left Vieques.

She stood over Orlando as he carefully unwrapped the coarse fabric. Inside was a leather satchel with a brass buckle. It was so ancient that it looked as if a stiff breeze might cause it to fall apart.

He looked hesitant. "This really should be done in a laboratory."

"You don't have one," she reminded him.

He couldn't argue with that. Instead, he reached into his pocket and withdrew a pair of disposable blue plastic gloves.

"Why didn't you tell me you had those?" said Ainsley.

"Oops, my bad," he said, grinning.

With great finesse, Orlando's fingers gently unlatched the brass buckle. Then he carefully opened the leather cover. He slid his fingers into the pouch. Ainsley watched his eyes as he worked intently. A bead of sweat dripped from the tip of his nose.

At last, he gingerly pulled out the treasure of Olayinka. Ainsley cocked her head in disbelief.

It was a sheaf of papers.

"Documents?" he said. "Papers? After all your raids, Olayinka? This is the most valuable thing you had to give to posterity?"

"You can keep them in your archive," said Ainsley.

But Orlando was hopping mad. "I already *have* thousands of documents in my archive," he replied. "Goddamn it, I need some *money*. This is *not* what I was expecting."

A universal problem, thought Ainsley. She watched him peel off the rubber gloves and throw them down onto the ground.

"I need to think for a minute," said the pirate scholar. "Just give me a minute."

She watched him hobble away, hands thrust into his pockets. Ainsley wasn't sure what there was to think about. He seemed to be in the midst of an emotional crash. Ainsley looked over at Sherman. He was dozing against a tree. Even in repose, he seemed somehow ready for action.

She was alone with Olayinka's documents.

57

Ainsley kneeled down in the clearing, amidst the remains of the motorcycle. The blue tarp was a short distance away. She turned her back on both of those things.

Then she slid her hands into Orlando's gloves and picked up the documents.

They were yellowed but still intact. Ainsley marvelled at the quality of the paper, which was nothing like the high-acid pulpy stuff that modern paperbacks are slapped together with. Instead, the papers felt more like bedsheets, which is maybe why they had lasted for so long. They had been intended to survive.

She thumbed through them, looking for something, anything, to catch her eye. Then, near the bottom of the stack, something did.

It was a baptismal certificate.

The ink had smudged or even worn away in some places, so was difficult to make out. But she could recognize that it was an official document, notarized, and even partially typeset.

As her eyes went back and forth across the page, she tried her best to translate. It appeared to be dated seventeen hundred thirty-four. Near the bottom of the page she found the name of the child.

Francisco Fernando Cestero Cruz II.

Ainsley chewed on her lip. She knew that name. That was Doña Pilar's ancestor, the one whose wife had owned the pearl brooch, the one who had chased Olayinka and killed her to retrieve it. Ainsley had written it down in her notepad.

Why would Olayinka put the birth certificate of her own murderer in her most treasured items?

Ainsley looked at the next line. What she read next was unbelievable. In fact, she read it three times before it began to sunk in.

Next to the word *madre*, there was a single word listed.

Olayinka.

Her mental wheels spun but couldn't gain any traction. It took a while before they finally did.

Olayinka had birthed Francisco Fernando Cestero Cruz. The man who supposedly had killed her.

Ainsley sat back on her heels. She felt her lungs tighten in her chest. This is what stress did to a person. She knew why people died of heart attacks upon hearing bad news. She'd feel even worse if this were her own family.

The next question: Why would Olayinka have named her son Francisco Fernando Cestero Cruz? That was the name of the man who'd supposedly killed her.

She felt a presence over her shoulder. It was Orlando. "Find anything interesting?"

"Yes," she said. "It's a baptismal certificate. What do you think?"

The fat pirate scholar put on his reading glasses and peered over her shoulder. "So Olayinka was a mother. Huh. We always thought she died childless."

"Look at the child's name."

"Francisco Fernando Cestero Cruz II."

"That was the man who supposedly killed her," said Ainsley.

"Says who?"

"My employer. She's his descendant." Ainsley was confronted with the unthinkable, and she said it aloud. "Do you think Olayinka was killed by her own *son*?"

"It's not likely." Then he noticed something else. "Oh, this is fascinating. Look at the bottom."

The scholar's finger pointed to the margin, where a spindly hand had hastily added the words *libre, cincuenta y ocho*.

She translated that. *Free, fifty-eight*. "What does that mean?"

"For much of our history," explained Orlando, "anyone with both money and a conscience could buy a slave baby's freedom at the baptismal font. They negotiated a price with the owner. I've seen hundreds of baptismal certificates like this."

Then he peered closely at the addendum. "I even recognize the handwriting. That was Father Manuel Soto. He lived on the west side of the island in the early seventeen hundreds."

"So does this mean—"

"Yes," he interrupted. "Somebody bought Olayinka's baby its freedom."

"For fifty-eight pesos."

"Yes."

"Who would do that?" she said.

He shrugged. "If the mother was a slave, then typically it was the slaveowner. He was usually the father too. They enjoyed certain privileges, you know." Orlando peered at the document again. "What was the name of your employer's ancestor?"

"Francisco Fernando Cestero Cruz."

"This isn't him. This is Francisco Fernando Cestero Cruz the *second*." Orlando pointed at the two Roman numerals. "His son."

"So what are you saying?"

Orlando raised an eyebrow. "It probably meant that he owned Olayinka. He impregnated her. And then he named the baby after himself and purchased its freedom."

Ainsley rubbed her temples. "This makes absolutely no sense. Olayinka *escaped* slavery and became a pirate."

He stroked his pointed beard. "You're right, she did. She was executing raids in the late seventeen-twenties. But this baptismal certificate is dated seventeen thirty-four."

"So she went *back* to slavery?"

"Yes."

300

"Why the hell would she do *that?*"

"Not by choice. I would bet my paycheck that she was recaptured. Probably by her baby's father. It would fit in the time period."

Ainsley's mouth had dropped open. This was a revelation. It meant that, during the arc of this remarkable woman's life, Olayinka had travelled from slave to feared pirate ... and eventually back to slave. It also meant that even if Olayinka had stolen the crab brooch from Francisco Fernando Cestero Cruz, he *hadn't* killed her, the way Doña Pilar had told the story—he'd just made her into a slave instead.

Most importantly, it meant that Doña Pilar, the island's most virulent defender of Spanish European culture and values, was herself descended from a black slave.

Ainsley felt her stomach clench. She knew that it would be her job to break the news to Doña Pilar.

58

IT WAS MIDAFTERNOON BY THE TIME Ainsley had packed up the documents and picked their way back down the trail to where the horses were tethered.

One the group had remounted, Sherman led the trio back down the trail. Ainsley leaned back in her saddle, the way you're supposed to when going downhill, and thought about the documents.

Olayinka had been a slave not once, but twice. She'd given birth to the man whom Doña Pilar claimed as a full-blooded Spaniard ancestor. At some point, probably soon, Ainsley would have to confront the old racist with the truth of her ancestry.

She wondered what other secrets were being kept from her.

At last Ainsley shook off the daydream. She sat up straighter in the saddle, squared her shoulders, lifted her head. This had undoubtedly been an interesting day trip. But she hadn't come to Vieques to watch a man on a motorcycle get blown up, or to become an amateur archaeologist.

She had come here primarily to find Roman Galarza, the man with the pearl brooch.

The trees fell away and the horses squeezed back through the hole that had been sheared in the fence. The briny scent of ocean water floated into Ainsley's nose, and soon the crystal-blue water was visible again.

Up ahead, Ainsley saw Orlando pluck a pink flower from a bush and smell it.

"It's nice here," she said.

Orlando tossed the flower onto the ground with a dainty flutter of the fingers. "I don't really want to leave. This is much better than my stupid little pirates' lair above the bar in Old Town."

"Except for the land mines."

"I can deal with that. I don't do much walking anyways. So what are you going to do about your other mission? That person you're looking for?"

"I'm going there as soon as we get back," she replied. "I already wasted most of the day doing this."

"It wasn't a waste. We watched a man blow himself up and we learned that Olayinka was a mother."

"But you didn't get rich."

There was a long pause. "Being rich isn't everything," he said quietly.

303

Soon after, they broke out onto the beach, and the three horses were riding side-by-side across the golden sand. Ainsley looked over at Sherman.

"What should we do about the motorcyclist?"

"I'm going to call that in when we get back," he said. "I'll say that I was up there alone and discovered his body."

"You won't get in trouble?"

He shook his head. "People owe me a lot of favors at the Fish and Wildlife Service." Then he angled his head and looked Ainsley up and down in the saddle. "You're handling the horse well," he said. "You relaxed your hands."

"Please don't lie to make me feel better."

"I never lie," Sherman said. "These animals smell fear and react accordingly. You don't have any."

"Oh, I'm still afraid," she said. She patted the horse's neck.

By the time they arrived back at Esperanza, the sun was starting its long descent into the horizon. Ainsley helped Orlando hoist himself off the horse. When he hit the ground, he clutched his leg.

"What's the matter?"

"It hurts," he said. "Too much activity." Then another coughing jag hit him.

"Back to the *casa*?"

The fat pirate scholar nodded. They called over Jim Sherman, paid him the balance, and then turned the horses back to him.

"Do you need help walking them back to the stables?" said Ainsley.

"There are no stables," he replied.

Ainsley was confused. "Then what do you do with them?"

He shrugged. "Just let them go. They never wander too far." He smiled, then glanced at the water. "Gotta run. I can probably get one quick dive in before sunset."

There was a quick handshake, and then the munitions expert was gone.

Together, Ainsley and Orlando hobbled back into the town of Esperanza, along the esplanade, past the same stone picnic bench she'd sat at this morning. A couple hundred people were lined up on the street, sunburned and chatty, most holding tall tropical drinks. They were waiting for the sunset. That seemed to be the highlight of the day here on the southwest side of the island.

Ainsley noticed a hush as she passed. There were tugged sleeves, head nods, furtive whispers. Maybe she and Orlando looked worse than she'd realized. Navigating through a forest of land mines had probably killed whatever lazy island vibe she might've had.

"Have to stop," Orlando said suddenly. "I can't walk anymore."

Ainsley noticed that his breathing had become more labored. He dropped onto a stone bench and greedily sucked at his inhaler.

"I'll be okay," he said, gasping. "I just need some time to rest."

"Well, I have to find Roman Galarza," she replied. "The sun is going down."

He nodded.

"But you can't come with me."

He shook his head sadly.

"That's okay," said Ainsley, "I can go alone."

Orlando le Grand took the inhaler out of his mouth. "Listen, if you're not back in two hours, I'll call the police."

"That's nice of you," she said. "You're going to be okay here?"

He looked at her incredulously. Then he gestured out to the sunset, to the purple, pink, and orange washing across the sky. The dappled blue surface of the ocean rippled below. "How," he said, "could anything *not* be okay here?"

Ainsley smiled. "I have another idea. Don't move."

"Funny."

She crossed the street to a small store and returned a minute later. She put a cold bottle of Medalla on his picnic table. "My gift," she said, "to enjoy the sunset."

A big smile decorated his face. "You really want to be my wife, don't you?"

"Never."

"If you change your mind, there's one more thing you should know."

"What?"

"I can't drink just one."

"I knew you would say that." She pulled the rest of the six-pack out from behind her back, and laid it on the table in front of him.

He looked up at her with adoring eyes. "I was kidding about becoming my wife before. Not so much now."

"You've been a big help," she said. "I'll be back soon."

As she walked away, Ainsley glanced back. The fat pirate scholar, silhouetted against the sinking sun, had unlaced his shoes and propped his bare feet up on the low wall. He was holding a bottle up to the setting sun.

A toast to happiness.

59

Ainsley was striding briskly through the languid crowd on the esplanade. Heads turned as she passed, but she barely noticed. She was too intent on finding Roman Galarza.

She pulled the tracing paper out of her purse and looked at the address one more time.

Casa de Bohio, Esperanza, Vieques.

She stopped a passerby. He was wearing board shorts and flip-flops. A severe red sunburn had been whipped across his chest like the label of a Jamaican beer. He carried a fruity cocktail in a collins glass.

"Do you know where this place is?" she said.

He looked at the tracing paper. "No street number?"

"No."

"Well, it's my fourth season here, and I've noticed they don't always use street numbers. Especially not the older places."

"So this is an older home?"

"Yeah." He waved his arm generally to the east. "Maybe that way? The older places are all over in that direction." He looked at her empty hands. "Hey, where's your sundowner?"

Ainsley didn't have time to be drinking. She thanked him and continued travelling along the esplanade until the cement ended. The road now became an uneven ribbon of dirt. She kept walking, navigating the ruts and bumps, her thighs hurting with every step. She was looking for some sign.

Then she saw it. An old-fashioned signpost, with a vertical stack of arrows pointing in various directions. She scanned them quickly. One of the arrows read *Casa de Bohio 1/2 km*. It was pointing uphill, away from the ocean.

Ainsley took a deep breath and turned up the road. It was a dirt track, running straight up to a small cluster of houses and trees halfway up the slope. Not a single switchback to relieve the climb.

The back of her head was throbbing, her knee was stinging, her back was aching, and now her shins were killing her. Ainsley ignored them all and attacked the incline. After all, Roman Galarza, and the pearl brooch, lay only a half a kilometer away, at the top of the hill.

The orange sun sank lower, and she climbed higher. Other than a few shrubs tickling her ankles, the slope here was completely exposed. More sweat beaded on Ainsley's upper lip. She wiped it off on her shoulder sleeve. She was surprised there was any moisture left in her body at all.

What would she say when she found Roman Galarza? Would a direct approach work? *Excuse me, you've stolen a pearl brooch and I'm here to demand it back.* Maybe an indirect approach would be better. She could play it like she had the wrong address.

Whatever the decision, she'd have to make it quickly, because she had just reached the top of the dirt track. She paused for two gulps of water from her bottle, then turned towards the cluster of houses.

There were four bungalows, arranged in a small circle. In the middle of the circle was a garden area with chicken fencing, sprouting leafy vegetables, and a lemon tree. The community plot of land.

She studied each home. The first house was tidily kept, freshly painted. A small boy in cute overalls was playing with a bucket and pail in the front yard. Ainsley guessed that wasn't a likely hide-out for a jewel thief.

The second house looked to be totally abandoned, cobwebby and boarded-up. It'd probably been a vacation home for a family on the main island who'd hit a hard patch, and couldn't afford to keep it up.

The third was as plain as a bologna sandwich, cement porch, simple shutters. It was unmarked. She guessed that the Casa de Bohio would at least have a sign.

The fourth was huddled behind the others like a shy younger sister. Ainsley ventured quietly into the circle to see the bungalow. It was wreathed in an enormous cloud of bougainvillea. The flowers even extended out on a trellis, all the way to the street.

Ainsley stealthily approached the front of the property and fingered some of the purple flowers. At the heart of each bloom, a white bud was nestled like a secret.

To her right, overgrown by the blossoms, Ainsley noticed a wooden placard. She pushed the growth aside. Etched into the wood were three words.

Casa de Bohio.

Her breath caught in her throat. She took an involuntary step backwards. This was the hideout of Roman Galarza. Ainsley looked at the front door. She didn't have the courage to brazenly rap on it. She would do some reconnaissance first.

Pressing her bag under her arm, Ainsley slinked quietly around the side of the bungalow. There were two open windows, curtains drawn. The stiff weeds crinkled beneath her feet. She tried to tread lightly.

She stopped at the corner, flattened herself against the stucco wall, and peered around the corner. In the back of the house was a sliding glass door, which led to a brick patio. A few pieces of dirty white outdoor furniture sat on its bricks. In the grass, a barbeque grill was covered in a thin layer of dirt.

The Casa de Bohio looked like somebody's rental cottage.

Then a sound caught Ainsley's ear. A hissing, popping sound. It was familiar. Then the fatty smell wafted into her nostrils, and she knew.

Bacon.

Inside this house, Roman Galarza was frying bacon. He didn't seem to be hiding out as much as seemed to be on vacation. The smell of bacon took her back to her first morning on the island, at Doña Pilar's house.

Then she heard an obnoxious burp. Suddenly Ainsley felt a heat come over her face, a white-hot knowledge of who was frying bacon inside the house.

Keep watching, a voice inside her head told her.

No, she replied.

Keep watching.

Ainsley forced her eyes to stay fixed on the patio. Her fingers clung tightly onto the edge of the house. She watched the glass door slide open. She knew who was going to step outside, even before he did exactly that, carrying a bottle of rum in one hand.

It was Luis Cepeda.

60

AINSLEY PULLED BACK FROM THE CORNER of the bungalow, dropped her head, and silently mouthed several obscenities. Part of her refused to believe that this could be happening.

Luis had been holding out on her. He'd led her on a wild-goose chase all over the main island, from Ponce, to the *centrale*, to the *parranda*—and now it seemed that he had known exactly where Roman Galarza was all along.

The more she thought about this, the more furious Ainsley became.

Soon she reached a tipping point. Anger got the better of her judgment. She found herself turning the corner of the bungalow and striding across the backyard. She saw Luis notice her. She saw his mouth drop open. It all felt like a dream.

"How did—" he said, as she stepped onto the patio.

"Shut your mouth," she replied, "and don't say a goddamned word until you're told to."

"But—"

She snatched the bottle of rum from his hand and threw it onto the grass. He was so stunned that he didn't even go after it.

"Where is Roman Galarza?" she said.

"I don't know."

"That's bullshit. He's here. His wife wrote down this address on her notepad. You helped me get to his house."

The poet just stammered in response.

Ainsley stepped closer to him. She was up in his face now. "For someone who loves words, you'd better start using them."

"You just told me to shut my mouth—"

"I changed my mind. Any language is fine. Try me."

The poet edged backwards, his hands up in supplication. "I really don't know. He's gone."

"Roman Galarza is gone? What does that mean?"

"He went somewhere."

Luis' eyes were dancing all over. There was not a doubt in Ainsley's mind that he was lying. It was useless to pursue this.

"I'm going inside to look for him," she said. "You sit down and wait. This is only the beginning."

"Of what?"

"Of a very uncomfortable evening."

314

His brow furrowed. Ainsley could see him scheming for a way to get out of this.

Ainsley opened the sliding glass door and stepped into the house. The floors were made of white linoleum and were clean enough for surgery. Except for the greasy frying pan cooling on the stovetop, the kitchen was empty in that certain way that rental condos and houses have. In the living room were pieces of ugly wicker furniture with floral cushions stuffed with styrofoam.

"You can look all you want," said Luis, "but he's not here."

"I'll be the judge of that," Ainsley replied.

She passed the bungalow's main bathroom and peered inside. There was only one toothbrush on the holder.

Of the two bedrooms in the back, only the master was occupied. The left side of the bed had been slept in. The right side of the bed was untouched. Not that she'd expected two full-grown men to be sharing a double bed.

Ainsley stepped back and blew air out of her mouth. She'd now seen every room in the house. A terrible feeling was tightening in her abdomen. It was attributable to a single thought.

Luis was here alone.

There was no sign of Roman Galarza. Part of her wondered if there ever would be.

Ainsley stepped onto the outdoor brick patio again. Down the hill, the blue expanse of the Caribbean was turning purple in the deepening dusk. A few degrees above the horizon, a single planet glowed like a pinprick in space.

315

Luis was sitting at the dirty white table. He'd retrieved the bottle of rum, found two glasses, and poured two shots of rum, one into each. He gestured to the chair opposite his own.

"Let's talk," he said.

"That chair is filthy."

"Then I will clean it for you." He leaned over and wiped the seat with the sleeve of his shirt.

Ainsley approached slowly, then lowered herself to the seat. She could feel its plastic slats bend beneath her weight.

Then her eyes bored into his. "You need to tell me what the hell is going on."

"There's no rush," Luis said, stretching out casually, lacing his hands behind his head. "This is Vieques. Nobody does anything here."

"Listen, I'm serious. I've trusted you with everything here. And now I find out you've been lying to me."

Luis hoisted his glass of rum. "I propose a toast."

At this moment, Ainsley had no patience for conviviality. "A toast to what?"

"To keeping your temper."

Ainsley watched his glass clink against hers. She watched him drink his rum. She had zero interest in sharing a drink with this failed poet and handyman.

"You're an impossible personality," she said.

"So I've been told." He leaned back in his chair. "Now, are you ready for the truth?"

"I've only been demanding it for the last quarter hour."

"And you promise not to get upset?"

"Luis, just tell me."

A cunning expression came across his face. His eyes fixed upon hers like a cobra's.

"There is no Roman Galarza," he said.

61

AINSLEY FELT THE REACTION BEGIN IN her ankles. It was a strange feeling. It spread up her legs, through her backside, shot up her spine, and crinkled her forehead. She could feel her face twitching. It was hard for her to meet Luis' eyes.

"You told me," she stammered, "that he worked at the Ponce Museum of Art."

"I did."

"And we met other people who knew him."

"So you think."

Ainsley spun the story backwards in her head. "What about that guy in the Yankees cap? The one we met at the poetry reading? You didn't know him at all, and he gave me Roman Galarza's name."

Luis smiled. "He's my friend Tomás."

"You *knew* that guy?"

"We worked it out on the phone while I was in the bar in Ponce. Remember when you wouldn't come inside?"

Thinking back, Ainsley remembered perfectly. Her nostrils flared. She was feeling more and more duped with every passing minute.

"So you collaborated with Tomás to make up an imaginary person named Roman Galarza who stole the pearl brooch."

He just smiled.

"So how did Pacheco know about Roman Galarza? You hadn't even seen him in years."

Luis waved it off. "That was an act too. He's my best friend."

Ainsley facepalmed herself. "Oh my God." She put her head between her knees and said it again.

Then she sat up, feeling aggressive. She was determined to find a single way that she hadn't been misled, if only for the sake of her own ego. "But what about the *parranda*? I was inside Roman Galarza's house! I met his wife!"

Luis poured another shot of rum. "That," he said slowly, "was my house. And the woman you met was my wife."

Ainsley sat there, staring dumbly at him. Her mouth opened and closed several times. Trying to grasp the sheer audacity of the ruse that had been played upon her.

He continued. "We had to clear all our personal photos out of the house before you arrived with the *parranda*."

"Which is why you joined it late."

Luis nodded. "My wife wasn't happy. Especially when you left your phone and showed up the next morning and stole that pad of paper. How did you read the address?"

"Someone helped me do a rubbing."

Ainsley thought back to the pad of paper. Luis had written the address to this casa on the notepad and left it for his wife.

Luis leaned back in his chair. He was looking at Ainsley with the distance you give to something you respect. "I tried to lose you, Ainsley Walker. I tried to tire you out. But you *just ... kept ... going.*" His fist accented every word on the table.

That sounded familiar to Ainsley. She knew that the word "persistence" was going to be etched on her tombstone someday.

"But you utterly outsmarted me," she said.

He shrugged. "You're an outsider. It really wasn't that hard."

"But I'm supposed to be *smart*," Ainsley said.

"I am too. I outsmarted two ex-wives and four kids."

Ainsley exhaled mightily. She was trying to conduct an orchestra of clashing emotions within her soul. "But there is something else."

"I think I know what it is."

"Tell me."

"You want to know where the pearl brooch really is."

Ainsley nodded.

His eyes danced mischievously in his face. "I was wondering how long it would take for you to ask."

"I bet you don't know where it is."

"I do."

"Then keep talking."

Luis glanced around, as if for eavesdroppers. Then he leaned forward and lowered his voice. "I have it."

She had suspected this. "How did you get it?"

"That is a secret."

"Tell me."

"I can't. But it's not here."

That sounded like it could go either way. Everything Luis said now was to be treated with suspicion.

She thought about it a bit more. Why on earth would he have fled the main island of Puerto Rico, to hole himself up in a rural rental house in Vieques, if he didn't have something to hide? It made even more sense given that Luis had just admired her persistence.

She decided that her doubt was well-founded. He was keeping the brooch somewhere on these premises.

"Fine," she said. "Play your games."

"They're not that fun."

"Tell you what. Try to think up another one while I use the bathroom. I'm looking forward to getting duped again."

Ainsley rose to her feet and walked back into the rental house. She hadn't asked permission. She could feel his eyes watching her back.

Once inside, she strode quickly down the hallway. She knew exactly what she was looking for.

The master bedroom had grown darker with the creeping dusk. She flipped on the floor lamp in the corner. Her eyes scanned the room. Bed. Desk. Dresser. Open suitcase.

Then she spotted it.

The purple velvet sack with gold trim. Luis' colored poetry pencils. The ones that she'd thought were so cute back at the *malecón*.

Behind her, Ainsley heard the sliding glass door open. The poet was coming after her. Quickly she went to the bedroom door and closed it. Her fingers scrambled for the door lock. She prayed that there was one.

She found a deadbolt. She twisted the small rod a quarter turn to the left. The door went stiff. She thanked heavens for whatever paranoid soul had installed a deadbolt here, on the island of Vieques. Maybe theft was a bigger problem than it seemed.

She walked back across the room to the small purple bag. She picked it up and felt its heft in her palm. She opened the golden cinch ribbon.

Luis was pounding on the door. "Ainsley, let me in. I will show you where the pearl brooch is. Just let me in—"

She turned the bag upside down onto the bed. Out spilled a jumble of colored pencils, purple, aquamarine, magenta, ochre. She estimated thirty total. Except for the green pencil, none had been sharpened. These had been for show. He didn't really need colored pencils to write his poetry.

"Ainsley Walker, if you don't open that door—"

A weight in her palm told her that there was something else left in the bag. She could tell that it was oddly shaped. Angular.

She peered inside. Something glinted back. She reached inside and grasped the object with her fingers and pulled it out.

It was a crab-shaped pearl brooch.

62

AINSLEY STOOD THERE, GASPING. SHE FELT like the oxygen had just been sucked out of the room.

The brooch was surprisingly small, maybe half the size of her palm. But the pearl occupied most of the setting. It was exquisite. A beautiful sphere, exceptionally large, it possessed the finest lustre she'd ever seen.

The door shuddered in its frame. Luis was throwing his shoulder into the wood now. Ainsley thanked her lucky stars that he didn't know it was more effective to kick a deadbolt.

She studied the handiwork closely. Two claws were drenched in diamond pavé all the way to the tips of their pincers. Four smaller legs were dotted with sapphires on either side of the body. On the head, two tiny ruby eyes peered out at the world.

Ainsley gaped at the craftsmanship. The word *vintage* didn't do this piece justice. It was older, and more spectacular, than that.

As she stood there, weighing the brooch in her hand, Ainsley felt herself coming to an important realization. It was welling up from the pit of her stomach, where all her most important decisions originate.

She didn't want to give the pearl brooch back to Doña Pilar. The woman was an unrepentant racist with nothing but cobwebs in her purse. But neither did Ainsley want to let Luis keep it. He'd stolen this pearl from his employer and had probably been wondering how to sell it. Plus, he'd constructed that torturous wild goose chase that had devoured the better part of Ainsley's week. He'd made her feel like an utter chump.

Ainsley chewed on a knuckle. She knew what she would do. She would take the pearl directly back to the museum in Ponce and negotiate with them directly.

The door shuddered in its frame again. She glanced at it. She didn't want to open that door, especially not now that the tables were turned, and she was the little thief.

Then she saw the bedroom window. It was open. The glass had already been lifted. There was nothing but a screen between her and escape.

She prepped her leg, took two quick steps, and kicked the screen. It popped out of its frame. That was overkill, actually. She could've used her hands just as easily.

She could hear Luis panting outside the door. "Ainsley?"

Damn. He'd heard it. And he was smart too. He'd be dashing outside any moment now. Ainsley had only a few seconds' advantage.

She dropped the brooch into her purse, zipped it shut, clutched it against her body, and ran across the room towards the window. She tucked her head down and threw herself, right shoulder first, through the wide-open window.

She tumbled through the air and landed in a bush. It was a rose bush. She thrashed and flailed, feeling the thorns scratch her skin.

At last she broke free of its fragrant grasp. She heard the door to the house slam. Ainsley scrambled to her feet, picked up her bag, and tore off running down the hillside.

She could hear Luis yelling behind her. It didn't matter. He couldn't catch her. Ainsley ran as though someone had lit her shoes on fire. She reached her arms out, pulling on the invisible handrails, the way she'd been taught long ago. With the downhill momentum, she could barely keep up with her own legs.

At the bottom of the hill, she slowed to a walk, and finally stopped. She held her arms above her head, taking in great gulps of air. Above her, the sky had been blotted a deep indigo. Soon the points of starlight would wink themselves on.

Ainsley allowed herself a moment of back-patting. She had won the game. The pearl brooch was in her possession. Luis had been proven both a liar and a thief. It was a weird perspective, but Ainsley couldn't help thinking that she had been the force of righteousness in this stinky situation. And she had triumphed.

She glanced back at the cottage. It was almost impossible to see in the darkening landscape. But she could still glimpse a rotund figure standing silhouetted by the light, hands on hips. Watching her.

But his body language didn't seem angry. He exuded a sense of calm, even from this distance.

Ainsley turned away. She began walking back down the road to Esperanza, turning over the events in her head.

She may have won the battle, but she couldn't shake the itchy feeling that, somehow, she had not yet won the war.

Ponce

63

A DAY LATER, AINSLEY OPENED THE pouch and
turned it upside down. The crab-shaped pearl
brooch tumbled out.

She was wearing a visitor's badge and sitting
across the table from Juana Barbosa, the senior
projects administrator at the Ponce Museum of Art.
The museum executive was still dressed beautifully,
in a sleeveless green silk ensemble. Now, though,
the black woman's strong arms were crossed protec-
tively over one another. The gorgeous toothy smile
that Ainsley had admired a week earlier was now
replaced by a look of suspicion.

Ainsley had woken on Vieques that morning,
showered, then met Orlando le Grand for a breakfast of mango, pastries, and coffee. On the other
side of the small table, the fat pirate scholar had

seemed different. There had been a new twinkle in his eye, new color in his cheeks.

In short, he'd looked *happy*.

She hadn't wasted any time. After breakfast, she'd taken the first available ferry back to the main island, rented a car, and sped around Highway 53, then 52, at breakneck speed. She'd made it to Ponce in about three hours.

She'd been burning with a fever to show off her accomplishment to the one professional who would appreciate it most—and who would reward her for it.

Now, deep within a warren of offices in the curator's department of the museum, Ainsley switched on the gemologist's light. The small crab glittered and glowed. It was a lovely piece of work.

"That's it," said Juana. "The craftsmanship is astounding."

Ainsley nodded. To her surprise, though, the senior projects administrator didn't make a move to touch it. Her arms remained crossed.

"Don't you want to inspect it?" said Ainsley.

"I don't need to," came the reply.

Ainsley was perturbed. She'd been through hell and back to find the pearl brooch. Juana Barbosa knew that, too, because Ainsley had just finished explaining all the events of the past week—the poetry reading, the *lechonera* at the abandoned sugar refinery, the *parranda*, the dangerous afternoon in Loíza, meeting Orlando le Grand, the horseback excursion on Vieques, the blond idiot who'd blown himself up on a land mine, the treasure trove of Olayinka, and her discovery of Luis's trickery.

"I thought you'd be more excited," said Ainsley.

Juana didn't say anything. There was another moment of awkward silence. Ainsley felt the hair on her neck start to rise. She could feel unspoken words below the surface.

She decided to dispense with the personal stuff and cut straight to business. "So who do I see for the reward? You said you were offering three thousand dollars."

Juana's eyes flicked around. "We are, but it's going to take a while. There's a lot of paperwork."

"Why?"

Juana's tone changed. She sounded like a scold. "This museum is an institution, Miss Walker, not a criminal syndicate. The reward must go through proper channels."

"Look," said Ainsley, "finding this thing took a *lot* of work. Can't you just do it outside the official budget? You must have a small slush fund."

Juana picked her words as though she were measuring ingredients for a cake. "I think it's best if I speak with my superior first. Excuse me."

The executive stood up abruptly and disappeared into the maze of workspaces. Ainsley felt confounded. Maybe coming here had been a mistake. Maybe she should've gone directly to Doña Pilar, explained what Luis had done, then negotiated a reward. At the very least, it would be easier to grapple with an addled old lady than with a savvy museum executive.

Ainsley stood up and cautiously peered across the room.

Several feet away, Juana Barbosa was in an empty workspace, sitting in her chair. She wasn't talking to her superior at all. She was staring at her hands.

That decided it. There were other agendas at work here, and Ainsley wasn't cooperating with this institution any longer. She would head to the house of matchsticks and demand compensation from Doña Pilar instead.

She snapped off the desk light, put the pearl brooch back into the pouch, and stowed it safely in her bag. Then she moved quickly out of the long room.

Juana Barbosa was already walking over just as Ainsley reached the door.

"Excuse me, you can't leave, we haven't finished—"

Ainsley didn't hear the rest. She didn't need to. She removed her visitor's tag, flung it at the security guard near the door, and walked outside.

It was two o'clock pm, the hour for naps in Ponce, and the heat and the light were overwhelming. Ainsley shaded her eyes with a palm. She was starving, and not just from that day's work. She estimated that she had accumulated at least a ten thousand calorie deficit over the last few days. It was time to grab a good lunch. Then she would leave.

As she hurried around the corner from the museum, Ainsley glanced backwards. Juana Barbosa had come outside the museum with two security guards. She looked upset. She was motioning to them to sweep the area.

These people had no power over her, no authority. Still, Ainsley had no desire to tangle with anybody, not even harmless museum staff.

She would leave Ponce, quickly, and drive back to Caguas. It was the final step of her mission.

Ainsley put on her sunglasses and strode quickly back to her car.

Caguas

64

THREE HOURS LATER, AINSLEY WAS DRIVING past the broken-down storefronts of Caguas, past the auto repair yards with the hand-painted signs and piles of tires.

She'd stopped for lunch at a roadside restaurant along the way. Her intuition had served her well. The slow-roasted pork was juicy and tender. The *plátanos* were crispy and salted. But the real star of the meal was the rice with pigeon peas, *arroz con gandules*, which was unbelievably flavorful. The waitress had told her that it had been seasoned with annatto oil, brown sugar, and coconut milk. Ainsley had sworn to buy a Puerto Rican cookbook whenever she finally got home.

Which appeared to be drawing closer. On the car radio, she heard that San Juan International

335

Airport had reopened the previous day. Ainsley thought back to her pretty seatmate, Amaryllis, the woman who'd started this whole ball of insanity rolling a week ago. It felt like Ainsley had lived several lifetimes since then.

The rolling hills reappeared, and her fingers tightened on the wheel. She remembered the turn-off that Tomás had taken, cranked the wheel, and a moment later was speeding down the two-track dirt road. It was still lined with the tall silk cotton trees, their red branches splayed high above. They'd survived the tropical storm.

As had Ainsley.

She passed over the low-lying portion of the road that had been flooded a week ago, the one that Tomás had splashed through in his truck. It was bone-dry now.

Then she swept around the final curve and saw the house. Doña Pilar's weather-beaten pile of kindling had been brought to its knees by the tropical storm. Several more boards had fallen onto the lush grass. Parts of the roof had been ripped off. A window was broken. One more good rainfall, and it would be condemned.

Then something caught Ainsley's eye. It was a pair of vehicles, parked in front of the plantation house. One was a battered Ford Fiesta. A lump formed in Ainsley's throat.

Luis was here.

Of course he would be. He would be fawning over the elderly woman, trying to butter her up in preparation for the shitstorm that Ainsley was bringing.

The other vehicle was a stylish white sedan, a Lexus. Ainsley hadn't seen that one before.

She parked her own rental car, shut off the engine, and stepped outside. It was a delightfully sunny day, so different from the weather a week earlier.

As Ainsley walked across the grass towards the plantation house, she thought about what exactly she would say to Luis. He'd lied to her for a week, then confessed, then lied to her again. Anything that came out of his mouth she would assume was just more bullshit.

Ainsley tried to picture her next few movements. She wouldn't even look at Luis when he confronted her. Instead, she would march directly upstairs to Doña Pilar's bedroom. She would lock the door behind her. She would pull out a small chair and sit beside the old lady. She would hand over the pearl brooch. And then she would describe, using textbook Castellano Spanish, just how deeply Luis had shafted her.

It was a good plan. She wouldn't knock on the front door either. She wouldn't have to. The treasure riding inside her purse like a little princess gave her the authority to do anything.

As Ainsley approached the porch, the front door opened. A rotund figure stepped out of the darkness within.

It was Luis. He was wearing an inscrutable expression on his face.

"Ainsley," he said, "we've been expecting you."

"Am I that predictable?"

"No, just smart."

She wondered why all this unnecessary flattery. Maybe it was to mitigate the anger that she was going to stoke in Doña Pilar.

"Please step aside," she said.

A quizzical smirk appeared on his lips. Then the door opened again. A female figure stepped out, her strong arms highlighted by a sleeveless green silk ensemble.

It was Juana Barbosa.

Ainsley stepped back in surprise. The museum executive must've driven to Caguas immediately after their meeting. Ainsley's leisurely lunch had guaranteed that the woman would beat her to the old woman's bedside.

She felt her heart palpitate. What if the senior projects administrator had just fed all sorts of lies to Doña Pilar? She could've floated any number of whoppers. That the brooch was lost permanently. That it'd been damaged. That Ainsley herself had absconded with the prize.

"Miss Walker," said the museum executive. Her voice was a lovely purr.

"Miss Barbosa," replied Ainsley.

Juana and Luis were standing side-by-side on the porch. Something about their body language made Ainsley grow suspicious. They looked too comfortable with one another.

"Do you two know each other?"

Luis shrugged. "No, I only met her once, last week. You were there."

The senior projects administrator laid a hand on his forearm. "Don't bother, Luis." She turned to Ainsley. "Maybe you should sit down."

"I'm comfortable standing."

"Are you sure you want to hear this right now?"

"Hear what?" said Ainsley.

Juana Barbosa straightened up. She seemed to carry an air of power. "That Luis has been working for me."

65

Ainsley cocked her head. She wasn't sure if she'd quite heard that right. "Could you repeat that?"

Juana nodded. "Luis is working for me. I hired him a month ago."

"To do what?"

"To steal the pearl brooch."

Ainsley opened her mouth, but nothing seemed to come out. She stood there gasping like a fish before managing to croak a response. "But you didn't *have* to steal it. Doña Pilar *donated* it to your museum."

Juana grew very serious. "Didn't anybody inform you of Señora Pilar's conditions for the exhibit?"

Ainsley thought back. "Maybe."

The black woman's lips curled. Ainsley saw her struggling to contain herself. "Allow me to remind you. Doña Pilar demanded that the story of the pearl brooch be told in a manner that we felt did not reflect the historical record."

"What manner?"

Luis stepped in. "Doña Pilar is an ugly racist."

Juana touched his arm again. "Calm down." To Ainsley: "She demanded an inaccurate perspective of Olayinka in the exhibition. She wanted to rewrite history."

"So you agreed to that?"

Juana shrugged. "We really wanted that brooch. It's historically significant. It's a rare surviving link to one of the forgotten stories of our Puerto Rican past." She smiled to herself. "Olayinka, the black female pirate."

Ainsley started to guess what had happened. Juana Barbosa had made a bullshit deal with the old lady, pretending to acquiesce to her racist demands—and then, on the sly, hired her handyman to steal the pearl brooch.

"So," said Ainsley, "what was the point of stealing it?"

Luis was blunt. "We were going to hold the pearl brooch until she died."

"The strategy was to delay—" said Juana.

"—until she hired you," finished Luis.

The two of them were staring at the visitor. Their faces showed both frustration and admiration. Ainsley suddenly understood her place in this story. She had been an unwelcome irritant, a wrench tossed into the gears of the story.

Then she thought of an even better metaphor. She was a grain of sand inside an oyster. Ainsley smiled to herself. The oyster had attacked the irritant, but the irritant had refused to leave, and it had gained layer upon layer of experience until it had transformed into a pearl.

"I had *no* idea about any of this," said Ainsley.

"Of course you didn't," said Juana. "But we couldn't tell you the truth, either."

"Then why are you telling me now?" Ainsley pointed to the second story of the house. "Doña Pilar is right there. She's probably listening. I can tell her *everything*, if I wanted to."

Neither one responded. Luis looked at Juana; she looked back at him. The exchange of glances was not lost on Ainsley. She suddenly grew tired of being the caboose of the conversation.

"You two have so many goddamned *secrets*," said Ainsley. "I know there's something else you're not telling me. I can *smell* it."

Luis looked towards Juana again. "What do you think?"

The black woman had cast her eyes downwards. "I think we let her find out for herself."

Ainsley felt herself standing on the edge of an even bigger unknown, if that were possible. This sat poorly with her. From a surprise birthday party in the third grade to a disappeared husband twenty years later, Ainsley had always *hated* to be played with. And even though she understood Luis and Juana's motivation, the fact was that they were batting her around like a pair of cats with a toy mouse.

"Look," said Ainsley, "I learned all about Olay-inka, and I agree with you. However, I just made it through a huge shitstorm and deserve some compensation. Give me three thousand dollars, and I'll hand over the brooch. I'll play along however you want."

Juana looked at her feet. Luis couldn't meet her eyes.

"Fine," she said. "I'm coming in to see Doña Pilar."

She stepped between the two and opened the Spanish-style front door. Inside the living room, the tatted, yellowed lace curtains were still hanging over the windows. The credenza was still flung against the wall like an unwanted memory.

Ainsley found her way back towards the staircase. She placed her left hand on the railing and slowly ascended the narrow steps, placing her feet diagonally. The floorboards squeaked beneath her shoes.

At the top of the staircase, Ainsley stopped. Despite the stifling air, she felt a chill down her spine. It was a creepy feeling.

She turned and walked down the hall towards the old lady's bedroom. She passed her previous bedroom, with the short bed. Then she passed the library, with its cracked leather chair and old books, where she'd read about the history of Puerto Rico.

Then she reached the master bedroom. The door was closed. She knocked firmly. There was no answer. She opened the door and stepped inside.

The bedroom hadn't changed since her first visit. The large, Spanish-style four-poster bed was still parked majestically in the center of the far wall. And on the bed lay the old woman. She was still wrapped in her bejeweled nightgown and swaddled in hand-stitched quilts.

As far as Ainsley could tell, only one thing *had* changed.

Doña Pilar was dead.

66

AINSLEY WALKER WAS NO STRANGER TO death.

Looking at the body carried her back in time to her own father's death. She remembered being in the room when he'd had passed away. She remembered the black hole where the mouth had once been. The vacant eyes. It wasn't something a ten-year-old girl could ever forget.

That same look was on Doña Pilar's face.

Ainsley heard footsteps behind her and turned. Luis was standing in the doorway, Juana behind him. "I found her when I arrived this morning," he said. "It probably happened in her sleep."

Meanwhile, Ainsley was struggling with her own conflicting feelings. She felt upset at the presence of death, a natural mammalian response. She felt grim satisfaction that such a revolting person had passed away. And she felt anger that nobody was here to pay her for all her efforts.

She stood there, grappling with all of these things. Then she heard Juana clear her throat. "At least it was an easy death, God bless her," she said.

"No suffering," added Luis.

"Yeah," croaked Ainsley.

Juana stepped into the room. "You should look more closely at her."

"I already am."

"No, look even closer. Come here."

She took Ainsley's hand and pulled her towards the bed. It happened too quickly to protest.

As they approached, Ainsley saw the dead woman's gnarled, veiny hands had been pulled up her chest, the coverlet clutched in her final grasp. Her eyes had been closed.

"What should I look at?" said Ainsley.

"Her face. Do you notice anything different?"

Though unnerved, Ainsley peered directly into the face of death. Something was odd. Then it dawned on her. The old lady's skin had changed. A week ago, she had been about five shades lighter.

"I'm not sure," said Ainsley, "but she looks darker somehow."

Juana nodded. Then she reached forward and lifted a piece of Doña Pilar's dyed lemon-yellow hair. "Touch it."

Ainsley hesitantly rolled the hair between her fingertips.

"Is it soft?" asked Juana.

"No, it's coarse."

"One more thing," said Juana. "Do you remember what color her eyes were?"

Ainsley did remember. It was hard to forget
that vivid green—an intense shade that had grabbed
her visitor's attention by the throat.

"They were green," she said.

"What are they now?"

"I don't know."

"Open one and find out." Juana saw Ainsley's
disgust. "Don't worry, she's dead. She can't see you
anymore."

Ainsley slowly reached out her hand. Her
innards were quivering like children hiding inside a
trunk. She placed two fingers on the ridge above
the eyebrow. The old woman's skin was already
cool to the touch.

Then, using her thumb, she gently lifted an
eyelid. A lifeless orb stared back. Ainsley sucked in
her breath.

The irises weren't green. They were *brown*.

"Do you understand now?" said Juana.

Luis had pulled out the drawer of the old
woman's vanity. He carried it across the room and
placed it on the foot of the bed. He began item-
izing the various toiletries. "Skin whitener. Hair
relaxer. Box of twenty custom-made green contact
lenses. Saline solution."

Ainsley finally understood. Doña Pilar had
obvious African roots, deep in her genetic makeup,
enough to be visible. And she'd taken great pains to
disguise that very fact.

It wasn't as shocking as it could've been. After
all, Ainsley had found Olayinka's buried documents.

She knew the true history of this woman's ancestor. She knew exactly where that African blood had come from.

She was both fascinated and disgusted. Suddenly the whole situation—the corpse, the room, the lies, the brooch, the racism—all became too much for Ainsley. She wheeled around and ran out of the bedroom.

67

SHE WATCHED HER FEET FLYING ACROSS the hallway floorboards. She watched the steps disappearing below her shoes, two at a time. She heard Luis
shouting her name. None of it mattered. Ainsley
wanted out of this plantation house, off this island,
away from liars.

In the living room, she felt a hand catch her
arm. It was strong. She tried to shake it off.

It was Luis. He whirled her around and
grabbed both of her shoulders. She allowed him.
Part of him wanted to hear his words.

"She was a sick woman," he said. "Her heart
was twisted against itself. Do you see why I had to
deceive you? Why I made up an imaginary thief?
Maybe you have to be Puerto Rican to know how
important this is."

"No," said Ainsley, "I get it."

"Here, look." Luis pulled her to the picture of Doña Pilar's family on the wall. It was the same one that Ainsley had studied a week earlier. "Have you seen this?"

"Yes."

"Did she tell you that was her family?"

"Yes."

"She was lying. That isn't her family at all."

It made perfect sense. Still, Ainsley was stunned. These revelations were coming faster than she could handle them.

He continued. "I knew Doña Pilar when I was a little boy. She used to take care of me and my sisters when my mother was at work. Her real family wasn't this white. But they had disowned her anyways."

"Why?"

"Her dark skin. She was the black sheep." He eyed Ainsley. "It happens in Puerto Rico. The darkest child in a family has the most problems. Usually it's drugs. I've known many like her."

All of this was news to Ainsley. She felt a lot of pity for the dead woman upstairs. It seemed that Olayinka's genetic material had lain dormant for three hundred years, then exploded in a single descendant.

"So she made a new life for herself," Luis continued. "I remember when she first bought this picture and hung it on her wall. That's when the stories started flowing out of her mouth. How all her ancestors were perfect white *peninsulares*. We laughed at her. It was all bullshit."

Luis paused. "But she lived long enough that the lies became the truth."

Ainsley didn't know what to say.

Suddenly Luis grew frustrated. "The hardest part was that the rest of us had to play along, or she would get furious."

No wonder nobody had stuck around her life, Ainsley thought. Then she said, "What about this house?"

"It's always been derelict, even sixty years ago. She bought it for a kiss and a smile."

"So it wasn't passed down several generations in her family?"

Luis shook his head. "That was a lie."

"And the studying in Spain?"

"More lies. She never stepped off the island."

"And the pearl brooch? How did she get that?"

"She took it from her mother's jewelry box the day that she was disowned. It was the most valuable thing that her family owned."

Ainsley breathed out. Doña Pilar had also probably viewed the pearl brooch as a symbol of the African blood in her veins. It made sense. And she'd twisted its history to conform to her new European identity that she'd invented.

This was a lot to process.

Juana had come downstairs. Her skin glowed beautifully in the hazy afternoon sunlight that filtered through Doña Pilar's ratty old curtains. Ainsley suddenly knew why this woman had engineered this theft. Doña Pilar's twisted worldview ran counter to everything a sophisticated Afro-Caribbean woman stood for.

Then Ainsley remembered the pearl brooch, still riding safely in her white bag.

"About the reward," said Ainsley.

Juana grew detached. "There is no reward," she said. "I made up a reward to satisfy Doña Pilar."

Ainsley understood. This theft had been conducted off the books, motivated by the anger of a proud Afro-Caribbean woman against another woman who was ashamed and disgusted by the ethnicity and culture that both of them had sprung from.

This also explained why Juana had been so reluctant to speak at the museum earlier that morning. And it explained why Omar had said that Doña Pilar had such a bad reputation in his community.

"Then it's time for me to go," said Ainsley.

She turned to leave. She sensed Juana stiffen. They were down to the bitter truth now. Ainsley held the only remaining card, and that was the pearl brooch itself.

"We could call the police," said Juana.

Ainsley stopped. She could call the police. However, the more Ainsley thought about this situation, the more confusing it seemed.

Ainsley had stolen the brooch from Luis. Luis had stolen it from Doña Pilar. Doña Pilar had stolen it from her own mother. Who owned the item? Nobody stood on a moral high ground. Nobody had more claim than anybody else.

"Yes, you could," she replied.

Then she walked outside, onto the dilapidated porch. She stood at the far end, looking at the green tropical hillsides. Luis and Juana quickly followed at a respectful distance, like puppies trailing their owner carrying a food dish.

"Ainsley," said Juana carefully, "we'd like to find a resolution that satisfies everybody."

"I'm thinking," said Ainsley.

She stared out at the purple mountains. Clearly, there wasn't any money from the museum to be had—or, if there was, it wouldn't be worth the effort twisting Juana's arm. Neither, however, did Ainsley want to simply turn over the pearl brooch without a fight. She'd put a lot of work into finding this damned thing.

Ainsley thought about what she really wanted. If it was money, would it be possible to sell it elsewhere? Omar, the *vejigante* artist and jewelry fence, would be the logical person to turn to, but after her blackmail, she was sure that he wouldn't want to talk to her, much less give her a fair deal. She could take it with her back to the mainland to sell it, but that didn't seem right either. This was a Puerto Rican heirloom, a part of the island's history.

The more she thought, the more uncomfortable she felt keeping the brooch for her own profit. On the other hand, there had to be a way for *somebody* to profit from its recovery.

Then the answer hit her.

She turned around, a fire in her eye. "Have either of you heard of a man named Orlando le Grand?"

Luis shook his head no. Juana, however, touched her finger to her chin, thinking. "Yes, we met with him a few years ago regarding his archive of historical documents. He wanted to sell it to us."

"He told me that your museum turned down his offer."

"We didn't have the funds."

"He said that you wouldn't even negotiate."

"Maybe."

"Maybe you just didn't want to buy it."

Juana shrugged. That wasn't a denial.

Ainsley smiled. She finally had found the leverage. "Here's the deal, Juana. If you can find both the desire and the funds to purchase his archive, the pearl brooch"—she took it from her purse and held it up, glinting in the daylight—"is all yours."

She held it there for a moment. Luis looked like he was salivating. For half a second, she thought that he might leap across the porch and attack her.

Then she stowed it into her bag again, threw her bag across her other shoulder, and hopped over the railing. She walked off, across the grass. Halfway to her car, she turned around and cupped her hands to her mouth. "By the way, don't try to call him. He'll call you."

Ainsley stepped into her rental car, started the engine, and pointed the vehicle back to the road. In the rearview mirror, the two figures stood on the porch, watching her leave.

The nineteen-century plantation house grew smaller and smaller in the mirror, until finally it disappeared completely.

68

THE NEXT AFTERNOON, AINSLEY DROPPED OFF her rental car, paid the fee, and stepped onto the free shuttle that was transporting her to the San Juan International Airport.

She sank back into the cushions. The air-conditioned interior was a relief from the humidity, which had returned with a vengeance. She watched the other riders step onto the bus bearing large suitcases, duffel bags, strollers.

By contrast, Ainsley was carrying only one item: her white Marc Jacobs purse. It'd never deserted her.

Inside that bag, of course, lay pretty much everything she needed except for money. Not only had she not been rewarded for finding the pearl brooch, but this Puerto Rican adventure had actually cost her some change. Not to mention a few layers of skin.

She clutched the boarding pass in her hand. It'd felt good there. The airline had at last provided a ticket home, more than eight days after the ill-fated emergency landing at this very airport.

She'd spent the morning doing three final activities. First, she'd called Orlando le Grand to report the happy news that she'd nicely blackmailed the Ponce Museum of Art to purchase his archive. After the whoops of joy had subsided, she'd dropped the other shoe: he would need to take delivery of the pearl brooch to complete the transaction.

"So when will you be back on the main island?" she'd asked.

"Never," he'd replied. "Vieques is my home now."

"Really?"

"I'm serious. It's my heart."

She'd laughed at the sudden shift in provinciality. "Then I'll have to ship it to you, because my flight leaves in a few hours."

"That's fine. Send it to our hotel. I'll be here."

"Listen, don't run off with it. You won't be able to sell it anywhere without word getting back."

"Can't you see I've changed?" he'd boasted. "All I want now is cocktails and sunsets and my lungs back."

"Two out of three isn't bad. Watch your mailbox."

"Are all Americans as generous as you are?"

"I wish that we were."

He'd laughed. Ainsley knew that the money he would shortly negotiate for the sale of his archive would keep the fat pirate scholar in cocktails and sunsets for a little while longer. And after everything that he'd done for her, she was glad to help him.

She'd spent the rest of the morning carefully packaging the treasure. Before sealing up the box, she stopped to admire the crab-shaped pearl brooch one final time. It was truly lovely. Sold at an international auction, it could probably fetch at least twenty thousand dollars. Part of her regretted not exploiting this situation for her own personal gain. That part of her, of course, was the same part that opened her credit card statements every month.

Still, Ainsley knew that the item didn't deserve to be collecting dust in some private collection in London. It belonged to Puerto Rico. She'd driven to a UPS center near the airport and paid for delivery—with insurance, confirmation and all the trimmings—to Orlando's *casa* on Vieques. When she'd stepped out of the building, she'd felt good about the way everything had wrapped itself up.

Now she was here, on the shuttle. It pulled up alongside the airport curb. "American Airlines," said the driver.

Ainsley stepped off the shuttle and walked into the San Juan International Airport. She did the security striptease, collected her things, and strolled down the long concourse. The high window alongside the moving walkway provided one final glimpse of green palms bending against blue skies.

It didn't bother her. She was happy to be going home.

At her gate, she gave her boarding pass to the man behind the scanner. "Welcome back," he said.

"Thank you."

He passed the item through the red bar code. His screen beeped. He glanced at it. "Ah. It looks like we're going to send you up to first class. For the inconvenience you suffered last week."

Ainsley felt a little wary. She remembered what happened the last time she was told to sit in first class. "Okay."

She walked down the long accordion gangplank to the airplane, ducked her head as she entered the door, and found her wide leather seat. It was on the aisle. A woman with dark hair was already seated next to the window, looking out at the tarmac. Then she turned her head.

It was Amaryllis.

"Oh my God," she squealed, unbuckling her seat belt. "Ainsley, I wanted to call you but realized you never gave me your number. How did everything go? My uncle couldn't find you either! Did you find the missing jewelry?"

They hugged. Ainsley didn't know quite how to answer her question. "It's been a hell of a week."

"I can't wait to hear all about it. Sit down, please!"

As Ainsley settled into her seat, her beautiful seatmate signalled the flight attendant. "Two glasses of white wine, please."

Then she turned back to Ainsley. "There are no hurricanes anywhere between here and Miami. I checked. We're making it *home* this time."

Ainsley grinned. "Thank God. What did you do all week?"

"Oh, eat and drink, eat and drink. That's all people really do here, you know?

Ainsley laughed ruefully. She sincerely wished that had been her experience. Then she heard her phone beep once. That was the signal for a missed call.

She pulled it out of her purse. As the flight attendant handed Ainsley the glass of white wine, she pointed at the phone. "I'm sorry, but all electronic devices must be powered off."

"I'm just checking one quick thing," said Ainsley.

"You have one minute," came the reply.

That was damn strict. Reading the screen, Ainsley saw that someone had just left her a voicemail. One minute wasn't enough time to access it. Instead, she opened her missed calls log.

There it was. An unfamiliar number had just called her—and it was more than ten digits long.

Ainsley showed her seatmate. "Do you recognize these numbers?"

The pretty woman studied the screen. "+351 218. That looks international. There's a country code and city code."

"Where is it?"

"I don't know. But I'll check for you."

Amaryllis pulled out her own phone and tapped some letters into the browser. "Hurry," said Ainsley, "or you'll get yelled at too."

Amaryllis giggled. "I'm really trying, my phone is just slow. Oh, here it is." She paused. "Did you say +351 218?"

"Yes."

"That's Lisbon."

"Lisbon?" said Ainsley. "In Portugal? Who could've been calling me from there?"

Her seatmate turned off her phone. "You'll find out in a few hours when we land. Now let's toast a week in Puerto Rico."

They clinked glasses as the airplane lifted into the sky.

Turn the page for an excerpt from the next
AINSLEY WALKER GEMSTONE TRAVEL MYSTERY...

The

PORTUGAL

AN AINSLEY WALKER GEMSTONE TRAVEL MYSTERY

SAPPHIRE

J. A. JERNAY

The Portuguese woman drove the Toyota up the short lane, around a few blind curves, and up a twisting road lined with granite statues and sweating tourists hiking uphill. Ainsley sensed that this road was leading to something spectacular.

She was right. With little warning, the road turned into an area crowded with people snapping photos. Ainsley followed their lenses. To the right side of the car was an imposing façade of a white-washed palace, topped with red terra cotta roof and a tall white cone. It was fronted by a cobblestone square.

"The Royal Palace," said Rita. "That's where the kings used to spend their summers. You should see the inside, if you have time."

"I'd rather learn about your assignment."

"Of course," Rita replied, "you're right. The villa is on the other side of town. Five more minutes."

They passed through the heart of Sintra, a blur of pastelerias, cafes, restaurants, gift shops, jewelry shops, and small museums. Then the road entered a grove of green pine trees, the shadows dappling on Ainsley's lap. She rolled down the window and inhaled deeply. The air was fragrant with pine resin and salt water.

"Sintra is the best place in the world," Rita said. "During the fifteen hundreds, the nobles built their summer homes here. In the seventeen hundreds, the tourists started to arrive."

"It's magical," said Ainsley.

They swept around a curve in the road, and Rita suddenly braked. The car slowed to a stop before a tall reddish wooden gate. It was smoothly lacquered, brand-new construction, no more five years old.

Rita fumbled in her purse for a remote control. She clicked the button. The smooth gate began to slowly roll open, revealing a double-tracked gravel driveway that curved into the tall pines beyond.

"I hope you're ready for this assignment," said Rita.

"Why?"

Rita didn't answer. She took a drag off her cigarette and blew the smoke out the sliver of open window. Then she popped the clutch, put the car in gear, and pulled into the property.

The car pulled into an old forest, and headed slowly down a long, dark tunnel formed by the craggy trunks of pines, the slender trunks of euca-

lyptus. The trees felt old and mystical, living repre-
sentations of historical Portugal itself.

"The Souza family lives in Oporto," said Rita.
"Their quinta is in the Douro Valley, of course, with
all the other port wine producers. This is their third
residence."

As they came around a bend, the trees fell away,
and the house was suddenly displayed before them.

Ainsley's eyes widened, a small gasp issuing
from her lips. For nearly two days, she'd had been
trying to imagine what the Souza property looked
like. She'd envisioned a traditional neoclassical
mansion—alabaster columns, long white balus-
trades, old glass running down the windows. A
stone cherub spitting a stream of water into a
fountain. Lines of green moss between the granite
steps.

This villa was nothing like that.

The Souza house was ultramodern. Perfectly
contemporary.

It was a white box. The exterior was painted
a blinding white, as pure as angel breath. Black
railings clawed across the side of the house like
demon's talons. The corners were sharply perpendicular. It was as gorgeous as a modern white box
could be.

Ainsley stepped out of the car, gaping. Rita
watched her closely. "It's a summer home. They
built it ten years ago but hardly ever use it."

"So it's empty."

Rita shook her head. "Not quite. Two years ago, the Souzas decided to begin offering it to the public. Now it's a vacation rental."

"How much do you list it for?"

"Five thousand euros a week."

"That's kind of insane."

"We haven't had too many clients." She shrugged, then took another drag on her cigarette. "Follow me, and you'll find the problem that's giving me a rash."

Rita guided them up the front walk. Ainsley paused at a black, shallow pond, in the center of which floated a single, perfect, green lily pad. The trickling sound of water issued from somewhere nearby.

Peaceful.

Rita unlocked the front door and held it open. "Please, enter."

Ainsley stepped into a tall atrium. The walls painted the same angelic white, the same slashes of black railing indicating indoor balconies overhead. Further on was the living room, filled with low-slung gray sofas, white arch floor lamps, and reddish-brown wooden floor.

Ainsley whistled low. Rita nodded towards the patio. "The outside is even better."

She opened the sliding glass door, and Ainsley stepped onto a beautiful granite patio. A narrow outdoor lap pool, a gorgeous rectangle of electric blue, stretched alongside the home. Slingback canvas deck chairs circled a modern firepit.

And then there was the view.

Ainsley was standing over an unbelievable vista—a rocky slope strewn with gray boulders, green bushes, and brown brambles. At the bottom she could see the red-orange roofs of a town, at the edge of which washed a jagged line of white surf.

Beyond the froth, all the way to horizon, was the deep gunmetal blue of the Atlantic Ocean. The sublime view paralyzed Ainsley. From the edge of this mountainside, she could see at least fifty kilometers out, enough to notice the curvature of the earth. She understood why medieval Europeans had referred to Portugal as the country at the end of the earth. From this height, the ocean must've terrified average medieval Europeans. It was still awe-inspiring to Ainsley now, in the twenty-first century, despite the fact that she had just flown across that stretch of water in an airplane.

She turned to Rita. "I take it back. Four thousand euros a week is nowhere near enough."

Rita nodded. "Sintra down the road. The beaches of Estoril below. It's incredible. This is one of the most desired properties in Portugal. You can see why there have been homes on this site for more than five hundred years."

"So where is the scene of the crime?" said Ainsley.

"Over there."

The property manager pointed to the left, towards a narrow green lawn, bordered by some modest hedges and orange trees. At the far end of the grass, backed into a small rock outcropping like a cornered warrior, sat a small white chapel. It was about the size of a large shed.

"What is that?"

"The *capela*," said Rita.

Capela was the Portuguese word for chapel. Ainsley knew that this was where the phrase a capella had originated, since musical instruments hadn't been allowed in Catholic churches for most of recorded history.

"Show me," she said.

Rita nodded, then moved down the steps, her head hung low, as if carrying a heavy burden. Ainsley followed her across the lawn, the salty ocean breeze at her back, driving her across the ground, towards the chapel, into the mystery.

"The capela was built in 1534," explained Rita. "We don't know who built it. But we do know that in the seventeen hundreds, a rich trader in Oporto bought this property. He'd just returned from a decade trading gemstones in Brazil. To honor the founders of Portugal, he commissioned an azulejo mural to be built inside this old chapel."

They were at the capela door, a wooden number that had been bleached by the sun. Ainsley noticed an alarm system next to the handle. Rita's fingers punched in a code on the keypad, and the small device beeped. She pushed down on the handle and pushed the door open.

Then Rita turned to Ainsley, a weird fire in her eyes. She pulled out her phone and produced a picture. "The *azulejo* mural this trader commissioned was of the Knights Templar as they triumphed over the Moors. It's an important event in our history. It's the moment Portugal was born. Here, look."

Ainsley peered at the woman's phone. On the small screen, she could see a photo of the azulejo mural. She squinted and studied the photo hard. It depicted a group of frightened Arabs, on their knees before a Christian crusader, a famous cross on his chest. His robed arm was outstretched above them, and in his hand was something glittery and beautiful. It was bright blue, and even in this photo, it was throwing the light in a hundred different directions.

That was no tile. "Is that a gemstone?" asked Ainsley.

Rita nodded.

"Is that a sapphire?"

Rita nodded again. "The trader wanted something so beautiful that he would become famous. So he had the sapphire baked into the azulejo."

Ainsley whistled to herself. It was a gorgeous piece of art.

Rita moved aside. "Please see the bad news."

Ainsley stepped into the chapel. The thick stone walls kept the temperature chilly, even on a temperate day. Medieval builders knew insulation.

Soon her eyes adjusted to the darkness, and Ainsley saw that the room was empty except for something on the far wall. She took two steps forward, and it came into focus.

This was the mural itself, the one that Rita had just showed her. It was larger than the picture had indicated, at least three meters across. Ainsley saw that the craftsmanship was better than the photo had transmitted—the blues were more brilliant, the figures more compelling. She gazed at the frightened Moors, the proud Knight Templar, the outstretched arm. A shaft of yellow sunlight fell across the tile where the knight's hand holding the gemstone was supposed to be.

But the gemstone was gone.

So was the tile. In its place was an empty square of dried, chipped cement.

From the doorway behind Ainsley came Rita's voice. She spoke softly, as though from a great distance: "Do you see my problem, Miss Walker?"

Ainsley turned and looked at her. "Somebody has stolen the sapphire."

Get every AINSLEY WALKER
GEMSTONE TRAVEL MYSTERY title ...

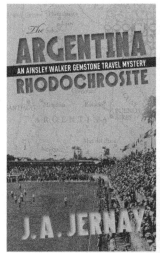
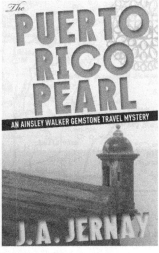
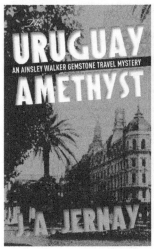
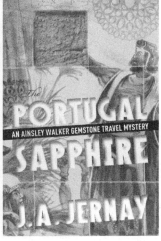

**Don't miss the JAKE LOGAN
PRIVATE TUTOR MYSTERY series....**

**And don't forget titles by
Jonathan Feldman...**

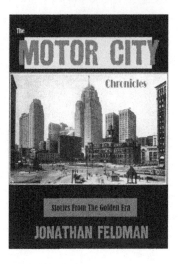

Made in United States
North Haven, CT
08 October 2022

25176684R00232